A
CHOSEN
NOVEL

WIND
CATCHER

JEFF ALTABEF & ERYNN ALTABEF

SECOND EDITION SOFTCOVER

ISBN: 1622533070

ISBN-13: 9781622533077

Editor: Megan Harris

Interior Layout & Formatting: Mallory Rock

Printed in the U.S.A.

www.EvolvedPub.com
Evolved Publishing LLC
Cartersville, Georgia

Printed in Book Antiqua font.

OTHER BOOKS BY JEFF ALTABEF

Shatter Point

WINNER: Pinnacle Book Achievement Award, Fall 2014 – Best Book in the Category of THRILLER

What Others Are Saying about *Shatter Point*:

"An original gripping, saga. From genetic manipulation and twists of fate to cold-blooded murder, scenarios change with a snap but succeed in bringing readers along for what evolves into a wild ride of not just murder and mayhem, but social inspection."

- Donovan, eBook Reviewer, Midwest Book Review

"The book combines my favorite aspects of my favorite authors into one. James Patterson – the master of the psycho killer who kidnaps girls, Patricia Cornwell – scientific thriller, and Dean Koontz – really spooky plots."

– Kat Biggie, No Holding Back

"*Shatter Point* is an exciting novel of suspense, action, drama and even a little bit of horror…. It's definitely one of the best novels out there right now."

- Next Page Reviews

"When I reached the last 100 pages no one was going to be able to stop me reading until I knew the ending!"

- Olivia's Catastrophe

"An amazing read.... This is one of those books that no reader will be able to part with until they reach the end, I guarantee it."

"If you enjoy a great suspense novel, I would HIGHLY recommend this book. It will get your heart pumping and have you hoping the craziness will turn out for the good of everyone involved. You won't want to put this story down till the very end."

For my wife Karen, both my daughters, and for my mom who, through her love and talent as a storyteller, has sparked that passion in me.
— JA

For my wonderful family who has inspired me throughout the process of writing, and for my best friend Mary, who reminds me that anything is possible with a little faith.
— EA

PROLOGUE

Sicheii told me this story only once, which was odd because he always repeated his stories a half dozen times. Every time he told a story it changed—often in subtle ways. Other times, he switched around important events or characters. When young, I pointed out the inconsistencies as if he'd been caught cheating at cards, which he also did quite often. My grandfather never flustered. He patiently explained that his stories were living stories. That's what he called them—*living stories*. As such, they changed on their own from time to time. He never explained what he meant. Now I know.

Three years ago....

Sicheii opened my bedroom door and waved me inside. The taste of chocolate birthday cake swam in the back of my mouth and happily back flipped over my tongue where it swirled among my teeth. Mom stopped me after eating two pieces, but the rest of the cake was safely tucked into the freezer—a spoonful away.

Only the three of us celebrated my thirteenth birthday: Sicheii, Mom, and me. Other kids had big birthday parties, but for me, it was only evers three. As usual, Mom was talking to her boss downstairs in her office so Sicheii and I were left alone.

He pulled me into my room, closed the door, and sat me on the bed. He rolled my desk chair over and bore his penetrating gray eyes into mine. That expression could only mean one thing. He liked to tell me stories when Mom wasn't listening. I know he told her the same ones when she was young, but this way, his stories were like secrets we shared together. Besides, Mom wasn't a fan of his tales. They weren't *modern* enough for her.

"Are you going to tell me another story?" I asked him.

He smiled and nodded. The lines of his deeply tanned face turned upward and his white hair shifted against his broad shoulders. "Yes, Juliet, but this is not just *any* story. This is the story of your birth."

"Mom's already told me all about how my life began."

He frowned. "This story is about your birth, not your beginning. The beginning of your story starts when the First World was new, as it does for all of our people."

"Troy says the same thing."

"He's right. Your friend enjoys a strong connection to the spirit world." Sicheii inched the chair closer to the bed, his eyes intense and his voice stoic. His mood had turned dark as suddenly as an unexpected storm.

"Your arrival into this world was... difficult. Your mother had been admitted into the hospital the prior afternoon. She had already endured eighteen hours of labor when we all clustered about her bed. Sweat and strain clouded her face. My eyes never strayed far from the heart monitor, which measured both of your heartbeats. It was three twelve in the morning."

"Were you angry that Mom wanted to go to the hospital?" A small smile snuck across my face. I've always wanted to ask him about that. As the Tribe's medicine man, he helped dozens of other women deliver babies, so I imagined he was probably sore that Mom wanted to deliver in a hospital instead of under his care.

"Your mom is headstrong. She puts too much faith in *white medicine*. It's better to look deeper into the state of someone's spirit than treat symptoms, but that's not the intent of this story."

I pushed one of my pillows against my headboard and tried to get comfortable. When I punched the pillow a few times to get the shape just right, he shot me a sharp look.

Once I was done fidgeting, he continued. "Tension filled the small room. At first, there were only four of us — your mom, the doctor, one nurse, and me. But more people started to squeeze into the small room and the activity buzzed like a beehive. Your mom pushed when the doctor told her to. Her entire body strained with effort. She screamed in pain. She had refused any painkillers. The intervals between your heartbeats lengthened. First, ten seconds, then fourteen, then twenty. I grabbed the arm of the nurse standing next to me.

"'There's something wrong. Something from inside,' I told him.

"He frowned. 'Everything's fine. She's just in active labor,'" Sicheii smirked. "The arrogant man thought he knew more about childbirth than me. My fingers dug into his thin arm, past muscle and tendon, until my nails pressed against bone. He had to pry them loose with considerable effort."

3

Sicheii's eyes burned white hot. Often, he used funny voices to enliven his stories, but his tone was flat, as if he wanted to tell these events exactly as they happened instead of how he wished they had.

My pulse quickened and butterflies swirled around the ice cream in my stomach.

"My eyes narrowed when your heartbeats stretched to thirty seconds. I locked eyes with the doctor. She was a friend of mine.

"She stared back at me, and at that moment, she suspected something was wrong also. Everyone looked at us.

"'Prepare the OR,' she ordered. 'We're doing a cesarean.' One nurse ran from the room. The nurse who had doubted me started to protest when a scream escaped your mom's lips. It sounded like a hawk's hunting call, loud and shrill. A chill raced up my spine.

His voice quickened. "Blood appeared where it should never have been. Doctors and nurses whirled around the room. IVs were injected into your mom's arm. The heart monitors were disconnected. New worried looking doctors appeared wearing operating gowns. An orderly wheeled your mom into the operating room. Stark white light burned my eyes, and I was left on the outside to pray." He took a deep breath.

"How come you didn't go inside?"

"That operating room was no place for me. What good could come of my presence? Praying was better. You know there are many spirits to call upon."

I nodded. Sometimes he made me recite all the spirits and what type of guidance I should seek from them.

"I called upon all of them, but focused on my favorite two— your grandmother and great grandfather. Time slowed as if the world spun more slowly than it had ever done before. I drifted between worlds and spent time in the shadow lands with my wife

4

and grandfather. They told me much about you. They said you would be okay and sent me back. When my eyes opened, your mom's obstetrician stood before me, her face grim. Spider webs crept from her eyes and canyons burrowed into her forehead.

"She told me that you and your mother were out of danger. I waited for the bad news written in her sad eyes and downturned lips.

"'But?' I prodded her.

"She sighed. 'But your daughter's uterus ruptured. The damage was extensive. We've repaired the organ, but she won't be able to have any other children.' She leaned against a chair, exhausted from the delivery and operation.

"I nodded, and she retreated from the room."

I expected the story to end. Mom had told me most of this before, but Sicheii leaned closer to me. Only a few inches separated us. He smelled of incense—amber and cinnamon. His eyes were wide and sweat dotted his brow. My hands turned clammy. I'd never seen him worried before.

"After the doctor left, I thanked the spirits and slipped from the room. The nursery was on the same floor as the birthing room, but that wasn't my first stop.

"The time was early and the floor deserted. Unseen, I glided through the staircase door and found a plain tan backpack waiting for me with a blue hospital gown and an identification card hidden inside. One of my friends had left it for me."

"Who?"

He shook his head. To say he had many friends was the same as describing cotton candy as sweet. One of his friends always seemed nearby.

"Disguised as a nurse, I strolled to the nursery and avoided the gaze of the few sleepy doctors and nurses who lingered on the floor. One nurse was on duty—another friend. We shared a look, and she left. Three newly born babies slept in bassinets. All three were quiet. You were easy to spot. Even then you looked like your mother. I lifted you in my arms, kissed you on top of your newly born squished head, and unwrapped the white cotton blanket that bound you."

He touched my knee, and I held my breath. "I took a leather pouch from my pocket, removed an ancient needle blessed by the Great Wind Spirit, and found the sole of your right foot. I asked the Wind Spirit for strength before blessing your foot with the needle. You screeched, but your scream quickly died away when you stopped breathing. Your face turned blue and my heart raced, worry bubbling up inside of me. Time ticked past. I counted fifty seconds before I breathed life back into you.

"You began to breathe and cry again. Relief washed over me like a river over smooth stones. I wrapped you back in the blanket, returned you to the small basinet, turned, and left." He squeezed my knee and lifted his hand back. "We are the only ones who know this story. You need to remember it." Watery tears filled his eyes.

"Why would you do something like that? Were you crazy? Who does that?"

He stood without looking at me. The chair rolled away from the bed and bumped into the desk. He spun and strolled from the room, leaving me alone without answering any of my questions. I followed him downstairs, still peppering him with questions. *What was in the needle? Where did you get it?* He acted as if he didn't hear me and walked out the front door without saying goodbye to Mom.

When he left, I raced to the kitchen and asked Mom about his story. She bristled. Their relationship was best described as a seesaw, one end frosty and bitter, the other warm and loving. They argued often then, the seesaw tilting firmly in the frosty direction. She told me he had made up the story and for me not to worry about it. I wasn't sure what to believe.

That night, I took a flashlight and stared down at my right sole. I brushed fuzz from my sock away and found a small star-shaped scar.

CHAPTER

Everything about me is a lie.

My entire life is a leaning tower of lies that threatens to collapse at any moment and bury me so deep I may never climb out from under the rubble.

I slam the bathroom door and my hand trembles as the old-fashioned steel bolt slides into place.

Click.

The locked door offers no real safety. Locked doors can be broken, but it does give me a moment of privacy and a chance to breathe. So much has happened over the past few days. It's like I've become a totally different person—a stranger, someone unrecognizable.

The adrenaline that had been pumping through my veins has completely melted away now as I lean against the wooden door. My breath comes fast and ragged. My body feels heavy and weary and my legs weaken. Gravity pulls me down. Too tired to resist, I slide down the length of the door until the white marble floor rushes up to meet me.

I work hard to steady my breath and focus on taking in fresh air, expelling the old. It's a simple process, yet it takes all of my concentration. When air starts to flow, my eyes close. Time slows and drifts by erratically.

Images flash through my mind—an eclectic group of memories: childhood birthdays, second place in a spelling bee, hanging out with Troy, rock climbing with Sicheii. Most are happy, but they're all tainted now. The lies spoil them. They were never true. They were just part of a story, one that's changed forever.

My weary mind reaches for sleep, but I resist. Too much time would be wasted. There's too much for me to do. Too many loose ends need to be tied, so I open moist eyes and wipe away tears I don't recall crying.

When my vision clears, crimson-streaked fingers flutter near my face as if directed by someone else. I thought blood looked like ketchup, but it's darker and thicker than you would think. My hands spin in tight circles. Each finger is stained with thick, mud-colored smears.

Whose blood is on them?

A cold sweat coats my back and my chest tightens. This blood must be scrubbed away immediately. It starts to burn as if it's alive, as if possessed by dark spirits, spirits that want to harm me. It freaks me out. I have got to wash them clean now, this second, immediately, before....

I turn the faucet and hot water tumbles over my skin. I frantically rub my fingers together and hope friction and water alone will make the blood disappear. The water in the sink turns red and then pink, but traces of blood stubbornly stay behind. A bar of soap rests on the edge of the porcelain sink. Lather squishes between my fingers—twisting and turning, scrubbing and rinsing. My skin turns raw from the rubbing, and when the water has lost all its warmth, I turn the faucet off.

Hard to find specks of blood cling to my flesh, but I still see them and feel them.

Will they ever wipe clean? I don't think so.

A silent scream builds deep within me, which so desperately wants to be released it practically hurts, but no sound slips past my lips. I'm too tired to scream.

A square mirror hangs over the sink, but it's an enemy. I don't want to see who I've become, so my gaze stays fixed down toward the sink. Unfortunately, the blood-smeared faucet is shiny, stainless, and reflects back an image of myself anyway. I glare deep into my eyes, leaning close to the faucet to study them. They look familiar, but as I pierce them more deeply, a hollowness appears that has never been there before. It scares me.

People change. Sometimes they change over the course of a lifetime, and other times change happens swiftly because of a single momentous event. I'm not the same person I was just a few days ago. Too much has happened, too many lies revealed. Truths, solid and real, have crumbled away before me and left behind falsehoods, shadows, and a future as uncertain as a prisoner on death row waiting for a pardon.

The pendant Sicheii gave me flops out from underneath my shirt. It was supposed to protect me. I grip it until my knuckles turn white.

Knock! Knock! Knock!

"Juliet, we've got to talk, Love. We need to come up with a story for the police."

Just a few days ago, I was an average girl who looked forward to her sixteenth birthday, hoping for a little freedom and a chance to get a driver's license.

Being average is a joke. I will never be average. I was never average....

CHAPTER 2

A few days earlier...

Moms invented mornings to torture their daughters. It's the only thing that makes sense. Nothing worth doing needs to start at seven in the morning. Weekends are awesome mostly because I can sleep late and linger in bed until eleven or later. Most days, I'd like to sleep until afternoon, but Mom never lets me stay in bed past twelve. She thinks I'm wasting my life away. Still, this is a school day and sleeping late is not an option.

"Wake up, sweetheart."

The words drift toward me, alien at first until my sleepy brain puts them in the correct order and makes sense of them. Realization dawns on me. I stuff my head under my pillow and seek safety, hoping to shield myself from this awful affront.

Mom's voice turns stormy. "Wake up!" *Sweetheart* vanishes as she wraps razor-sharp barbed wire around her words.

I moan, roll over, and peek at the alarm clock. The fuzzy orange numbers read 5:30. She has to be kidding. The sun's not even up yet.

Argh!

I jam my head back under the pillow and wish I had something larger and soundproof to block her out.

When can I go back to sleep?

Light floods the room when Mom flips the switch. Suddenly, I remember why she's waking me up. She needs to catch an early flight for business, so she woke me earlier than usual to make sure I would be ready to take the bus.

"Don't make me take *extreme measures*." Her voice sounds serious and rich with tension. It's her no-nonsense voice, the one she uses for work.

I've missed more than my share of school busses over the years, so she's quick to ratchet up her terrorist-like tactics *to extreme measures*. Usually she starts by ripping off my sheets and twice has escalated to putting ice cubes down my shirt. She's serious, so I groan something unintelligible, push my pillow to one side and crack open my eyes, which is practically heroic under the circumstances.

She's already dressed and hovers beside the bed in a plain white silk blouse, gray slacks and hands clutched to her hips.

I promise to get up, but the words get tangled up with sleep and sound practically unrecognizable. Still, it placates her enough that she stalks out of my room after tossing out a final warning about me falling back to sleep.

For a second, sleep pulls at me. I start to doze off when I remember the last ice incident. Not pleasant, and Mom's anxiety over her business trip will only make this one worse.

I open my eyes with an impressive amount of willpower, stagger to my feet, bump into the bedpost, stub my toes hard against the doorframe, see stars, clutch my damaged foot, and hop into the bathroom. Luckily, I didn't break my foot—nothing but a red bruise—so I turn the water on in the shower.

Hair still wet, I search for my school uniform under a pile of clean clothes that never made it into the dresser. Despite my best intentions, they never do.

A light buzzing sound hums in my head as I yank out a fresh Bartens shirt. I do my best to ignore the noise. It just started one day. At first, it sounded like static, but since then it has grown louder and has begun to sound like voices. I think the voices want to tell me things, possibly important messages, but they make no sense.

It's annoying. No one else knows about them. Mom would definitely overreact if she found out. My plan is to ignore them. It might not be the best plan, but it's better than seeing Dr. Schmidt, our family physician, and being attacked by the Old Spice cloud that hovers around him, answering his stupid questions. Hopefully, the voices will either tell me something important or go away on their own, so I shake my head and busy myself with getting dressed.

When I go downstairs, no one specific thing seems out of place, but the air feels heavy, as if tension is spinning away from Mom in precise circles. She's headed out of town for two days to a convention in Scottsdale. She works as a lawyer who helps rich people avoid paying taxes. I'm sure there's much more to her job than that, but the details are a blur. She's great at what she does, but spends way too much time at work and should, in my opinion, have more fun and find a nice guy. I tried to set her up with a teacher from my old school two years ago, but that went nowhere.

She rests one hand on the black granite island in the kitchen with a mug of hot coffee perched in front of her. Her day never starts without two cups, always black. A crossword puzzle rests next to her mug. She never has problems with them, but this time she's only finished two thirds of it, and her letters look as if she carved them into the paper with a chisel.

Her pretty oval face is tense with lines around the edges of her eyes and lips. She twirls her long black hair in tight circles, a sure sign she's worried about something. My internal alarm goes to yellow alert. This is the first time she's leaving me alone. I'm almost sixteen. *What could happen in a few days?*

"What do you want for breakfast?" Her eyes flicker to the time on the kitchen wall clock.

"I'll have some peanut butter and apples." I start to head for the refrigerator.

"Sit. I'll get it for you." She swings the refrigerator door open and grabs an apple and a jar of peanut butter.

She hasn't made me breakfast in years. Yellow alert turns orange. I eye her suspiciously when she places the plate in front of me.

More hair twirling and another glance at the clock. Orange turns a light shade of red! "Mom, relax. Everything is going to be fine while you're away. Two days is not a long time. The house won't be destroyed."

She smiles thinly. "About that, *sweetheart*." She pauses.

It might be early, but self-preservation kicks in. The return of *sweetheart* sounds ominous, and that pause means trouble. Something is wrong.

I narrow my eyes. "What did you do? You didn't hire a college kid like last time." I cross my arms over my chest. "That was a disaster. She had friends over until two in the morning. They smoked and ate all the food."

"No, Juliet." She averts her eyes and stares down at her coffee mug as if she's found a miniature boat floating in her morning drink, and it's the most interesting thing in the world.

My heart thumps, and my alert turns deep red.

"Your grandfather is coming over to spend a few days while I'm gone. He'll be here by the time you return from school."

My stomach lurches. The buzzing in my head turns into a loud screech that makes me wince. "Not Sicheii! The college student would be better." I rise from my seat. I'm tall for my age, but she's still an inch taller. She glares down at me, ready for the fight, her eyes hot and her face flushed with color.

"I can't believe you're doing this to me!"

"Juliet Wildfire Stone, there's nothing wrong with your grandfather! You can spend a few days alone with him, and it won't be the end of the world. He loves you and that's final."

I cringe when she uses my full name. A story about an out of control wildfire played on all the news stations the day after my birth, so "Wildfire" became my middle name. I shudder to think what would have happened if there was a garbage strike. Only a few people even know about it.

"Sicheii's weird. He's so...."

"Native American." She clutches her hands against her hips. "I don't understand how this happened. You were such good friends when you were younger. He taught you how to rock climb and swim. You used to spend so much time together."

"That was years ago. Before we moved here and you made me switch to Bartens."

"What does Bartens have to do with your grandfather?" She scrunches up her nose and squints her eyes, the same look she gets when she tries to help me with my algebra homework. Usually I feel sorry for her when she looks like that, but not now.

"Really, Mom?" I say through clenched teeth. *Can she be this clueless?* My trouble with Sicheii has *everything* to do with my new exclusive private school. I don't care if his beliefs are old fashioned. Old doesn't make them wrong. But they pull me in the opposite directions of Bartens. He doesn't care about Ivy League colleges, or fancy vacations, or high paying jobs. Not like they do at my new school. Sometimes I feel like a rubber band, pulled in two different directions. At some point, the band snaps.

I can't explain this to Mom now, especially because I'm pissed, so I take the easy way out. "I'm the only one with Native American blood in the whole place. It's impossible for me to fit in. I didn't want to move here in the first place and leave my old school. Bartens sucks. Home schooling would be better."

She rolls her eyes in that annoying dismissive way she does that drives me crazy. "We moved two years ago, and you're not the only one with Indian blood at Bartens. Besides, it's a much better school than your last one. There were too many *undesirables* at your last school."

Undesirables is Mom's code word for my friends.

"You just need to become more involved. Why don't you play lacrosse? You're a terrific lacrosse player. The school team could certainly use you."

"You don't get it! I'd be the crazy half-blood Indian girl playing lacrosse. They'd never let me hear the end of it. You don't understand how hard it is for me over there. Everybody is so... white and rich."

Mom's face softens. Her skin loses a little of its angry red hue, returning to her natural copper color and her brown eyes widen. Under normal circumstances, her eyes are large and beautiful, but when she gets all motherly and widens them, they take over her face until it's impossible not to become lost in the rich, coffee colored swirls. I'll never be as beautiful as she is. My nose is longish and pointy, and my eyes aren't nearly as wide as hers.

16

"How many Native American partners do you think there are at Dormit and Will?"

I turn my back on her. It's so annoying when she gets like this—all factual and logical and right.

She's trying to trap me, but I won't fall for it, so I return to my best argument with my back still turned to her. "Why can't you trust me? I'm old enough to be on my own for two days. I don't need Sicheii doing his weird stuff around here." Panic strikes. I spin in a tight circle and lean against the table with both hands. "He's not going to pick me up at school, is he?" Air sticks in my throat.

"No, Jules, he'll just be at the house. None of your friends at school will even know he's here." She manages a weak smile.

I can breathe again. "I don't have any friends at Bartens except Katie." I look away, my head hung low.

"What about Tiffany and Ashley and what's her name?"

My jaw drops. Could it be that she hasn't listened to a word I've said over the past two years? "Do you mean *Morgan*?"

"Yes, that's her name. They seem nice."

She must be kidding. Bartens teams up each new student with a mentor. In my case, by some cosmic stroke of bad luck, they choose Morgan—the super popular, Barbie look alike, head cheerleader with a giant trust fund who wants plastic surgery on her perfectly fine nose for her sixteenth birthday. She invited me to a party during my first month at school where she made it clear that I wasn't her *kind* of girl. To her, Native Americans had no place at Bartens.

No one spoke to me at that party except Katie, which put her on the outs with the *popular* crowd almost immediately. But that wasn't the worst part. The party had a Native American theme, including a viewing of *Pocahontas* in the giant-sized media room. *Pocahontas!* I hate that movie. It's the white man's version of the perfect hot Native American girl.

I stayed all night and even choked down some of the tepee shaped cake they wheeled in on a cart with "welcome" written across it. They weren't going to get the satisfaction of running me off, even if that was the longest night of my life.

"Mom, those girls are like a pack of super mean spoiled sharks. They're the last girls I'd be friends with." *How could she be so clueless?* Besides, it might sound lame, but I was looking forward to two days of freedom. I didn't have any particular plans except for catching up on a few television shows and maybe having Troy over.

Mom's lips purse in that way she does when she feels sorry for me, and then a horn honks from the driveway. "I'm sure you can find other girls who would make better friends at the school. You just need to be more outgoing." She checks the clock on the wall. It's 6:15, and she sighs. "I've got to go. We'll come up with a strategy about Bartens when I come home."

She loves strategy sessions. They never work.

She bends down to kiss me, but I strategically step back out of reach, and she scowls at me instead. "Do what your grandfather says. Be respectful." She walks to the front door where her Tumi carry on bag waits.

"I'll call you later." She opens the door. "Love you."

She waits for me to say I love her back, but I'm still angry and won't do it. She shuts the door, strolls down the walkway, and slips into the silver sedan that waits for her without looking back. The sun is out, and the day promises to be steamy. As the car motors away, my anger increases in intensity.

I'm old enough to take care of myself! Sicheii will be a disaster. He doesn't need to watch after me.

The edge of my iPhone digs into my leg. I'm dressed in the Bartens uniform—blue slacks and a white collared shirt with the stupid logo on the chest, which only makes me angrier. I reach into my pocket, remove my phone, and speed-dial Troy.

By the time the phone rings twice, I'm about to hang up when a sleepy voice answers, "Hey."

I hesitate, but there's no backing out now. "Want to cut today? It's too sunny to go to school."

"It's six in the morning."

"Pick me up in two hours. We can go to Slippery River and hang out."

Troy hates school so he'll be happy to spend the day at the river.

"Okay, I'll pick you up," he says, his voice still gravelly.

I hang up and stuff my phone back into my pocket. I've never cut school before and instantly regret my decision. Still, she should have trusted me. She forced me to do it. I stomp my right foot and pain stabs my heel.

It's a searing pain in the shape of a small star.

CHAPTER 3

Troy sees the world in black and white. Sometimes his certainty makes me jealous. My world seems filled with grays—some dark and others light, but rarely any certainty.

Both of his parents are Native American, and he looks the part with caramel skin and long, straight, raven-colored hair twisted in a braid that falls past his shoulder blades. He has never cut his hair. One time, I waved a pair of scissors at him and threatened to lop off his braid. He got angry. He believes long hair is a sign of power and spiritual strength. He'll never let anyone touch his.

Even though he knows the password to enter our gated community, the security guard calls to confirm he's a *wanted* guest. He'll be pissed. He takes slights like that worse than I do, so I wait for him on the edge of the driveway and worry our day will start off on a bad note.

I hear his bike, a 1980 Honda CX motorcycle painted in the original royal blue, before it rolls into view. He found it at a junkyard and worked on it for six months until he got it back on the road. Now the bike runs better than it did when new, but it's loud. He likes it that way.

He pulls the bike three quarters of the way up my driveway, and the tires stick to the hot pavement. He kicks down the kickstand, pulls off his helmet, and slides from the seat. Faded blue jeans cling to his legs and an extra-large, plain white t-shirt fits tightly against his chest and shoulders. Troy is big. He doesn't have a sculpted physique like you'd find on workout shows, but muscles grow on his body like powdered sugar accumulates on funnel cake.

"Outstanding security guard you've got. Does he treat all your guests the same way, or only the brown ones?" Fire blazes behind his eyes.

I smirk in hopes of dousing the flames. "Only the ugly ones with loud bikes." Troy is definitely not ugly, and he knows it. His chiseled jaw and deep set, almond colored eyes give him a pensive expression, as if he's really listening. Girls love him.

"Right." His tone is chilly, but the edges of his lips turn up and form the beginning of a smile so I know we're out of the woods.

My neighbor, Mrs. Jones, pulls back her living room curtains and stares at us through her front window. She's the neighborhood gossip and one nasty drunk. She's probably fifty years old, but looks like a hundred. Too many drinks and too much sun have sucked the joy and life from her. Rumor has it she was *Miss Arizona* twenty-eight years ago. It's hard to see her in the pictures on the web, but it's possible. I had hoped to sneak out without her knowing, but Troy's bike is too loud and she has a sixth sense for snooping.

She wasn't happy when we moved in — a single mother, and even worse, a single Native American mother and her teenaged daughter. But for the last two years, we've given her nothing to gossip about. Now a sharp guilt pang stabs me in the ribs. She'll tell everyone about her truant teenaged neighbor and her wild looking friend. She'll say she knew we were no good all along, that we were trouble, that our kind can't be trusted.

I shouldn't care what she does, but heat flushes my cheeks anyway.

Troy follows my eyes and glances at Mrs. Jones. Her stare deepens into a glare. She clutches a phone in her right hand and a glass that's probably filled with something a lot stronger than orange juice in the other.

He blows her a kiss, and she flips him the bird.

Troy smiles. "I like her. She's a nasty shriveled up person, but at least you know where you stand. There's no phony garbage with her."

"Great."

"So what gives? It's not like you to skip school."

I manage my best shrug with a backpack strapped on my shoulders. "My mom is out of town, so why not have some fun? Why waste such a great day by going to Bartens?"

"What's the rest of the story, Jules? You told me last week that your mom was going away for a few days. We could have made plans then and avoided the early morning wake-up call." He shoots me a knowing look. This is the problem with best friends. Even though we don't hang out as often as we used to, he still knows me better than anyone else. "What happened?"

I sigh. "Mom's got my grandfather staying with me for a few days. She should trust me." I hope to escape with a half-truth. He doesn't need to know about my problems at school. He'll take them poorly. He'll say I should be proud of my roots and tell the others to piss off. He might even stop by Bartens with some of our other

Native American friends just to make a point. He could be like that sometimes—full of surprises, a little dangerous.

"Right," he says in a tone of voice that tells me he doesn't really believe me. "I don't understand what the problem is. Your grandfather is cool, way cooler than mine."

"Let's roll." I step past Troy and toward the bike. "Slippery River is calling us."

He tosses me his heavy all black behemoth of a helmet with a plastic face shield.

I catch it, but keep it at arm's length. "Where's the other helmet? I'll use that one." I wrinkle my nose at the odor. Troy's spare helmet is small and light and doesn't have a face guard or the sweaty smell.

"The chin strap snapped on that one." He smiles. "I need to fix it. This is all I've got."

"You wear it." I shove the monster in his direction. "You're the one who's driving."

He jumps on the bike and melts into the seat. "The way I see it, your grandfather will kill me if anything happens to you anyway. At least one of us will survive if we crash." He starts the bike with a kick. The engine roars as he revs it with a sly grin on his face and a glance at Mrs. Jones. "Put it on or we can hang out here all day with your neighbor gawking at us. It's your choice." He beams a smile at me.

A tickle climbs up my back. Sometimes his smile does that to me. I reluctantly strap on the helmet and hop on the back of the bike.

Troy blows Mrs. Jones another kiss and glides us out of the driveway. We leave the gated community behind and travel in the opposite direction of Bartens. I love the rush that comes with riding Troy's bike, so my arms wrap around his waist and a smile slowly sneaks on my face.

Anything is possible on a day like this one.

CHAPTER

Freedom has a certain smell—sweet and fresh like dew on a spring day. It lingers in your nose and lungs and fuels your soul. I sniff a heavy dose as we reach Slippery River and the promise of a lazy afternoon. It chases away the guilt I feel over cutting school.

Twenty-five years ago, the Tribe owned Slippery River. The town took over the land to increase tourism and pays the Tribe only a third of what they make in admissions fees during a year. A bad deal, but the judge ruled in the town's favor. The weather is supposed to turn hot, so tourists flock to the park in disorderly groups of loud, sunburned, flip-flop wearing beer guzzlers.

Troy drives us through a little used side entrance to avoid the main gate and the fifteen-dollar entrance fee. He parks the bike off the pavement on the far end of the lot and secures it to a tree with a heavy chain. Dozens of tourists meander toward the middle of the park. A mild expression of disgust sprouts on my face. One twenty-something-year-old guy, wearing a ripped Black Sabbath t-shirt, huffs along while dragging a dented cooler I imagine is crammed full of beer for him and his two buddies. All three look pale like ghosts and will burn within the hour. As locals, we have the right to feel superior to tourists, so we shoot them one last disdainful smirk and flee northwest in the opposite direction, away from the marked trails and the main part of the park.

A mile upstream, Slippery River turns wide, deep, and lazy. As the river approaches the park, the water carves a path through a canyon, narrows, and picks up speed. It's called "Slippery River" because the moss-covered riverbed makes the footing slick. Most visitors start upriver and let the water pull them downriver like a natural amusement park ride, screeching the entire way.

Sicheii took me to the main part of the park a long time ago, but we came at night during a full moon when no one else was around. We never told Mom. She would have thought our sortie was too dangerous. Sicheii's definition of dangerous is different from hers.

My legs start to burn as we squeeze our way along a narrow game trail, and I scrape my elbow on a rock jutting into the path. When we reach a particularly steep stretch, Troy pulls me up effortlessly with one strong hand. Fifteen minutes later, we find our favorite spot underneath a soapberry tree with just enough leaves to shade us from the worst part of the morning sun.

From the lofty perch, we stare down at the river far below. I glance at Troy and let him decide if we should keep going since I dragged him out of bed this morning. We can continue to the top of the cliff, but the rest of the climb is steep and it's not worth it.

"Why don't we stop here? There's plenty of room to stretch out under the tree."

I nod, toss down the backpack, and settle under the soapberry's branches. "What's the latest between Ella and Marlon?"

"They're still in *love*." He shakes his head, flopping his braid from side to side on his back. "They're the most unlikely couple in the universe of unlikely couples. Ella is still on track to be valedictorian and Marlon's majoring in shop. And *majoring* is being generous."

I smile and time slows. Since we don't see each other in school every day, I miss these conversations. "What's the latest about the casino? Are they paying bonuses this year?"

"My dad says the casino is packed every night, but you know the management company." He rolls his eyes. "Somehow they always just barely break even, so they never have to pay bonuses. We should have listened to your grandfather. He said they'd steal from us. They're supposed to give the Tribe part of the profit, but we haven't seen a dime in five years." He unzips the backpack and takes out a bag of Doritos and a tin of chocolate chip cookies.

I grab a handful of chips before he munches through them all and look out across the canyon. Devil's Peak spirals dangerously high in the near distance on the other side of the river. No one's ever climbed the soaring collection of red rocks. My mouth drops a little as it always does when I gaze at it. It's beautiful and dangerous at the same time. I point to the crest of the formation. "It looks like Satan is watching us today."

When I was a young girl, Sicheii showed me how the rock formation changes with the light. When we climbed to the top of the cliff opposite Devil's Peak, he pointed out the profile of the

Devil's face carved into the rock, complete with horns at the peak. Then he made me close my eyes and told me a long winding tale of how the Great Wind Spirit defeated the Devil when time began. At the end of the story, he told me to open my eyes and pointed to the rock formation with a sly smile on his face. The Devil's face had vanished only to be replaced by ordinary rocks.

"The Great Wind Spirit was victorious again," he pronounced with a wry smile.

Troy huffs. "I don't know why we call it Devil's Peak. The face looks like Coyote to me."

"What's the difference, Coyote or Devil? Either way, it's a dark spirit."

"They're different. Coyote is *our* dark spirit. The Devil has nothing to do with us." His voice has an edge to it. He grabs another handful of Doritos and glares out into the distance.

Troy is right. Coyote is different from the Devil. He's a dark spirit who tricks people into bad behavior, but he's not all bad. Sometimes he protects animals and Mother Earth from humans, but it seems like he's fallen down on the job lately. Either way, I'm not going to challenge him on dark spirits. They're all the same to me.

I pull a sketchpad from my backpack and notice a handful of fishermen by the base of the rock formation. Among the fisherman, a father teaches his young son how to cast a rod. I start drawing them both while Troy closes his eyes and listens to his iPod, which is really my old iPod. Mom bought me a new iPhone for Christmas.

Time stretches on quietly while I sketch. A smile sticks to my face as a warm sensation fills my body like the inside of a jelly donut. "What has Ms. Combs been up to?"

"She's been promoted to the principle of the middle school."

I drop my sketchpad in my lap. "No, it can't be. She was a horrible teacher! She never liked me."

"She didn't like me any better. At least she won't be dividing kids into reading groups and sorting some in the D group like she did for us. What did Matt Flynn tell you again?"

I chuckle and answer even though he knows exactly what he said. "He said *D* was for dummies, so I told him *K* was for kick, right before I kicked him in the nuts."

Troy laughs a full body laugh, and I can't help but join. His laugh is contagious.

"He was twice as big as you. If I didn't jump on him, he might have sat on you and squashed you."

"Yes, you were my hero." I playfully bat my eyes at him.

"That's not the only time I've saved you from fights." He starts ticking off names with his fingers and chuckles as he goes. "Joyce Janice, Michael Rivers, Michele Mason, Jason Hill—"

"You had better stop right now, or we're going to have a problem. It's not my fault they pissed me off."

He lifts his fists in a play-fighting stance. "I'm ready for you." We both burst into combustible laughter. It feels good to laugh with him, like I'm wearing my most comfortable sweatshirt. I can just *be* when we're together. *Why is it so hard for me to be that way with other people?*

I turn back to my drawing before the fishermen leave, add some finishing touches, and close my eyes to enjoy the warm sun on my face. The heat overpowers me as I slip into a daydream.

I'm in a cave, standing close to a small fire. Flickering firelight swirls along the cave walls. Jagged rock configurations appear and disappear with the fire's dance. White wisps of smoke spiral upward and vanish into an opening in the craggy ceiling. Next to the fire sits an old man, cross-legged, a stoic expression on his lined face. Sweat coats his face and bare chest. He wears only a leather wrap connected at his waist, and his long gray hair is tied behind his neck. His back is straight and stiff, but his eyes dance around the cave nervously. Still, strength lives in him, in his sharp jaw, bright eyes, and broad shoulders. I sense movement and know we are not alone, but I can't turn.

The old man speaks, his voice strong and clear. The language is old and weathered, like something Sicheii might say during a ceremonial feast, but I've never learned the old language, so the words drift toward me, meaningless sounds in the flickering light.

A long metal brand emerges from the fire, glowing angrily. The unseen guest must be holding it. Smoke swirls around the end of the marker, masking its shape. The old man tenses but does not budge. The brand inches toward his chest. Violet colored eyes, intense and demanding, reflect off the long metal rod. The brand scorches the old man in the chest. It sizzles when the marker kisses his skin, but he doesn't cry out. Tears flow from his eyes, but they don't look sorrowful. The stench of burned flesh fills my nose. It smells rank, like death and responsibility.

I jolt awake, body trembling, breath rapid and glance around me, relieved to find the soapberry tree and Troy and Slippery River, all as they should be. People say you can't smell while you sleep, but I don't believe them. Smells often linger after my daydreams, like they do with this one.

I push the last vestiges of the daydream from my mind with a mental shove. Luckily, they fade quickly. One time, Sicheii suggested I study my daydreams to understand my ancestors' messages, but I'd rather push them from my mind. Who wants messages from their ancestors like texts from the grave? Life should be lived in the present and the future, which, as far as I can tell, has little to do with my heritage or my ancestors.

An empty bag of Doritos rubs against Troy's sneaker. His head rests against the backpack, eyes closed as he listens to his music. The light bounces off his hair, which has grown longer from the last time we were together almost two weeks ago. I miss seeing him every day and knowing the important things going on in his life that we never text or talk about—whether his father is hassling him, or which girls have crushes on him.

For a moment I imagine him with short hair and in a Bartens uniform. The fuzzy image refuses to focus in my mind mostly because he would never cut his hair or wear the stupid uniform. I shake my head and frown. I'm being selfish. He'd be miserable without the Tribe or the rush of wind on his bike that ruffles his hair or his mysterious camping trips.

I yank one of his ear buds from his ears. He's not listening to music, but an audio book instead.

"Hey!" Troy swivels his head toward me.

I frown, and he pulls off the other ear bud.

"Still having a difficult time with the dyslexia?" Even with the reading disorder, Troy is incredibly smart. He can perfectly recall everything he hears, but his teachers give him a hard time about his reading, so he constantly struggles in school. If his family was rich and he went to Bartens, the school would find a way to get around his learning disability and he'd be an *A* student.

He shrugs. "If I listen to the books, at least I'll pass English."

"You need to work on those exercises the school counselor gave you." I shoot him my most disappointed scowl. He can be so pigheaded. He spent three months finding the exact original color paint to fix his bike, but he refuses to work on his dyslexia. "You're not going to make it through college by listening to books on your iPod."

"I'm not going to college, Jules." He glances farther up the rock canyon away from me. "We both realize it. I'll work as a mechanic in town with my uncle. There's not a car that's ever been made that I can't fix."

"You're too smart to give up on school. If you do the exercises, you can overcome the dyslexia. Other people get past it." We've had this argument in one fashion or another dozens of times over the past five years. He deserves a future brighter than anything this small town could offer him. *We* deserve something better, and I can't imagine my future without him in it.

"I've tried, but the letters mix up. There's nothing I can do about it." He balls his hands into fists and pounds his right hand into his thigh.

I'm about to start round two of our fight when a high-pitched shriek startles me. A red shouldered hawk circles through the air currents high above us. This type of hawk is Sicheii's animal guide. He believes hawks warn him about pending trouble, so I always pay close attention to them. Something about the call strikes me as odd. A bush sways awkwardly in the ridge above us, but there's no wind. A biting chill runs through me.

No one else can see us from our remote location, and no one knows we're at Slippery River. Suddenly, I feel vulnerable, like we've strayed too far from the herd. "Let's get out of here."

Troy squints at the sun, which has traveled well past midday. "Sure, it's getting late. I've got to help my uncle in the garage later anyway." He rises and stretches with a soft groan.

The hair on the back of my neck stands on end as I stuff our trash into the backpack and cram my phone into one of the waterproof pockets. I feel a weird pull from the top of the cliff, as if something's watching us, and hear faint noises that sound like footsteps from the ledge above us. I swing the backpack on my shoulders and walk to the edge of the cliff. Something or someone is closing in on us. It might sound ridiculous, but Sicheii taught me to trust my instincts. He believes they come from spirits we cannot see, and right now, my instincts are barking at me. We need to get to the river fast, and the trek down will take too long.

"Lets dive." I smile at Troy. It's forced, but luckily he doesn't notice.

He peers over the cliff and shrugs. A deep river pocket sits right below us where we can safely land. "We'll have to dive over seventy feet to the river."

I know the jump is good with him. He's a great cliff diver, but the shrug leaves the window open for me to back out.

Another high-pitched hawk call shrieks from above. I glance to the top of the cliff and my heart skips a beat. A weird dog-like creature stands near the edge, drool dripping from its powerful jaws. It's hard to see the beast clearly in the afternoon glare, but it looks big, and instead of fur, black leather skin stretches tightly against a lean muscular frame. It snarls at us, and I see a mouth full of sharp teeth. Vile. Deadly.

It moves along the edge while keeping it eyes on me and seems to hobble a bit. Its front legs are noticeably shorter than its back ones. The sun glints off something shiny on its side, and it looks like it has small claws and two leathery bat wings folded against each side of its body. That has to be my imagination and the sun playing tricks on me.

Troy turns and notices the creature for the first time. "What in the world is that?"

"I don't want to find out."

The beast howls and the high-pitched wail pierces my every fiber.

"It can't get us down here," says Troy, but there's no certainty in his voice.

A heartbeat later, the creature leaps from the cliff, and I swear those creepy wings fly open for a second as it lands on our ledge not more than twenty feet from us. It smells like rotten fish.

It takes a second to gain its footing. I'm sure it'll race past the soapberry tree and launch itself at us any second.

Troy pushes me toward the edge. "Go!"

I run, heart hammering in my chest, and leap with a screech. I'm suspended in air for a second, and then plummet to the river. Wind whips through my hair as my legs knife into the cool water. Two kicks and I break the surface.

Troy follows with a loud splash.

When he clears the water, he says, "That was the freakiest dog I've ever seen."

I look back toward the cliff where we jumped, but don't see it. "Did you see any wings?"

He smirks and that makes me feel silly. "Wings? All I saw was the foam coming out of its mouth."

I must have been seeing things. Besides, it's on the cliff and we're in the water, so I let go of my fear and tease him. "Were you worried it was going to eat you for lunch?"

"Both of us," he says. "It must have been rabid."

"Well that explains it, then."

"Explains what?"

"Only a rabid creature would want to eat you." I splash him, and he chops water at me with both of his hands.

I laugh and counterattack with a two-handed splash of my own.

All is good until the hawk calls one last time.

I glance into the sundrenched sky, expecting to see the bird.

All I can make out is a black shadow, but it looks larger than a hawk, and then it suddenly disappears.

CHAPTER 5

We splash the river at each other for a few more minutes, but the frigid water bites our skin, so we swim to the bank. Without a towel, the sun will have to dry us. Luckily, it's still hot as we follow a trail toward the parking lot.

When we near Troy's Honda, we turn a corner in the game trail and hear beer cans crunch, rock music blare, and something that sounds like water flowing from a hose—all signs drunk college students are hanging out by his bike.

We share a look, and he says, "Crap" right before he sprints ahead.

I race a step behind. Drunken college kids are worse than nasty raccoons, and our town collects them like a cactus does needles.

Three students have surrounded Troy's bike. Crushed beer cans have been tossed about and a small, gross looking puddle sits right by his back tire. The student closest to the puddle fumbles with his fly.

"Hey, move away from my bike," Troy shouts as he slows into the clearing.

All three guys appear sloshed with flushed faces and unsteady gaits. Two stand off to the right and one farther from the rest to the left nearest to the bike. They all have "State" t-shirts on with different designs. Of the three, the middle one looks the most dangerous. He seems the steadiest with beady, calculating eyes.

The guy farthest to the right is the largest, his thick arms bulging with muscles. The extra-extra-large white and red t-shirt he's wearing says "Rugby" on it and barely fits over his barrel-chested frame. "Cool bike," he mutters with a smirk. He must weigh fifty pounds more than Troy.

The beady-eyed fella sweeps his vision over Troy and sneers. "I want to take it for a ride. Tell me the combo for the lock."

Troy tenses, the vein in his neck pulses, and his body coils. He looks explosive. "No one needs to get hurt." He lifts both of his hands above his head. "Just step away, and we'll take off."

The student on the left wobbles toward me. His greasy hair hangs down to his shoulders. Sunburns blotches his face and arms and he grins stupidly. He's thin, about my height, and reeks of beer and stale cigarettes.

"You're cute. Why don't you come with me and leave the *chief* with them?" He stumbles a half step toward me.

His two friends snicker.

I turn to face the greasy haired idiot. He's only a little wider and heavier than me. His dilated eyes look glassy and he smirks like a spoiled child in an ice cream shop. I smile at him and wave him closer. "Boy, you're a real prize, aren't you?"

The dope doesn't hear my sarcastic tone and continues to stagger unsteadily toward me. Beer in the form of sweat pours down the sides of his face. He stops five feet away and flashes me crooked, yellowish teeth. He's only one step away.

I glance at Troy and say, "K."

He shrugs. "Is for kick."

I turn back to the drunk and boot him right in the balls with all my weight behind the kick. He seizes up into a fetal position and collapses on the dirt. One hand grabs his privates while the other pounds the ground. He mutters something. It's hard to make out, but it sounds like he wants his mother.

When I turn, Troy has already grabbed Rugby Shirt by the arm and twisted hard. When he squeals, Troy drives his elbow into his arm. The bone breaks, but Beady Eyes lands a right hook against Troy's jaw when he isn't looking. The punch sends him spinning.

I don't like Beady Eyes's confident swagger as he stalks after Troy. My chest tightens. I move toward him ready to jump on his back when my foot kicks the ridiculously large and slightly smelly helmet.

Troy straightens himself and darts at Beady Eyes, clenching his arms around his waist. I grab the helmet and step toward them. Beady Eyes hits Troy with another right, this time in the side, and Troy grimaces.

I narrow my eyes. The helmet feels heavy in my hand. I focus on the back of Beady Eyes's head and swing it down hard, bashing it into his skull. He goes limp and tumbles to the ground.

I turn to face Rugby Guy who's holding his right arm gently with his left. He's sweating profusely and fear fills the white portion of his wild looking eyes. He speaks fast and groans a little at the end. "We're just messing around. We didn't mean *nothing*. I think my arm's broken, man."

Troy moves next to me. "Step away from my bike."

"No problem. Just keep away from me." Rugby Guy joins his greasy haired friend who's still groaning and squirming on the ground off to the side.

Troy unlocks the bike while I watch over the two drunks. In a minute, he starts the bike and spins the back tire, spraying loose stones at Beady Eyes, who starts to moan and throws up.

I jump on the back of the bike and glance at the sky. I'm not sure if I'm looking for a hawk or that weird dog creature. Either way I feel uneasy, as if something is wrong, something big. Something nasty.

CHAPTER 6

Troy navigates the bike along the narrow side road that leads out of the park. Tension knots his back.

"I wish we could ban drunk college kids from our town," I yell in his ear. "Now I've paid you back for Matt Flynn."

He chuckles and the rigidity vanishes. "That still leaves Janice Joyce, and—"

I punch him on the shoulder. "What did I say about that on the cliff?"

We both laugh as he turns left on Route 100. He opens the throttle, and the wind embraces me and distracts me from the horrible things I'm sure Mom will do once she learns that I skipped school. My distraction is short lived because sirens wail behind us and I jump.

Troy glances in the side mirror and grumbles under his breath. "What now? I hope my dad hasn't done anything else."

Troy has a sketchy relationship with the sheriff's department. Nothing seriously bad, but his dad gets into bar fights, so they like to know what he's up to. Small towns suck that way. I want to live somewhere big like New York or Paris or London, a city where no one knows my family tree or his, and we can be free to be ourselves without the past getting in the way.

When he slows the bike, the two police cars scream past us with a *whoosh*, sirens blaring. "I wonder what that's about?" I shout, trying to compete with the wind. "When was the last time two police cars raced in the same direction?"

"Let's find out. That's Sheriff Daniels's car." He twists the accelerator, and the Honda spurs forward. The wind roars and I'm flying. I tighten my arms around his waist and my body bends toward his. I can feel his heartbeat through his t-shirt, and he smells like summer.

Within a few miles, the squad cars turn right onto Canyon Avenue. "They're headed into the Reservation," Troy says. His body stiffens, and the knot returns. He lives in the Reservation.

The Reservation isn't technically a *real* reservation. It's paradise when compared to the real Rez, which is 50 miles away in the middle of nowhere. Many families on the Rez don't even have electricity, and only half the kids graduate from high school. Broken down cars and trucks litter the yards like weeds. There are no chain stores or malls or Starbucks. Only a few mom and pop stores are permitted on the Rez. It seems like a third world country stuck in the middle of Arizona.

Sicheii goes there often, bringing supplies and help when he can. I used to go with him, but that was a while ago. Last year, Mom and I only went during the harvest celebration to see the tribal dancers.

This Reservation is actually a run down neighborhood where most of the residents are poor and have some Native American blood. Troy swings the bike on Canyon Avenue and follows as far behind the flashing lights as he can while still keeping an eye on them.

We pass dozens of ranch-style houses clustered close together with peeling paint, slanted walls, and weed infested, rock-filled yards. The difference between this neighborhood and my gated community is stark. They might as well be on different planets, which brings a guilty lump to my throat. We have so much and they have so little. As we move farther from Route 100, the houses become more dilapidated, some with missing windows, and one front door leans against a porch.

Troy slows the bike as the police cars turn left on River Road. "This is a dead end," he says. We crawl along the winding street, turn a corner and find three police cars their lights spinning parked in front of the last house.

He swerves to the curb a few hundred feet from the cruisers and turns off the bike.

I squint at the home in front of us. "That's Old Man Roundtree's house. Why would three cruisers stop at his place? How much trouble could Roundtree get into? He's as old as dirt."

"Maybe one of his potions backfired. Jack bought a sickness curse from him last week and cast it on Mr. Stevens our chemistry teacher. He was out for a week with strep throat."

"Rumor has it you've been buying love potions again." I poke him in the ribs with my elbow.

"He's been making potions and casting spells for a long time, Jules. Science can't explain everything." Troy jumps off his bike. "Come on, let's take a closer look."

I groan. "Do we really need to snoop around?" I'm in plenty of hot water for skipping school already, but he ignores me and jogs toward Roundtree's house. Why look for trouble? But what choice do I have? So I slink after him, trying to stay in his shadow.

Roundtree's house is set back fifty yards from the road. It's older than the other houses on the street, a small clay ranch-style home with a red-tiled roof. At least the walls are sturdy and all the windows and doors are intact.

A wooden sign by the front door proudly proclaims *Medicine Men Make the Best Lovers*. A small smile spreads across my face. Sicheii would not be happy.

Troy scoots toward the right side of the house, bent at the waist, stopping behind an ash tree. I run behind him, doing my best to keep up. Roundtree's property stretches all the way to Fishkill River. An old chicken coop leans precariously behind his house and directly in front of us. A few bushes, four trees, and a discarded lawnmower separate us from the coop. Patches of green dot the yard, although there's little grass. At least not the type you'd find in my neighborhood.

I tug on Troy's shirt. "Let's turn back. We'll find out what happened soon enough through the rumor mill."

He shoots me a mischievous look. "Come on. We can run along that line of trees and hide behind the coop." He points to three trees, which make an uneven line toward the coop. "If the coop doesn't collapse on us, we should be able to see what's going on in the backyard. No one's going to catch us."

He races out from behind the ash tree before I have a chance to protest. He knows I want to go back, but once he starts, he also knows I'll follow him. Best friends can really be a pain in the ass sometimes.

We run from tree to tree, trying to be as quiet as we can, but the rocks crunch under our sneakers. When we reach the coop, we're breathing hard. Sweat soaks my shirt and my heart pounds. Luckily, no chickens are home.

A surreal quality fills the air as if I'm standing in the middle of a photograph. It's hard to explain. Something just seems weird, as if the world is not quite right, and I should notice what's wrong right away, but nothing jumps out at me. We hear Sheriff Daniels's muffled voice, but other than that, it's quieter than it should be. The air is crisper, the colors brighter.

When we shuffle to the back of the coop, we edge along the rotten wood until we see Sheriff Daniels and the rest of the backyard. Three goats graze together along the river's edge. They watch Daniels and the other officers who stand in a loose circle around the base of a wide maple tree.

I strain my eyes to check out what they're looking at, and then Deputy Johnson moves. I wish he hadn't. Roundtree is tied around the trunk of the maple by his arms, his bare chest smeared with blood, his body slumped lifeless against the rope. We are too far away to see him in detail, but the blood pooled at the base of the tree tells the story well enough.

I want to pull my eyes away, but they're stuck. I've never seen a dead body before. Sure, there are tons of television shows where dead bodies are as common as sunrises, but it seems a lot different in person. I'm struck by the complete lack of motion as Roundtree's body pulls against the ropes. Even when you sneak up on someone who's sleeping, his or her chest still moves up and down. Here, there's nothing.

Troy flattens his body against the back of the coop, which leans with his weight and creaks a little until it steadies back in place. "Who could have done that?" He looks at me and all I can do is shake my head.

"We'd better sneak out of here," he whispers. "They're not going to be happy with us snooping around a murder scene."

Finally, we agree, but a sharp pain knifes through my skull and the buzzing I hear turns into a waterfall of noise that crashes in my head. I bend over at the waist. My head's dizzy and I gasp for breath. My lungs explode. The coop sways against my back. Images flash in my mind—close-ups of Roundtree's body: cuts ripped into his chest, a jagged gash down his face, purple bruises mar his neck, his open eyes lifeless, blood everywhere.

I squeeze my eyes shut tight, but the visions only intensify. He has a tattoo on his chest of two arrows twisted together with a circle around them. Both arrows have different arrowheads and feathers. I know this tattoo. My grandfather has the same one.

I gasp for air, chest tight. Short bursts of oxygen spurt into my lungs. The ground sways under my feet. My mind turns fuzzy and my head's on fire. My stomach churns and bile fills my mouth. The ground rushes up to meet me when Troy grabs my shoulders and steadies me.

"Argh." I clasp my head because it feels like it'll shatter if I don't hold it together.

The images linger for another heartbeat and then vanish. I lean against Troy and breathe deeply. Air fills my lungs, and my legs feel stronger. I open my eyes and concentrate on Troy's face. It looks fuzzy and then focuses.

"Are you okay?" His eyes are wide and his lips are turned down softly.

"I'm fine." I shake my head to clear it. *Fine* is definitely not the right word to describe how I feel. I've never experienced pain like that before, but at least I didn't toss my lunch. My hands tremble as air begins to flow more smoothly into my lungs.

Movement catches my eye. Deputy Johnson wanders in our direction. He hasn't seen us yet, but if we move he'll spot us for sure. "We've got to wait," I whisper. We push flat against the coop. A pointy piece of wood stabs me in the back, and I shift away from the jagged edge.

Only a few yards away, Deputy Johnson's steps are slow and cautionary. He hesitates and stares at something on the ground. My skin crawls. He's sure to catch us. He squats low and picks up a broken piece of stone in the dirt. Holding it close to his face, he turns to face Sheriff Daniels. "This is the tip from some type of ceremonial carving knife. It has blood on it. This could be from the murder weapon."

When Johnson stands up, he scans the area, looking for other clues. He glances toward the coop and looks right past us. Just when it seems that he'll definitely spot us, one of the goats darts toward him, grunting with its head down, brandishing its horns.

"Make sure that goat doesn't come near the body!" Daniels shouts.

Johnson curses as he dodges the goat's charge and races after the angry animal to keep it away from Roundtree.

With Johnson chasing the goat, I tug on Troy's t-shirt. "We'd better go." He follows me to the side of the coop, and we sprint back to the bike, no longer worried about staying behind the trees.

When we reach the Honda, his face is screwed together angrily and his eyes burn. "Do you think someone used a ceremonial knife to kill Roundtree?"

"Beats me, but why would it matter?"

"It matters to me." He starts the bike with a hard kick.

CHAPTER 7

People judge others by their appearances — their clothes, the color of their skin, whether they have tattoos. It makes no sense, but it happens all the time. When most people see me, they only see a Native American teenaged girl, and with that come a slew of judgments and prejudices having nothing to do with me. The baggage for Troy is heavier, and sometimes he gets tired carrying the weight.

Joe, the security guard, smiles at me from the little hut at the entrance to my neighborhood, but scowls at Troy. It's obvious what he's thinking. Troy's too wild-looking for him. He doesn't *fit* in our gated community. He could be a *troublemaker* and deserves careful scrutiny. Joe's attitude makes me angry, but I'm not going to say anything now. Roundtree was murdered. Bigger worries occupy my mind.

The same must be true for Troy because he grins back at Joe, and without a word, Joe presses a red button and the metal bar rises out of our path. Troy winks at him and continues on, pulling the Honda to a stop in front of Mrs. Jones's house. This is our second stop after leaving Roundtree's house. First, we visited the Dairy Freeze on the way home where I changed into my school uniform just in case Sicheii arrived home before I did.

I hop from the bike.

"Are you okay, Jules? Has your headache gone away?"

I had a hard time describing what happened to me by the chicken coop. I've never felt anything so intense before. It felt as if the usual buzzing in my head had become solid, and someone had pried open my skull and stuffed gory images inside. Not pleasant. The headache was real enough and simple to explain, so that's all I told Troy. Why talk about visions, which were probably just another product of my overactive imagination anyway? The blood pooling by Roundtree's feet must have caused my imagination to fly into hyper-drive, no doubt fueled by my NCIS addiction.

I yank off the helmet. "I'm feeling better now that this thing is off my head. It makes a better club than hat." I manage a weak grin. At least the noise in my head has quieted down to a manageable level. "I still can't believe someone killed Roundtree. Who would do that?"

Troy rubs his face with his hands and takes the helmet from me. "Beats me, but he must have really pissed someone off. I'll call you later. Maybe I'll find some clues when I dig around the Reservation." He dons his helmet, starts the Honda, waves, and motors away with a squeak of the tires.

I trudge up our driveway toward the front door. The door opens, but it moves only a few inches and jolts to a stop as the shiny metal chain bars entry. Sicheii is home. Why would he use the chain? We never use it.

"I'm home, Sicheii. Let me in." Thirty seconds pass. I tap my foot against the stoop and there's no answer. The day is still hot and sweat starts to coat my forehead and back. What weirdness is he up to now?

I drop my backpack with a thud, amble over to the three-car garage and peek into the windows. Sicheii parked his mint-condition, burgundy, 1973 Porsche 911 next to Mom's boring white Volvo. The license plate reads, "MED MAN." Wherever he goes, everyone recognizes the sports car as my grandfather's, which is only one reason I hate driving in the thing. It's also loud, has no cup holders, gets only AM stations, and smells like oil. Still, Sicheii loves the car. It's old, but he drives it fast.

I sigh—he's here somewhere.

Just then, Mrs. Jones pulls up in her silver Mercedes and screeches to a stop. She manages to keep two wheels on the pavement. The other two leave a skid mark on her grass. Stumbling out of the car, she slams the door shut, and weaves her way over to me.

Great! Could my day get any worse?

"Hey you! Janice. How was school?" A wicked grin flickers across her face. "I see you've put on your uniform." At least that's what I imagine she's saying. It's hard to make out the words because she slurs them.

I groan and walk toward her. "My name's Juliet."

She stops only a foot from me, which is good because for a second it appears as if she's going to crash into me. Her breath stinks of Scotch. "Right, Jane. I know education isn't high on your people's list of priorities, but listen to me—"

"My Mom's a partner at Dormit and Will! She's way more educated than you!"

She grabs my arm. "No need to shout, Jackie. You people are always so loud with the drums and... whatever. I'm just saying, tramping around isn't going to get you far. Once your... looks go, you'll have nothing without an... education."

Heat flushes my face and I pull my arm free from her talons. "Thanks. At least I have you as a role model."

Her mouth drops open far enough that a fly zips in. She doesn't notice. "You little—"

"*What?*"

She must see the fire in my eyes because the color drains from her face and she mumbles, "Nothing," before she turns and staggers away.

I watch her make the entire trek into her house before my breathing goes back to normal.

Now, where's Sicheii?

There's no place to walk to in my neighborhood, so that means he must be in the backyard. I plod my way to our gate, push it open and find him holding a shovel, plunging it into the grass, a mad grin across his face.

Argh! What's he doing?

Grass is rare and expensive in our town. Mom pays landscapers a fortune to keep it green, just so our lawn can have the same color as our neighbors' lawns.

When I swing the gate closed with a thud, Sicheii stops digging and glances up toward me. His white linen shirt is unbuttoned. Dirt splashes his Lucky jeans, and his soft leather moccasins are neatly placed off to the side near the stone patio.

"Welcome home, Little Bird."

I'm not sure why he calls me *Little Bird*. I hate it, but at least he doesn't call me Wildfire in public anymore.

My jaw drops once I get a better view of the hole he's dug in Mom's lawn. It's already five feet across. "What're you doing? You're destroying Mom's grass!"

He smiles, and his bright, white, perfectly straight teeth contrast with his deeply tanned skin. "I'm making a barbecue pit." He proudly points to a pile of rocks and a flat slab of stone to the side of his newly created hole. "I caught fresh fish for us."

He speaks casually, like it's absolutely normal for him to dig up Mom's yard; I have to suppress a grin. "We own a perfectly good barbecue right there." My outstretched finger points at our rarely used gas Weber grill. Everyone in the neighborhood owns an identical one.

He scowls at the grill as if it's an alien device. "I don't know what that is, but I'm not using it. That's not how *the people* barbecue. The fish were good enough to sacrifice their lives for us. I'm not cooking them on such a thing."

Sicheii refers to Native Americans as "the people." I shrug. This isn't my problem. Mom decided Sicheii should stay, so she'll have to deal with the new pit in the lawn. "You'll have to explain the hole to Mom. Maybe you'll dig up some gold nuggets? You'll need them."

He shoots me a disapproving glower with his slate gray eyes. Gray eyes are unusual among our people, and Sicheii's are bright. "How was school?" He locks his eyes onto mine.

Big red warning lights flash in front of me. I panic and do the only thing I can think to do—lie. "School was... fine." My voice wanes like a balloon losing its last bit of air. I glance down at my feet and scratch the back of my neck. The sun burns hot against my face. My feet seem to fidget on their own. What can I say? I'm a bad liar.

"Really, Little Bird?" Sicheii leans against his shovel. He wears leather deerskin gloves to protect his manicured hands.

I double down. "I had a test in English, but I'm sure it went okay." My hands shift through my hair, straightening it.

He frowns, and the lines on his face all move at once, conveying generations of disappointment at me. "Why don't you tell me the truth?" He tosses the shovel on the grass.

He's caught me, so I have no other choice but to come clean, and my face flushes warm. "I skipped school today." I feel better now that I've told the truth. In only that short moment, I've started to feel nauseous.

"I know. You went to Slippery Rock with Troy Buckhorn, didn't you?"

I take a half-step back and wonder which one of Sicheii's friends ratted us out. "How'd you know? Who told you?"

He smiles and flashes his pearly whites at me. "The wind told me."

I plant my hands on my hips. "Now who's lying?"

Sicheii's eyes narrow, but he isn't angry, only amused. The twinkle that sparkles in his eyes betrays him. "I heard Troy's bike from the street and can smell the river on you in the breeze. Besides, your school left a message. They were wondering where you were."

Of course Bartens would call. I'm an idiot.

"I'm sorry. Cutting school was stupid. But that place gets to me, and the weather was perfect." I twirl the ends of my long straight hair. "And I haven't seen Troy in weeks." He likes Troy, so I grab onto him like a life raft.

He pauses for a moment and rests his gaze on my face with a half smile on his. I give him my best, most remorseful frown, widen my eyes as much as possible, and bat my eyelashes at him. None of my antics will change his mind, but I try anyway.

He shoots me a sly smirk. "The rainbow trout is in the refrigerator. Clean the fish for dinner the way I taught you."

I dash toward the backslider when he calls after me.

"Don't forget to thank the fish for their sacrifice. I'll heat up the stones."

He gave me a break. I'm still worried Mom will find out about my skipping school, but there's still a chance she won't. Hope is a good thing.

I slide the backdoor open and try to remember how to thank a dead fish for jumping on my grandfather's hook.

CHAPTER

Sicheii's life is free from structure. He doesn't care about what the *right* time of day is to do things. For him, dinner isn't a particular time, but a desire to consume the largest meal of the day. He'll eat dinner whenever he decides he's hungry — often in the middle of the day, sometimes for breakfast, other times late into the evening. He calls it "Indian Time." It must be great to live that way — free from rules and other people's expectations. He bends life to his will instead of the other way around. Only the art gallery tethers him to conventional time and even then he'll close the store to do more *important* things.

The sun still lightens the sky, but the trout smells delicious as the fish sizzles on the thin, flat slab of blue stone, and my stomach growls. All I ate for lunch was a few handfuls of Doritos I snatched before Troy scarfed them all down.

We go inside to the dining table where he places a platter of fish and grilled squash between us. He doesn't like to use separate dishes. He thinks the proximity brings us closer together when we share food off the same plate. It's just more of his weirdness.

Before launching into dinner, fork primed in my hand, he says grace. "We thank the fish and the squash for their sacrifices for our nourishment. Their spirits will unite with ours, and we will forever be joined as one."

When he finishes, he closes his eyes, hums softly, and starts meditating. He expects me to follow along also, so I close my eyes and hum. I'm not sure what he wants me to meditate on: everything I'm thankful for, or the connection between our food and myself, or perhaps the sacrifice the fish and vegetables made for me. Instead, visions of Roundtree creep into my mind. They're still vivid enough to make me wince. *What did he do to deserve that?*

I'm not sure how long I hum with my eyes closed, but he has stopped first. He's staring at me and looks through me as if he suspects something is wrong. He doesn't say a word about it though—he respects my privacy with the spirit world.

I nod, and we begin eating. I'm not sure if I thanked the fish properly, but I shovel in heaping forkfuls and thank them now. There's nothing as tasty as freshly caught fish.

Sicheii is still watching me with a raised eyebrow and a weird twinkle in his eyes, so I start a conversation about something far removed from Roundtree and those visions. "How are things at the art gallery?" He owns a successful gallery in Old Town where he sells Native American art and antiquities. He lives in a modern, luxurious loft above the store. "Shouldn't you be at the gallery selling to the tourists?"

"Lisa is running the store for me. She is more than capable."

I roll my eyes. Neither Mom nor I like Lisa. She's young and beautiful and as phony as a politician on Election Day. We both suspect she's a moneygrubber, and we don't have any idea how they met. One day, two years ago, we entered the gallery and Lisa was working there. That wasn't surprising. He hires college-aged kids all the time, but we both noticed the ease in which she touched him on the shoulder and the friendly glances they shared. Six months later, she moved into his apartment.

He ignores my reaction and smiles. "So how are you doing at that school of yours?" He hates Bartens almost as much as I do. He never mentions it by name. At least we share that in common. He had epics fights with Mom when she decided to make me transfer schools. He wanted me to stay connected with the Tribe and be around a more *diverse* population. He argued that life shouldn't revolve around Ivy League schools and trust funds and materialistic things. Mom wants the best for me, and her definition of best is different from his, so I transferred to Bartens.

I shake my head. "Everyone is so perfect there. They all like horseback riding, and look the same, like they're clones. There isn't much color among the students. I mostly stick to myself." I shove a forkful of fish in my mouth.

He scrutinizes me, fork frozen in the air. "You're stronger than that, Little Bird." He places his fork on the table. "They will see your worth if you let them."

"They don't care about *my* worth. All they care about is what car they drive or whether they're spending the summer in the French Rivera or the Caribbean." I swallow. "I'm better off without them."

"Either you are a river or a rock."

"What?" I instantly regret asking, having unwittingly opened the door to another Sicheii lesson.

I can almost hear the door creak on invisible mental hinges as a grin sneaks on his face. "Both rivers and rocks existed on the

First World when time began. Rivers change with the conditions. Water will always find the least resistant path. Build a dam and the flow stops, or construct a canal and the river will flood the new easier path."

He pauses and I nod, so he continues. "The great rock formations are unchanging. They're unbending and have strength and value in their unique beauty and construction." He smiles knowingly as if he's made sense. "You don't have to choose between that school and your heritage. You're either a rock or a river."

I shake my head. He's definitely a rock. If only my life was as simple as his. Talk about rocks and rivers reminds me of the strange dog-like creature Troy and I saw at Slippery River. If anyone will know what it is, it'll be Sicheii, and he's the one person who won't think I'm crazy.

"When we were at Slippery River, Troy and I saw this really freaky looking thing. It was probably a dog, but it didn't have fur, just black skin stretched tight. It might have just been the sun, but I could have sworn it had wings on its sides. Have you ever seen anything like that?"

He stares at me for a long moment, and his eyes turn pensive. "Did you get a feeling from this... spirit. What did your heart tell you?"

I recall the moment and remember how I felt compelled to look at the cliff. *I did feel something.* "It radiated a strong energy that pulled me toward it. I had the feeling that it shouldn't be here, that it wasn't... natural."

He tents his fingers in front of his face and nods. "I've never seen anything like what you've described. However, the dark spirit, Coyote, can take many forms. He can even travel the stars and visit other worlds. Often he appears human, but other times

56

he will take on an animal shape. This is a worrying development. I need to know right away if you see this creature again. You are to avoid it at all costs. It's more dangerous than you suspect."

The doorbell rings and I jump.

"Are you expecting anyone, Little Bird?"

"Nope." I jump to my feet. No matter who's at the door, it must be better than another lecture from him about dark spirits and Coyote.

Daniels and Deputy Johnson stand on the front stoop and look through the small window in the center of the front door. I'm totally wrong. My heart leaps unevenly. *Do they know Troy and I were at the crime scene? Did the college kids file a complaint? How much trouble are we in?*

Sicheii appears behind me. I undo the chain lock and open the door. Sheriff Daniel's face is pinched tight, and his lips are turned down in a deep frown. Sweat rolls down the side of his face where he has a thin scar near his right ear. *Is he going to cuff me right now in front of my grandfather?* I'm so certain he's going to arrest me, I almost lift my wrists together and thrust them at him to make the entire process easier.

"Good evening, Juliet," he says as he looks beyond me and stares at Sicheii. "We need a moment alone with Jake." Daniels is tall and stocky with wide shoulders, but Sicheii's shoulders are wider.

"Of course, Sheriff," Sicheii answers. His legal name is Jake Clearwater Stone. I've always called him Sicheii, which is a Native American word for maternal grandfather. "Come right in." He casually waves Daniels and Johnson into the house as if he's expecting them.

Both men take off their hats and stiffly enter the foyer. They look nervous as they twirl their Stetsons. Daniels glances at me.

"If you don't mind, Juliet, we'd like to talk to Jake alone for a minute." He looks sullen and speaks softly, which I don't like. In my experience, the softer the voice, the worse the trouble. I stand up straighter and am about to tell him that I'm not going anywhere when Sicheii answers.

"Why don't we go into the living room, Sheriff?" Sicheii glances at me. "You should go back to the dining room and finish dinner before the meal gets cold. I'm sure this will be a brief visit."

Daniels shuffles forward with Johnson a step behind. They've never been inside our house before and their steps are uncertain.

Left with no real choice, I trudge to the dining room, but the expression on the Sheriff's face worries me. I swing the door mostly closed but keep it open a crack. The living room is on the other side of the house, so I really shouldn't be able to hear them, but what the heck? It's worth a try.

At first, only muffled sounds reach me, but when I concentrate harder, the voices become clearer and grow louder. Their husky quality tells me they're speaking in hushed tones, but they sound as clear as if they're standing next to me.

"I have some bad news, Jake," Daniels begins. "Charles Roundtree was murdered earlier today."

After a short pause, he continues. "Where were you earlier?"

"At the art gallery. Why?"

There's another pause, and then Daniels says, "One of Roundtree's neighbors said they observed you arguing with him yesterday."

"He said it got heated," Johnson adds in his gruff voice.

Sicheii sighs. "We've been fighting for forty years in the same way day battles night. You both know that, but I respected him and we had an understanding. He lived in balance with the world in his way. His way was different from mine, but I had nothing to do with his death."

A plastic bag ruffles. "Do you know what this is?" Sheriff Daniels asks.

"It looks like the tip of a ceremonial carving hatchet. I've never seen this one before."

"Can you identify anyone who could've harmed Roundtree or anyone selling Native American antiques like this one?"

The question is pregnant with suspicion. Of course — Sicheii is the most successful dealer in Native American antiquities in town, and everyone knows it.

"I don't have any idea who harmed Roundtree." Sicheii's voice sounds final and hard like stone. Heavy footsteps lead to the front foyer, so I push the dining room door open another inch to hear better.

"If I think of something, I'll call you." The front door opens and closes with a soft thud.

I scoot to the dining table and attempt to wrap myself around what they had just said. *Why did Sicheii lie about where he was earlier today?* He went fishing. He wasn't at his gallery. Roundtree's house abuts Fishkill River. We've gone fishing for trout from those waters before, but there are other rivers to fish also. He could have caught dinner at one of the other ones.

When Sicheii returns, his body is stiff. Tension bunches in his shoulders, and shows in the rigidity in which he walks, and the lines in his clenched jaw. "Roundtree was killed earlier today. You wouldn't know anything about that, would you?"

I try to display as much shock in my face as possible without overdoing it and shake my head.

He must have been fooled because he asks me, "Have you been feeling well lately, Little Bird?"

"Fine." It isn't the whole truth, but I'm not going to tell him about my recent headaches and those noises in my head. I can't predict what he'd do if he knew the whole story, but he certainly wouldn't like it, and I can't take the chance that he'll do something really weird.

He steps close to me, looming over me in my chair. A trace of his musky cologne mixed with the smoke from barbecuing the fish hangs in the air between us. He seems to gaze right through me. "Have you been experiencing any weird headaches?"

"Not me." I turn away and fiddle with my fork. Sweat beads on my forehead. Who would believe me? I am such a bad liar.

His face softens as if he feels sorry for me. The lines in his jaw disappear and the canyons in his forehead smooth. "The time is coming when we must stop lying to each other. Events are moving quickly. Soon, we won't be able to control the spirits. You must open your heart. You can't run from who you are." He lightly grazes my cheek with his fingertips. "I've got to go. I'll be home late. Don't wait up for me. Keep the door locked."

He looks worried, which is totally unlike him.

"Do you need help?" I ask.

His voice sounds stoic, sad even. "No, Little Bird. You can't help me with what I must do." He spins and strides out of the house. The Porsche starts up moments later and speeds away.

I'm left sitting in the kitchen feeling hollow, full of questions but no answers.

CHAPTER

I call Troy within five seconds after Sicheii leaves. "Sheriff Daniels and Deputy Johnson just stopped over. They questioned my grandfather about Roundtree."

He pauses for a second. "I'm sure they're talking to all the people who knew Roundtree. Jake has to be at the top of their list. How many other medicine men are there?"

"Yes, but they said someone saw Sicheii arguing with Roundtree yesterday. They showed him the tip of a ceremonial hatchet that was used to murder Roundtree. It's probably the same one Deputy Johnson found while we were at the house. They sounded suspicious."

"There's a long list of people who have argued with Roundtree. Don't worry about it, Jules. People here think his murder is connected to some type of drug deal gone bad. Maybe Roundtree stumbled onto a combination of roots or herbs he made into a new designer drug. You hear about them all the time on the news. He was known to dabble in things he shouldn't have messed with."

"I have a bad feeling about this, Troy. After the Sheriff left, Sicheii acted weirder than usual. He seemed to know about my headache from earlier in the day."

"You looked pale when I dropped you off. Did he ask you how you were feeling, and you said you were fine?"

"Yes, but he asked me specifically about headaches, like he knew I had been having some lately."

"We both know you're a terrible liar." He chuckles but it sounds forced to me. "And Jake has been a medicine man for a long time. He's like a natural lie detector. I'd never try to fool him."

Troy's not making me feel better, so I squeeze the phone harder. "He also said some weird stuff about spirits."

Ten seconds pass before he speaks. "What... did he say?"

"He mentioned Coyote and said something about running out of time." I try to remember what he said exactly, but the precise words don't come to mind. "That the spirits are going to take over soon or something odd like that. He took off in a hurry after the Sheriff left. He never explained what the heck he was talking about. But then again, he never does." I don't tell him Sicheii lied about where he spent the day. I'm not sure why, but it doesn't sound good when rummaging around in my head.

Troy hesitates again, which is unlike him. "It's probably nothing, Jules. Your grandfather lives a complicated life and believes spirits influence everything. He probably needs to... check in at the art gallery, or maybe he wants to break the news to someone close to Roundtree."

Both reasonable possibilities but they don't feel right. Sicheii didn't leave to deliver bad news and he wasn't worried about the gallery. He looked nervous and concerned about the *future*. I'm lost in a maze of possibilities, so I forget that Troy's on the phone until he says, "Juliet. Are you still there?"

"Yes. Why did you become so upset when Deputy Johnson found that ceremonial knife? Why does it matter what Roundtree was killed with?" That question had been bothering me since we left Roundtree's house.

"I know you don't believe in this stuff...."

"But..."

"But, the spirits didn't just die when Steve Jobs invented Apple. They still exist today, working their magic on us. We know *how* things work, but not the *why* so much. I think the spirits cause us to take action sometimes, whether good or bad."

"And the knife?"

"Ceremonial knives are dipped into the spirit world. They make the separation between worlds thin."

He wants me to agree with him or, at least, open my mind to the possibility that he's right, but I can't wrap my arms around spirits and spirit worlds. I won't lie to him, so I don't know what to say.

After a long pause that feels like two lifetimes, he says, "I've got to go, Jules. I have a math test tomorrow and I'm pretty sure the spirits aren't going to help me. Just chill out about your grandfather. I'm sure he's fine." Trace amounts of disappointment in his voice magically travel through cyberspace and brush against my ear.

"Sure. Good luck on your test." I hang up and go online to discover what torture, disguised as homework, my teachers expect me to complete. Bartens uses an online blackboard where teachers post assignments. I throw my pillow when the two-page Global History assignment pops on the screen.

Mom calls halfway through my homework. She sounds tired. "How was your day?"

"My day was fine." I'm determined to limit my lying, and let's face it *fine* could mean anything.

"Are you minding your grandfather? He didn't pick you up at school or embarrass you or do anything else you'll need therapy for, did he?"

"No, *Mom*." *Mom* stretches out in a kind of whine I'm not proud of. "Everything is good. How goes the conference?" I change the subject to avoid questions I don't want to answer.

"Great but exhausting." She perks up. "I moderated an outstanding panel on...." Her voice drones on. I'm not really paying attention, until she says, "Can you put your grandfather on?"

"He went... out to find a new... ice cream flavor from the Dairy Freeze. Something about... natural Indian corn." How lame is that? Especially since a wide assortment of ice cream takes up space in the freezer, but Sicheii is generally weird, so Mom has no problem believing he wants me to try a new "natural" flavor from the Dairy Freeze.

"Okay, Jules." She yawns. "I'm going to sleep. It's been a long day. We'll make up a strategy about Bartens when I come home. Love you, sweetie."

"I love you too," I say before hanging up and almost feel her relief through the phone that I'm no longer angry with her.

The rest of my homework takes me past midnight to finish. The orange numbers on my clock say it's 12:25, and Sicheii is still out. My thoughts are troubled, but my pillow is soft. Sleep finds me.

My eyes open, but I'm stuck in another dream. I'm outside on a clear night under a black canvas specked with dazzling points of light. The stars look brighter than usual, which means that no man-made lights from buildings or houses dim their brilliance. Sicheii would call it a new sky.

Four men are sitting around a campfire in a loose circle. Sharp peaks of red rocks jut up around them, creating a bowl effect as if they're in the middle of a crater. The campfire dances off of gemstones and crystals that litter the ground and reminds me of the old legend about Devil's Peak. The crown of the Devil's head is supposed to be covered with precious stones, but no one has ever climbed the peak, so no one really knows.

The men have long obsidian hair and wear leather shirts that are uneven on the bottom. Tan breechcloths hang from their waists. Even though the campfire is small, the gems glow red and purple around their feet, amplifying the light. One face is familiar—the man from yesterday's daydream. He sits cross-legged with four objects placed neatly in front of him. He's speaking the old language again. Even though I don't understand what he's saying, he's clearly in charge and has the full attention of those around him.

The other faces around the campfire are all different looking, with various ages and features, but they share the same expression. They look enraptured as if they're being told secrets that change everything. The leader lifts a small leather book and hands it to one of the men, who eagerly takes it from him. The process is repeated two other times with another journal and a small leather pouch.

My eyes strain to see the last item in front of the leader. It's hard to make out because it lies flat on the ground. The wind puffs. The campfire flickers brighter for a moment and reveals the item's outline. It's a crystal, sharp and beautiful, but it's still cloaked in shadows. A turquoise pendant dangles around the leader's neck. It looks familiar.

I've seen one just like it before, but where?

This meeting affects me somehow. I don't know how, but the feeling burrows deep into my mind. There's a connection between these four men and me.

What is it?

A shadow, lit by moonlight, appears in the night sky and circles the meeting. It flaps its wings, and I realize it's no bird; it has massive webbed bat-like wings and swoops lower toward me. It howls and the sound could break glass. The cry grows louder as the demon dives straight for me, and then I wake with a gasp, the rancid smell of spoiled fish in my nose, and realize my alarm has gone off. I try to smack the off button, but I miss and knock the clock off the bedside table and onto the floor. The buzzing stops when I pull the plug from the wall socket. I usually go through a couple of alarm clocks each year.

I stumble into the bathroom and start my day, brushing off the dream as just another byproduct from my active imagination. What could an ancient meeting among Native Americans have to do with *me*?

After a few minutes under a steady stream of hot water, the fog clears from my head. Memories of Roundtree, Sheriff Daniels, and Sicheii's hasty departure flash through my mind. I rush through my morning routine quicker than usual and scoot downstairs, wondering whether I'll find my grandfather.

Pueblo music, with its steady drumbeats and complicated vocals, wafts from the kitchen. I smell incense burning—jasmine and cedar wood. Sicheii has definitely returned. I open the kitchen door and he's standing by the island wearing a plush white cotton bathrobe tied around his wide frame. Steam spirals above a fresh mug of tea in his hand.

He flashes a full-faced grin at me as if it's a normal morning, as if Roundtree hadn't been murdered, as if the Sheriff never questioned him and he didn't race off in a hurry only to return this morning. "Good morning, Little Bird. What time does your bus arrive?"

I check the clock. "7:30." There's plenty of time. "When did you come home last night?"

He looks at me quizzically; both eyebrows arch upward. "Did you have any problems?"

"No, nothing happened." My face flushes with color. It's not my place to question him. *Besides, do I really want to know what he was doing?* So I drop it. He seems relaxed and unworried, which puts me at ease.

He claps his hands together. "Good, now let's enjoy our morning meal." He sweeps his hands at the kitchen table. A bowl of yogurt, fresh strawberries and blueberries, granola, and two glasses of orange juice await us.

I have no intention of sharing that meal with him. I barely eat breakfast as it is, so I walk into the pantry, grab a box of Kellogg's cornflakes, find a bowl, pour, and go to the refrigerator for some milk. When I return to the kitchen table, he's already sitting with a spoon in his hand. He shoots me an annoyed look, then closes his eyes and starts humming and meditating. I follow along and force my mind to go blank. I don't want a repeat of yesterday. I don't want to see Roundtree again. When he stops humming, I open my eyes.

I dive into my cereal with feigned enthusiasm and peek at him across the table. He starts singing along with the music, his mug held steady in front of him. His singing voice is rich and strong, but he can only reach two notes. It works when he performs ceremonies, but he'll never make it on American Idol. I told him this once, and he told me true music comes from the heart, not the voice.

I smile at him, but after a few minutes, his singing grates. "How's the art gallery? Was there an emergency last night?" I'm not sure why I start down this road, but once the words start coming out of my mouth, they keep tumbling out as if it's a jailbreak.

Sicheii glances at me, his expression blank. "The gallery is fine. All is as it should be." He deliberately places his mug on the table without taking his eyes from me. "Why don't you ask me about what is really on your mind, Little Bird?"

My chest tightens. "I was just thinking about Roundtree. Who could have killed him?"

"Roundtree was a complex person. He lived life in accordance with his own rules and the spirits he sought guidance from." Sicheii slides his mug away from himself. "He made many enemies. It's hard to say who could have wanted to eliminate his spirit. I'm sure the Sheriff will figure out who's responsible for his murder."

Normally, that explanation would be enough for me, but I'm still anxious and want more. "Sheriff Daniels seemed eager to talk to you." I gulped down half my glass of orange juice. "What did he want?"

"You have excellent hearing, Little Bird." He chuckles. "I'm sure you heard exactly what he wanted." He tosses a few blueberries in his mouth. "Why did your mother think I went out to buy ice cream?"

Of course she would try his cell phone. Sometimes, I can be so stupid. "She called and I didn't know what to say. She wanted to talk to you."

"The truth is usually best." A sly expression twists his lips and brightens his eyes. "She might be stuck in Scottsdale for a few extra days. She's meeting with a new client."

My heart sinks.

Sicheii glances at the kitchen clock. "You'd better catch the bus, or I'll have to drive you."

I leap to my feet. Sicheii driving me to school would be a major disaster. My head aches as I snatch my backpack from the floor and march out the front door. The smell of incense lingers in my nose as the morning sun temporarily blinds me.

This day is going to be a bad one. Sometimes you just know.

CHAPTER 10

Bartens uses the same beaten down yellow buses as my old school. It's the only similarity between the two places. Sure, they teach some of the same subjects, but that's in name only. Bartens specializes in AP or college level courses we'll never receive college credit for anyway. It seems like they want to skip high school altogether and make believe they're something they're not, a college. It's all smoke and mirrors — the illusion of harder class work to slip as many students as possible into the Ivies. The more Bartens students that go to Harvard, the more they can charge in tuition. You don't need to be a genius to figure that out.

I trudge my way on the bus, and tap George, the bus driver, on the shoulder. A storm cloud hovers over him, and a vision of the Suns game's score flashes in my mind's eye. The Suns lost big, and I get the feeling he bet a bunch on the game.

"Tough game last night?"

"Tell me about it." George closes the doors with a hard yank.

I glance down the length of the bus and a pit grows inside me. I'm used to the feeling by now. The same pit grows every time I step on the bus, *every* school day for the past two years. Only three other students take the ride. Each sits alone, and each looks as miserable as I feel. The bus could hold fifty students, yet the most it ever takes is five. No one wants to take the *Loser Limo* as the other kids call it. It smells — part sweat and part rotten food, as if old sandwiches are stuck in the seats. Katie sits toward the back. I sigh and plop down on the bench behind her.

"Hey, are you feeling better?" Concern is scribbled onto her round face in small lines that ring her eyes and mouth. "I texted you last night, but you never got back to me."

Guilt jabs me, and I smile weakly. "It must have been a twenty-four hour thing. My stomach feels much better." Katie is a straight arrow and would never have approved of my cutting class yesterday, so I fib to avoid the topic.

When the bus bounces along our way, she flops next to me, filling up her seat and overflowing into my space a little. She's slightly overweight. Nothing extreme, but in the perfect world of Bartens, she stands out, and no one wants to stand out. I've threatened more than one student about calling her names, like *Katie the Cow* or *Weighty Katie*. I haven't punched anyone yet, but I've come close.

Dark circles smudge underneath her bloodshot eyes, new tear tracks mark her cheeks, and she sniffles. This is bad. "What's up? Are you okay?"

She whispers even though no one can hear us anyway. "Channel Seven News did a special on my dad." She bites her nails — her nervous habit. They look like stubs. "The trial hasn't even started yet, and they've all but convicted my dad of these terrible crimes. They say he ran the largest Ponzi scheme ever." New tears brim her eyes.

I wrap my arm around her shoulders as fresh tears start dribbling down her face. "You shouldn't watch those shows. They're idiots. They'll say anything to trick people to tune in."

As the bus turns left through the arched brick entranceway into Bartens, Katie pulls out a tissue from her backpack. Going into school with watery eyes would be like spilling blood in shark-infested waters. The other kids are already vicious toward her. Some of their families lost a bunch in funds her father managed.

The bus lumbers toward the back of the main building past a half dozen different brick structures with tall windows, white wood trim, and even a round glass English conservatory where we eat lunch. The design might work for our sister school in England, but the Arizona heat makes it totally ridiculous.

We pull to a stop on the south side of campus, away from our lockers. A gust of hot air smacks us in the face when we hop off the bus. I check her face—all evidence she had been crying is gone, so we amble our way to first period, Global History.

Ms. Arnold stands in front of the classroom waiting for her students to arrive. She started teaching this year and bubbles with energy. Apparently no one's told her she's supposed to hate the students like the other teachers. She runs an art club and is the assistant tennis coach, has curly blonde hair that bounces to her shoulders, and looks like she's in great shape.

As I walk past, she asks, "Are you feeling better, Juliet?"

I sniffle, slump my shoulders, and frown slightly. "I'm feeling better." I add a slight cough for effect. "Yesterday was a little rough."

Small class sizes suck. There's no place to hide. Teachers always know who's absent, who didn't finish the homework, or who's distracted by some crisis or another. I hate it. I want to blend in the back of the room, be anonymous, but how can I disappear when the class only has three rows of seats?

She smiles and nods, but her eyes linger on me. She studied Native American culture at Arizona State, which explains why she stayed behind in our little town. A few months ago, she stopped in my grandfather's shop and talked to him about some of the antique tools. She stood in the back of the shop and pointed to a case with some arrowheads, a knife, and two hatchets.

I freeze and my throat tightens. *He had two hatchets.*

One of the kids on the football team bumps into me on the way to his seat, so I remember to keep moving as the rest of the students file into the room and class begins. Ms. Arnold wanders around the class, asking questions, prying open ideas and comments from students who'd rather keep them hidden. Global is my favorite class even if she gives a horrendous amount of homework.

The bell rings and she grabs my arm as I leave. "If you're still not feeling well, you should go to the nurse's office. I'm off next period and can take you."

I shake my arm free. "I'm feeling much better."

Katie and I leave the social studies wing, withstand another heat gust, march through the double doors, and enter the main classroom building to find our lockers. I pause for a second in the doorway, something is wrong. A vision of Tiffany's face with a sly grin flashes in my mind, and it makes me cringe. She's not visible yet, but she's up to no good. The bad vibes float toward me like a gust of wind.

I clear the doorway and a larger than normal crowd loiters in the hallway, which looks like a clogged artery. Four clusters of *cool* kids create an obstacle course down the tight corridor.

Between classes usually only a few people hang out near the lockers. Something is definitely up. A nervous energy fills the small space, so my antenna goes all the way up, and I look for Tiffany as we weave around pockets of students and head toward our lockers.

Tiffany, Morgan, and Ashley gather in a small circle across from our lockers, standing close together with smug expressions on their faces and smartphones in their hands. I hesitate for a second as a weird déjà vu feeling creeps up my back. Tiffany looks *exactly* as I imagined her only a moment ago. The Bartens uniform doesn't leave much room for improvisation, and Tiffany generally looks the same, her hair always perfect, as if a cosmic stroke of good luck blows her hair in the ideal place every day, but this similarity is uncanny. She *never* wears the same earrings twice. She must have a vault with them stacked inside. I doubt I've ever seen her wear these golden starbursts before, but I just saw her wearing the same ones in my vision. Weird.

I shake off the eerie feeling and focus on her and her shark pals. When they see us, she nods our way, and the rest of them snicker. She is the undisputed great white shark of Bartens, and it looks like she's ready to attack. I narrow my eyes. A piece of paper is stuck on Katie's locker, which is two down from mine.

Katie hasn't noticed the note yet. A distant look dulls her gaze, so, I grab her arm, pull her to a stop, and whisper in her ear, "Is that Tyler back by the door? I think he called your name." Tyler smiled at her last week, and that was enough for her imagination to weave stories of love, wedlock, a house, and a picket fence. He's one of the few nice kids, but I don't see any possible romance between the two. He's the star of the basketball team and smiles at everyone. *Still, why dampen Katie's imagination?* It's better for her to think about Tyler than her dad.

74

She squints and sorts through the thicket of students, which buys me just enough time. While she bites her nails, an explosive energy builds in my body and I bolt past her, dart forward and zip by the four groups of students in a blur. It feels like I reach the locker in one giant step, as though I'm fired from a gun.

A newspaper cartoon stuck to Katie's locker depicts a jail cell with her father's hands clutching the bars. A bald, beefy-looking inmate lurks behind him. The muscle-bound cretin blows him a kiss — a horrible thing to stick on her locker. She would have been devastated if she had seen it.

By the time she turns back toward her locker, I've ripped down the paper, crumpled it in my fist, jammed it into my backpack, and turn to face the great white shark. I'm not going to let them hurt her. They can say what they want about me, but Katie just can't take the ridicule right now. Blood pounds in my head.

Tiffany's face twists into a scowl and her nostrils flare out angrily. It transforms her perfectly symmetrical face into something misshapen, something mean. I sneer back at her when a sudden bolt of pain jolts through my head. She calls me *Indian Trash.*

I'm not going to let anyone call me that, especially not Tiffany, so red clouds my vision, and I run at her — straight through the pack of sharks in a blink. Before she reacts, I grab her shoulders and ram her into the lockers.

Clunk!

She crashes hard against the metal and grunts, but she manages to grab two fistfuls of my hair, and yanks me to her side. Pain shoots through my scalp. It feels like she's ripping out my hair, so I go for her throat and clasp my hands around her perfectly tanned neck. I squeeze and slam her head against the bank of lockers.

Clunk!

I let go of her throat as she slides down the lockers to the floor. I want to grab her perfect hair and rip out a handful, but the hallway bursts with teachers and commotion. Ms. Arnold grabs my arms and pulls me away from Tiffany while the shark staggers to her feet and bends over at the waist, grabbing the back of her head and wincing. I lunge at her, but Mr. Davies, my math teacher, stands between us and pushes me to the side, and Ms. Arnold increases her grip around my arms.

The entire pack of sharks point in my direction and shout. They scream out different things, but the brunt of their message is clear; I started the fight.

Tiffany smiles. Her face even uglier than it was with the scowl.

I sigh and let my arms drop to my side. This is going to be bad.

CHAPTER 11

I sit in the Headmaster's office in a small chair as far away from his mahogany desk as possible, my head hung low in my hands, pondering my fate. How much trouble am I in? How long will Mom ground me? The longest was two weeks when I got into a fight in ninth grade. I get the miserable feeling this time might stretch until my eighteenth birthday.

To distract myself from my impending doom, I study the office. This is my first time here. Cherry wood paneling stretches halfway up the stuffy walls. A tightly woven burgundy carpet covers the floor, and numerous portraits of unknown, disapproving, pasty-white men stare into the room with annoyed expressions as if they had somewhere better to go and are totally uninterested in what's going on around them. Twenty-two faces in total stare back at me. Who are these people, and why are they at my school?

The office smells old and dusty and a bit acidic, like corroded batteries. I'm not sure why. Maybe the smell comes with the paintings?

Forty minutes have passed since they dragged me here. Sicheii is supposed to retrieve me, but the time stretches on and seems like a dozen lifetimes.

The office door swings open and the Headmaster, Alistair Cordingly, strides into the room, followed by my grandfather. Cordingly matches the office, smells old and is imported from England.

He could not look more different from my grandfather, and for a moment I forget about my problems and smile. Cordingly's light complexion, thinning straw-colored hair, and general stuffiness are all England with no trace of Arizona. He wears a navy blue pinstripe suit with a gold tie and gold handkerchief as if he had just stepped out of a *Brooks Brothers* catalogue. No one likes him or understands what he does. All the students believe he has an expiration date stamped on his palm when he'll be called back to England or curdle like sour milk.

Sicheii rolls into the office a step behind him. His sky colored linen shirt billows around him and over faded blue jeans. His favorite straw, wide-brimmed hat with a lone hawk feather stuck into the band sits on top of his white hair. Confident and self-assured, he knows exactly who he is and why he's here. Neither Cordingly nor Bartens intimidates him in the least.

Cordingly uses short, brisk steps to retreat to the safety of his desk while Sicheii strolls behind him with easy loping strides. Safely behind his desk, Cordingly smooths his tie and settles into his leather chair, his smile fake, his small black reptilian eyes skittering around the office.

Sicheii makes him anxious. Instead of sitting in the chair opposite him, as I'm sure he expects, Sicheii saunters along the edges of the office while studying the portraits with a grim expression on his face. He's not interested in the paintings. He's sending Cordingly a message that he cannot be dismissed lightly. I sit up straighter. He's done the same thing to me many times. When I'm in a hurry and want an answer to some critically important question, he delays just long enough for me to realize he's in charge and will answer on his terms.

I smile now that Cordingly learns the same message. Time languishes for a few more uncomfortable minutes. Finally, Sicheii pivots on his moccasins and turns his attention to the Headmaster, who has been staring at him quietly, fidgeting in his chair and tapping his fingers on his desk.

"I believe the art someone surrounds himself with reveals much about his character." From his expression, it's clear Sicheii is unimpressed with the portraits.

"Yes, well, these are portraits of significant alumni from our sister school in England." Cordingly points to the largest portrait behind his desk. "That is Sir Godfrey. He served as Chancellor for England's High Court. He graduated from our very first class almost one hundred and twenty years ago. Some legal historians still write about his greatest verdicts today."

Sicheii regards the painting with his arms crossed against his chest. "I'm sure he was an impressive man in person." Switching his eyes to Cordingly, he bores them into him as if they were daggers. "I understand there is a misunderstanding involving Juliet."

Cordingly settles his gaze on me. He keeps if fixed on me probably because he's more comfortable looking at me than my grandfather. "Juliet instigated a physical altercation with another female student this morning." He frowns and taps on the desk. "I do not need to tell you how seriously we take this violation of our conduct code."

Sicheii's focus unwaveringly falls on Cordingly. He doesn't even blink. "In my experience, disagreements are two-way rivers.

The currents often travel up and down river. Perhaps the best way to fully understand the nature of this dispute is to ask both students what happened."

"In this case, all the witnesses report that Juliet attacked this other girl without provocation. This is not acceptable behavior at Bartens." Cordingly flattens his hands together, brings the tips to his lips, and glances at Sicheii. "I know she has a history of fighting in her other school. However, this is her first offense at Bartens. Is there some issue at home? Students often act out when matters are unsettled at home."

Mom is probably the only single mother at Bartens. For the first time, I'm happy she's out of town and Sicheii is here instead. She would have already buckled under the pressure and blamed everything on me.

"Who is the other student?"

"Tiffany Johnson, but I must repeat that all our witnesses confirm Juliet as the provocateur." Sweat sprouts on the Headmaster's forehead like weeds. He picks up an expensive fountain pen and twists the writing instrument in his hands. The Johnson family is an elite member of the privileged class in our town.

Sicheii flashes his sparkling white teeth. "According to your rules, both students involved in a physical altercation are supposed to be suspended for a week with a full hearing where the dispute can be heard."

When did he read the school's rulebook?

Cordingly sputters words so fast they bump into each other on the way out of his mouth. "Y-yes, those are the s-stated rules, but in this case I do not believe we need to follow the rules precisely. As I said earlier, this is Juliet's first offense and luckily it was a brief one. Today is Thursday. I suggest Juliet stay home tomorrow and ponder her actions. She can write an apology to Tiffany and return to classes on Monday." He glowers at me and slows his pace so the words come out measured. "Of course, we would have to take more severe actions if this behavior happens again. Perhaps even ex-pul-sion."

The last word takes forever from start to finish and sends a shudder down my back. I'd happily return to my old school, but expulsion would be bad — the type of offense that would stay on my permanent record and prevent me from going to a good college. If I don't go to a good college, I'll never get into a top graduate school. Without a top graduate school, there's no chance I'll land a high paying job and live in a big city in an apartment with river views and expensive clothes and Apple products and cars and vacations and all the other luxuries I'm supposed to want. At least that's what Bartens tells me, yet Mom makes a lot of money and I can't help but think she'd be happier with more free time and less stress.

"I'm sure there will be no more incidents like this one." Sicheii turns and saunters from the office without another word. He doesn't even glance at me.

I jump from the chair and race after him.

The Porsche is parked out front. Before I can buckle the safety belt, Sicheii pulls away from the curb with a squeak of the tires. His disapproval drapes over me like a wet blanket.

"What happened?" He speeds from school, working his way around slow moving cars.

"Tiffany stuck a nasty cartoon about Katie's father on her locker. I yanked it off before she could see it. When I turned, Tiffany called me Indian trash."

He keeps his eyes on the road as he works the manual stick shift. "Do you think you were doing your friend a favor?"

"Katie would have been devastated if she saw that cartoon. She was already upset over a news show from the night before that said her dad was guilty and going to jail."

He glances at me for the first time. "How is she going to feel when a new cartoon gets stuck on her locker tomorrow? Especially when you won't be around?"

"I didn't think about that." Heat flushes my face.

"A good friend helps those she cares about face their challenges, not hide from them. We must embrace our destinies. Did anyone else hear Tiffany call you Indian trash?" He turns down a side street, swerves the car to the side of the road, and stops so suddenly the seatbelt jabs into my chest.

"I heard her. It sounded like she yelled it to me, but no one else said they heard her say anything."

"Even Katie?"

I shake my head. "But I'm *sure* she said it."

Sicheii's white eyebrows arch for a moment and then turn downward as if they tired from the effort. "I thought we raised you stronger than this. You are special. Your blood is special, more special than you realize. How others view you is the least of your concerns. A rock doesn't care if others think it is a diamond or piece of clay. The rock is strong because of its nature." He frowns and appears sad; something in his eyes that's hard to identify seems melancholy. "You are special because of your nature. You must accept this. You must be the rock, not the river."

"I know they shouldn't bother me, but sometimes it's hard." Oddly, I think we're talking about two different things. With Sicheii, it's hard to know for sure *what* he's talking about. "Thanks for coming to get me."

Sicheii swings the car back on the road. "The spirits are not entities that lived a long time ago and have since died. The Wind

Spirit is as strong today as she was in our ancestors' times. She touches all of us, you in particular." He glances at me as if he is telling me a secret only meant for us to share. "I need you to think on this. I have errands to run today. I'm not sure when I will return."

Didn't Troy tell me the same thing last night?

CHAPTER 12

With nothing to do, I wander to my room, dive on my unmade bed, and pound my pillow a dozen times, making believe it's Tiffany's smug face. When feathers start flying about, I toss the Tiffany Face Pillow at my mirror, flip open my laptop, and surf the web. Googling Roundtree produces a number of hits that pop on the screen. The first three all relate to his death.

The Sentinel has the longest article with the headline "Mystic Slain at Home. " I skim the piece, looking for details, looking really for anything that would mean my grandfather wasn't involved in Roundtree's murder. I don't find what I want. The reporter quoted Sheriff Daniels as saying that he has no suspects in custody, but he's following up on a number of promising leads. The reporter raised the specter that the killing had something to do with the occult. He wrote that Roundtree had long been suspected of participating in satanic rituals.

Satanic rituals?

Roundtree was certainly weird, even stranger than Sicheii, but I can't imagine him involved in satanic rituals. The reporter probably made that up.

The last line of the article catches my eye. "Sheriff Daniels believes an arrest is imminent." *An arrest is imminent*? Did Daniels speak to the reporter before or *after* he came by last night? He didn't sound like he was close to arresting anyone then, unless that someone was my grandfather. But if he had any solid evidence against him, he would have taken him in for questioning. At least, that's what they do on the television shows.

Nothing else of interest appears in the current articles. All three local newspapers describe Roundtree as a secretive medicine man who had no family and lived an odd life. None hint at who might have committed the crime, or why, and nothing exonerates Sicheii. Only *The Sentinel* mentions anything about satanic rituals, which I dismiss as nonsense.

I glance at the rest of the search results and find some that go back over decades. Dozens of old stories show on the screen. Outspoken, he frequently criticized the town government and led a protest against the casino, claiming it was going to be built on a culturally significant site. The developers originally wanted to build the resort near Devil's Peak, but he forced a compromise. They moved the project to the other edge of town.

The protest made him unpopular with the developers and business owners in town who all supported the casino. A small blurb about him being arrested for disturbing the peace around the same time appears in a local paper. They probably tossed him into jail because of the protests against the casino. Still, fifteen years is a long time ago and the casino *was* eventually built. Now, it's the largest employer in town. Too much time has passed to connect his protest of the casino to his murder fifteen years later.

Since my news searches into Roundtree's life hit a dead end, I check the web for images of the medicine man. Most were snapped at one of our Native American festivals with him wearing traditional clothing. I hover over one image taken during a Changing Woman Festival, which marks thirteen-year-old girls as women. It's one of the most important Tribal ceremonies. It takes four days to complete and is full of dancing and singing.

We went to one when I turned thirteen. We've never lived on the Rez and have always been outside of the official Tribal structure, but Sicheii made me feel like I was part of the ceremony. He stayed with me the entire four days and explained all the ceremonies to me. I smile. He made me feel special; he made me feel connected to my Native American roots. Things seemed simpler back then, before Bartens

The other photos were taken years earlier when he protested the casino. One shows an angry Roundtree in handcuffs, long hair blowing in the wind, a twisted sneer plastered on his face. He isn't alone in the picture. He's in the center of a group surrounded mostly by Native Americans, but the other faces are fuzzy.

I scan further down the search results and notice a picture dated twenty-six years ago—a blurry photograph of a group of men around a campfire. I click on the photo and it enlarges. A caption underneath reads—Secret Native American Society Among the Shadows by John Dent, July 25, 1986.

Six men appear in the photo. Four are familiar: Sicheii, Roundtree, Samuel Brooks, and Joseph Hunter. Brooks's shirt is unbuttoned and reveals a tattoo on his chest. I zoom in on the ink, but the image becomes increasingly grainy. It could be the same two twisted arrows my grandfather and Roundtree have on their chests. Or, it could also be something totally different.

It's silly, but the photo reminds me of my dream this morning of the campfire and the ancient Native Americans. I can't put my finger on it, but when I study the expressions on the men's faces, I realize the connection. They share the same raptured look, as if they've been told an important secret, and a chill creeps down my spine.

I search for the article, which should be connected to the photo, but nothing shows up on the web. *Secret Native American Society?* I type the phrase into Google and Bing and then every other search engine I can think of, but nothing connected to Roundtree or our town comes up. I'm just about out of ideas when I Google John Dent's name. He wrote three articles, mostly about local events. None of the other articles were dated after July 25, 1986 — strange. It's as if he stopped writing altogether. I check for his address and find only one J. Dent nearby, and he lives in Old Town, not far from my grandfather's art gallery.

It's already past two when my phone pings. Katie has left me seven text messages, three emails, and one voice mail. I ignore them. She should have backed me up with Cordingly, so I toss my last pillow from my bed and go downstairs to the kitchen.

I gobble down a peanut butter sandwich and try to come up with a plan. I could ask Sicheii about this secret society, but without knowing any more facts, he'll likely just tell me something odd that makes no sense at all. Without more to go on, asking him will be a dead end.

My phone rings, and I glance at the number, worried it might be my mother, and find Troy's smiling face.

"What's up?"

"You're never going to guess what happened." He sounds edgy.

"I'm not guessing." He always wants me to guess at the latest news. It's annoying. "What happened?"

"There's been another murder in the Reservation."

An acidic taste burns the back of my throat. Two murders in two days can't be a coincidence. We might not live in the safest town, but two dead guys practically constitute a murder spree.

"You won't believe who they found dead this afternoon."

This time I take the bait. "Samuel Brooks." He lives in the same neighborhood as Troy and he's in the photograph with Roundtree and Sicheii. It's a silly guess, but the silence on the other end of the phone is deafening.

"How... did you know?"

I grip the iPhone hard. My hand turns red. "Something weird is going on. I'm worried Sicheii is involved in it."

Now that I've said the words out loud, I realize they're true and they frighten me.

"Stay put. I'll be right over."

CHAPTER 13

Troy arrives first on his bike, but Ella's beat-up white Ford Fusion pulls up right behind him. A fresh dent marks the front bumper where it looks like she hit a tree, and duct tape wraps around the side mirror, which dangles precariously from the door. That's not the only duct tape on the car — the right taillight and rear bumper both benefit from patches of tape to hold them together.

I open the front door, and Troy leads Ella and Marlon into the house. It's good to see my old high school friends again. I hadn't noticed how isolated I had become. It must be a couple of months since we last hung out together and that's too long. The fault is likely mine.

I march them toward the kitchen, grinning and shaking my head.

"What's the problem," Ella asks, a bite in her voice.

"I can't get used to you two together," I say. "You're barely half his size." She's just short of five feet and resembles a pixie with short brown hair, cream-colored skin, freckles that bunch around her cheeks, and wide, chestnut eyes. Marlon is quiet and big. He's slightly taller and wider than Troy, dark skinned, and round in a natural, puffy way like a human cheese doodle.

Ella shrugs. "You know what they say, opposites attract. Besides, I like my guys big."

"And we all know Ella's way tougher than Marlon," Troy adds, and more than a trace of amusement sparkles behind his eyes.

Ella chuckles. "Just don't call me—"

"Tinker." Troy and I complete the sentence for her.

We all laugh and it feels good. I feel a little more like the person I was before switching schools.

"Billy Trout will never be the same," Marlon says. We all smile and think back to eighth grade. A few of the older boys started calling Ella *Tinker*. She marched toward Billy, the largest of the bullies, kicked him hard in the shin, and pounced. Marlon and Troy pulled her off him, but not before she left the boy with a bloody nose, two black eyes, and one cracked tooth. No one dared call her Tinker again.

"He deserved it. Besides, he left me with no choice. No way I'm going through high school called Tinker. I'd rather cover myself with sugar and kick a beehive." Ella speaks in one quick burst.

When we reach the kitchen, Troy asks, "So how did you know someone murdered Sam Brooks? You couldn't have just guessed. What's going on?"

"I didn't know for *sure*." I lean against the center island.

"How did you guess, Juliet?" Troy rubs his hands together, his eyes suspicious, narrow slits.

"I was surfing Roundtree's name to find some clues why he was killed and came across an old photograph." After a few keystrokes on my laptop, the old picture pops up and I hand the computer to him. He holds it low so Ella and Marlon can see.

"Secret Society?" Marlon rumbles, his voice as deep as a desert well.

"I don't know what that's about, but my grandfather's in the photo, plus Brooks, Roundtree, and Joe Hunter. I don't recognize the other two guys."

"That one is Edward Taylor," Ella says. "I recognize him from old pictures at school. He died five years ago. I think he had cancer. He was also a medicine man."

"Another medicine man. What are the odds of that?" A nervous fluttering twists my stomach. We have a puzzle and the first pieces are fitting together, but a little voice in my head tells me it's going to be complicated, and I'm not sure I'll like the picture when all of the pieces fit together.

"This doesn't prove anything," Troy says. "It's probably just a coincidence."

"Did you find anything else about this secret society on the internet?" Ella asks.

I shake my head. "Nothing. Even when I Googled John Dent's name, only some old articles and an address for him in Old Town came up."

She takes the laptop from Troy. "Did you look through *The Sentinel's* archives?"

My blank expression tells her everything she needs to know.

"My uncle works at the newspaper. For their 50th anniversary last year, they placed all of the old editions on their website under archives so people can go back and look at them." She glances up from the computer. "It was in all the papers. They'll probably go totally electronic soon anyway. The cost of paper keeps going up, and they make most of their money on e-advertising. I'd be surprised if anyone prints a paper ten years from now."

Troy shrugs, and Marlon eyes the refrigerator. He's always grazing.

"Are you guys hungry?" I ask. "We have leftovers in the fridge."

Marlon swings his wide frame toward the fridge. "No need to trouble yourself." He opens the door. "I'll help myself."

Ella has *The Sentinel's* website up and clicks the Archives tab. "Do you remember the date of the photograph?"

Marlon carries a plate of fried chicken in one hand and a drumstick in the other. "Did you know there are more chickens than people in the world?"

"Where'd you get that from?" Troy asks.

"Snapple cap. And the date on the photograph was July 25th 1986." The words compete for space with chicken. When I shoot him a look, he shrugs. "I have a good memory."

"Like an elephant," Troy jokes.

"You're just jealous," Ella says.

My world goes fuzzy. One moment Ella is typing on the laptop and the next, my mind swims, my legs buckle and a splitting pain cracks open my skull. A jumble of voices all mutter at the same time. They don't make any sense. I try to block out the sound and shake my head from side to side. Worried I might fall, I lean heavily against the counter and luckily, the pain and noise vanish as quickly as they came.

Troy grabs my waist. "Are you okay, Jules?"

All three faces stare at me nervously. I don't like their expressions, especially Troy's, so I shake him off and lie. "I'm fine. I haven't eaten anything in a while. I got a little dizzy." Apparently, the new me lies constantly.

Marlon thrusts the plate of fried chicken toward me. The last thing I want is to eat something, but what choice do I have? I grab the smallest drumstick and bite into the chicken with fake gusto.

"You're sure you don't want to lie down or anything?" Troy asks.

"I'm good." To prove it, I finish the chicken leg in three bites and hope to keep it down.

Ella types in the date for the article and flashing red words appear - *Improper Date*. "That's odd." She tries the day before. The newspaper appears on the screen. "Hmm," she says, and tries the date after. Another newspaper pops on the screen.

"Someone's deleted the July 25th issue from the archives," she explains. "I wonder why. The issue before and after are both available online. Every issue *The Sentinel* has ever published is supposed to be on the archives. That's what they said."

"It's obvious," Marlon rumbles.

We all stare at him. This time, he holds a chicken wing in his hand.

"Someone doesn't want us to read what's in that paper."

I have a sick feeling he's right.

"We can ask your grandfather," Troy suggests. "I'm sure he would remember an article written about secret Native American societies with his picture attached to it. There's probably an easy explanation for all this."

"No way. We need to know more before I ask Sicheii. I have a feeling this is more complicated than a newspaper article. Too many coincidences are lining up, and I don't like the way my grandfather is in the middle of them. He could be in trouble."

I retrieve the laptop from Ella and type in a search for Dent. The address for J. Dent in Old Town flashes onto the screen. "We're going to have to visit Mr. Dent and ask him."

"Let's go for a drive," Ella says.

Marlon places the now empty plate into the sink. "I'm in." He takes Ella's hand and marches toward the front door.

I know it isn't right, but a twinge of jealousy stabs me in the side. I've never had a real boyfriend. I sneak a furtive glance at Troy, who follows the happy couple a step behind. He's always been around, but our relationship has never been more than just friends. I'm not sure why, or if I even want it to be more. He's had many girlfriends over the last couple of years, but we have an unspoken agreement. I never ask about them, and he never tells me.

How stupid is that?

CHAPTER

Ella zips through traffic on her way to Old Town, revving the engine hard, swerving around a slow moving station wagon and plowing across a light she claims had just turned orange. She drives the way she thinks: fast and on the edge of chaos. I try not to look out the window as we screech to a stop inches away from a truck stopped at a red light.

Troy sits in the backseat with me and we share a look. Driving with Ella is a little like riding a roller coaster without the safety features.

"How did you guys find out about Brooks?" I ask no one in particular, hoping to distract myself from the swerving and screeching of tires.

"Marlon lives a few blocks from his house. He saw police cars and his brother at the scene," Troy says.

"His brother?"

"Yeah. He started working for the sheriff's department a few weeks ago," Troy says.

"Good for him," I say.

"If he doesn't screw up, I'm hoping he'll get me a job after high school," Marlon says.

"With your brother, that's a big *if*," Ella shoots me a look in the rearview mirror. "He was late for his first day. He forgot to set the alarm."

"Could happen to anyone," I say. "Some of us aren't morning people. How did Brooks die? Was he tortured like Roundtree?"

"My bro didn't give me the details, but he looked white and his face puckered up like he was about to lose his lunch. I could tell from his expression Brooks was murdered. I don't know about torture."

"The two killings have to be connected." I sigh. A sick feeling tells me these murders are tied to the photograph and my grandfather. I just need to figure out how the pieces fit together before Sheriff Daniels or the killer.

Ella swings the car into a parking lot on the East end of Old Town and screeches to a stop between two white SUVs with out-of-town plates. Old Town consists of a collection of narrow winding cobblestone streets, which are too tight for cars. Locals rarely come to Old Town except to work. As a young girl, I used to go with Sicheii to his art gallery during the weekends when Mom went to her office. We spent many hours in the ice cream shop next to his gallery. I always got chocolate and rummaged through the red rock souvenirs they sold from large plastic boxes.

As we pile out of the car, I ask, "Do you guys know if Brooks had a funky tattoo on his chest?"

They all shake their heads.

"Why?" Ella asks.

"Roundtree had weird ink on his chest. I saw it in one of the pictures. Maybe it's a clue." I don't mention my grandfather's tattoo. I feel bad about withholding information from my friends, but I don't want to make my grandfather seem more like a deranged killer than he already does. After all, he's still my grandfather. There must be some explanation for these murders that doesn't involve him wielding an antique hatchet.

We walk mostly empty streets, it being that lazy time after lunch and before dinner. The address for Dent lists him on 3rd Street. While Old Town attracts mostly tourists, many of the old brick buildings still have apartments above the storefronts.

My legs grow heavy as we approach Sicheii's gallery on the way to Dent's place. We pass two restaurants and one t-shirt shop. I slow to a creep when we cross the street and onto the block with his gallery. I stop at the ice cream shop next door and feel a little foolish. My relationship with Sicheii has always been complicated. He's not like a normal grandfather who sits in a rocking chair, reads books, and goes to school plays. He has an edge, a wild side he's only shared with me in glimpses. He sees life differently from most. I worry that edge has gotten him into real trouble this time as I peek through the window into the gallery.

"Who's talking to Lisa?" Ella asks. "They seem to be having quite an argument."

Lisa waves her hands and leans forward aggressively. Ms. Arnold crosses her arms against her chest, her face flush.

"She's one of my teachers from Bartens. I didn't realize they knew each other, but they both went to Arizona State." I start to feel a little dizzy. I'm sure they're arguing over my grandfather, and the argument has something to do with these murders. I have no idea how or why, but I had better find out soon.

"Well, whatever they're fighting about, they certainly seem angry," Ella says. "I don't see any sign of your grandfather."

I don't like waiting around on the street by the gallery. I keep expecting Sicheii to jump out from behind me like he's done a hundred times before. I bite my lip to gain control over my imagination. The pain helps.

I'm about to suggest we move along when a wet, sticky, tongue licks my fingers. I look down and find a chocolate cockapoo staring up at me. My attention was so fixed on studying the gallery I didn't notice the dog sneak up on me. He's knee high, has beautiful chestnut eyes, curly fur, and a cute little soul patch of gray fur on his chin. He cocks his head to one side as if he's asking me to rub the fur on his head, so I oblige, and swear he smiles at me.

A middle-aged woman jogs toward us. "Come back, Charlie!" she shouts as she crosses the street.

"Don't worry, the Dog Whisperer has him," Ella tells the red-faced woman.

"I'm so sorry. He never runs like that. I don't know what got into him." She grabs the end of his black leash.

Charlie sits at attention and stares at me and drags a smile from me because he could be the cutest dog I've ever seen. "I just have this effect on dogs." I shrug. "They seem to like me." Dogs have always acted weirdly around me. I don't know why. Troy used to joke that I smell like a milk bone, but he stopped since I stomped hard on his foot and elbowed him in the gut the last time he said that two years ago.

Ella rolls her eyes. "I'll never go to a dog park with her again. One time, three dogs jumped on top of each other just so she could pet them. That's why we call her the Dog Whisperer."

"Do you have one of your own?" the woman asks.

"No, Mom's allergic."

The woman shoots me a sidewise glance and says, "Thanks" to me, and, "Come on," to Charlie. I watch as she leads the dog away. He keeps looking back at me, but she tugs him along.

"You could always walk dogs for a living," Marlon says.

"Really?"

"What? Dog walkers make good money."

"Let's keep going." I tug on Troy's arm.

We scoot past the gallery toward 3rd Street. We take a right onto Dent's road and stop at number 125, right next to Aunt Maye's Big and Tall Western Outfitter. A blue neon sign makes it clear where we are.

"This store is perfect for you, Marlon," I tease him.

He wrinkles his face. "I doubt they have my style."

I grin at his oversized t-shirt and loose fitting shorts.

"Marlon likes casual chic." Ella chuckles as she loops her arm around Marlon's. I chuckle along with her, but a new pang of jealously stabs at me. They seem so close. *Do they know how lucky they are?*

A glass door stands to the left of the storefront. I check the names on the directory. J. Dent lives in apartment 302. The walkup uses a buzzer system.

"How are we going to get in?" Marlon asks.

"Should we buzz Dent?" Ella suggests. "Or maybe we should buzz everyone else and hope someone lets us in. Of course, there's a third option."

All eyes turn to me. This is my show. "I vote for the third option. We should surprise him." I glance at Troy. "Can you pick the lock?"

He frowns, leans forward, and examines the lock. It's an old pin and tumbler, something that hasn't been updated for decades.

By the time he looks up, Ella has already grabbed a bobby pin from her hair. Troy grins, takes the pin, and removes his keychain from his pocket, which has an assortment of small tools stuck in it. He slides out an Allen Wrench and goes to work on the lock.

Troy twists the wrench, the latch clicks, and the door opens. "After you," he says as he holds the door open.

I lead us up the wooden staircase, and in a minute we're facing apartment 302. Only three apartments are on the floor. 302 faces the street and has a simple red wooden door with brass numbers toward the top. My pulse accelerates. Some of the puzzle pieces are behind this door. I rap on it three times, wondering if Dent is home, wondering what we'll learn.

We wait. Time slows. Marlon breathes heavily behind me. Anxiety surrounds us like moisture in a rain cloud. Just when I think no one is home, a rustling sound comes from inside the apartment.

As the noise gets closer, a high-pitched voice cries out, "It's about time. The toilet won't flush since this morning. I'm too old to wait all day!" The door opens and a thin, gray-haired woman stands on the other side. She twists her severe, gaunt face into a question. "Who are you? Where's Carlos, the Super?"

I'm in front, so I manufacture my sweetest smile. "We're looking for John Dent."

A sad shadow drifts across her face. The expression is fleeting, as if she's had much practice chasing it away.

"There is no John Dent living here. You have the wrong place. I'm Jane Dent." She starts to swing the door closed, but she moves slowly, so I walk into the apartment before she gets the chance. I don't know where this confidence comes from, but there's more to the story, and I need some answers. My friends reluctantly follow me.

"I didn't invite you in," the old woman protests, but she moves to the side as we walk past her. The apartment is nicer than I expect—exposed brick walls, hardwood floors, and tall windows with a view of Old Town.

She shuts the door behind us. Her voice lilts, fading at the end. "So why are you looking for my John?" Her eyes pierce mine and sparkle like emeralds.

"John Dent wrote a newspaper article we're interested in," I say. "We thought we could ask him a few questions. It's for a school project."

The old woman leans against a dark blue couch. Behind her is a fireplace with a plain brick mantel with family pictures placed on the ledge. The largest picture shows a middle-aged woman with her arm around a young man's shoulders. They have the same green eyes, her eyes. Other pictures flank that one - pictures of grandchildren and two women who also resemble her. They're probably her daughters.

"John wrote a few newspaper articles, but that was a long time ago." She crosses her arms against her chest. The sleeves of her thin yellow blouse droop from her wrists. "I can't help you with them."

"Do you know where he is?" I study her closely, trying to read her. "We need to talk to him."

"My John died some time ago. You need to leave, or I'm calling the police." She bites her lip.

I hesitate. There's more that she's not telling me. I can feel it. Troy has already started for the door, but I stay solidly in place. "When did he die?"

The old woman's eyes flutter to the floor. "Four years ago. Now please go. I'm sure Carlos will be coming any minute."

I nod, and we leave. When we reach the street, we bunch together in a huddle.

"That seems like a dead end," Troy says.

"Really, Troy?" Ella says. "She was hiding something. It was obvious from her body language. Something happened to her son that she doesn't want to tell us."

"She only had one picture of him on the mantel, and he looked like he was in his twenties," I say. "I wonder when he really died."

"There's only one way to find out," Ella snaps. "We'll go to the cemetery."

"Let's stop at Tito's Tacos first." Marlon licks his lips.

"I can't believe you." Troy jostles him with an elbow.

"What? I'm hungry."

CHAPTER 15

Packed as usual, a line stretches beyond the Tito's Tacos food truck at least ten customers long, and when one leaves, another takes his place—mostly day laborers that quit work early, but a few others with collared shirts and khakis who might work in Old Town blend in, too. No one from Bartens is here. I'm not surprised.

Do I belong, or have my two years at Bartens changed me so much I'm no longer welcome at Tito's?

I grind my teeth. I'm not as close with my friends as I was before Bartens. It's not any one thing, but the ease we used to have between us is not the same. I'm always one step behind, trying to catch-up. I should have known that Marlon's brother got that job with the Sheriff's Department, but now these things, small but important things, slip by without me knowing.

Which world do I belong in?

It can't be both. Sometimes I feel isolated, like I'll never belong anywhere. Troy and Katie are really my only two links to both worlds—the only two I can count on, but some days that's not enough. There's ice beneath my feet and it's cracking. I'm afraid if I fall in, no one will be around to help me out. Sicheii wants me to be a rock, but if I'm a rock, can I be comfortable in both places like he says, or neither?

What if I'm just not strong enough?

I take a deep breath and my lungs fill with a greasy, spicy scent that makes my mouth water. I imagine that odor lingers well after Tito's Tacos is gone. It probably lives in the trees, the soil, the rocks....

The smell helps cleanse my thoughts and snaps me back to the present. We sit on a picnic bench as far away from the food truck as possible. Marlon has already eaten three tacos and launched himself into his fourth without any loss of enthusiasm. He's a taco-eating machine.

"So what do we know?" Ella asks. "Someone killed Roundtree and Brooks. They both died violently, within a day of each other, so both murders are probably connected."

"Brooks, Roundtree, Hunter, Taylor, Juliet's grandfather, and one other person were in the photograph," Marlon adds between bites. "And that article was removed from the newspaper's website."

"Yes, and John Dent died, and his mom lied to us about when. I have a strange feeling his death is connected to these two new murders," I add.

"We don't know that she lied." Troy purses his lips. He looks frustrated and rubs his hands over his face, which is unlike him. "There may be no connection between the killings and the photograph. The picture was taken over twenty-seven years ago. That's a long time. Brooks and Roundtree were both old and knew each other. There could be many other explanations for the murders."

"True, but you have to admit it's strange that the only edition of *The Sentinel* not online is the one with the photo. Marlon is right." I frown at Troy. "Somebody doesn't want us to see the article."

Marlon beams a smile at me as he shovels the last bite of taco in his mouth. "Guess what's my favorite day of the year!" A small river of pepper sauce leaks down the side of his face and splashes onto his t-shirt.

Ella hands him a napkin.

"Christmas?" I say.

"Nope. October 4th."

"Why?" Troy asks.

"October 4th is National Taco Day."

"Great." I smile and shake my head. "Let's find John Dent's gravestone so we can discover when he died. I'm sure his mother lied about that, and if she did, something else must be going on."

"What about John Dent's Secret Society article?" Ella asks as she rises from the bench and stretches. "What could he have been writing about?"

Troy shrugs his shoulders. "Outsiders have always believed rumors of secret societies involving magic or pagan rituals among the tribes. He probably wrote some nonsense along those lines. I doubt there's much to it. If a secret society exists, they're sure doing a good job of keeping it quiet."

"That would be the point, Troy." Ella rolls her eyes.

"Your attitude is starting to bug me." I jab my finger at him.

"Why? Because I have a hard time believing there's a secret society filled with people we know that's been meeting for over thirty years. And this secret society has dangerous information that someone's willing to murder to discover?" He uses air quotes when he says secret society, and I want to deck him. I know it sounds far-fetched, but the pieces are starting to fit together, and there's more to this mystery that I need to find out.

"Actually, Troy, there have been many secret societies that have gone on way longer than thirty years." Ella ticks them off with her fingers. "There's the Skull and Bones, the Freemasons, the Templars, the Illuminati—"

"Don't forget about Area 51," Marlon interrupts. "We all know the government has an alien corpse hidden in Area 51."

Troy shakes his head and lifts his arms up in mock surrender. "I give up. Let's go find the gravestone and discover when John Dent died. Maybe he was abducted by aliens."

I walk briskly toward Ella's Ford. Moving feels good. Time is running out. The cemetery is huge, and the sun has started sinking. We don't have much light left.

Ella pilots the Ford into the cemetery's massive parking lot. The place is quiet—no more than ten cars are parked toward the entrance. All the locals use this cemetery, including the town's five founding families. I don't even know if there's another one around here.

As we walk through the gate, we hear the bubbling sound of the meandering creek that splits the burial grounds roughly in half. Narrow green bands dotted with grass and a few short conifer trees create a thin line on both sides of the stream. When the graves spread away from the water, clay, red rocky soil and random cactuses replace the grass.

"Let's split up in two groups," Ella suggests. "Marlon and I will cross the bridge and check the West side of the cemetery, and you two can stay on this side and search the East side."

Troy and I walk methodically down the rows of the dead. I spot a palm-sized piece of petrified wood and start tossing it and catching it as we go.

106

"I don't understand why anyone would want to be buried in a box," Troy says as he marches, head swinging from side to side. "I want to be cremated and returned to the earth, so my death will benefit other living things."

"You sound like Sicheii."

"That's not a bad thing. There's value in the old ways. You can't ignore them."

"The world has changed a lot since the old ways." I trudge up and down the rows and keep my head down while I study the names. I call out the unusual ones to pass the time. Most of the gravestones are simple rectangles half buried in the ground. "To advance, we need to evolve. No one hunts buffalo with bows and arrows anymore, Troy."

"You used to care more about our traditions before you went to that school." Troy kicks some loose stones.

He's right. I was closer to Sicheii back then and would spend lazy afternoons with Troy talking about Sicheii's stories and the different spirits. We don't do that anymore.

Troy romanticizes our past and believes the old ways are more than superstitions primitive people needed to get by. Technology replaces all those superstitions for me. Who needs the Wind Spirit to praise or Coyote to fear when we have Apple and the Internet and science and the super-mean spoiled sharks at Bartens to fight?

We wander into the oldest part of the cemetery, and a row of old stone mausoleums appears on our right.

Troy points to the crypts. "I'll check the newer section of the cemetery on the other side of the tombs. Call out if you find anything."

He doesn't wait for me to say anything and jogs off. He's still a little steamed. I don't blame him; he's been a better friend to me than I deserve.

Feeling like a slug, I weave my way among the tombstones when the wind gusts, and the stink of rotten fish spoils the air. My blood freezes. It's the same rancid odor the weird dog-like creature gave off at Slippery River. I absolutely never in a million years want to turn around, but the smell becomes stronger. They say what you don't know won't hurt you, but in this case it might chomp me into little bits.

I turn and a shadow stalks toward me, not more than a dozen paces away. Just because it looks like a demon from hell, doesn't mean that it means me harm. Maybe it just wants to play?

"Nice demon," I say in my best dog voice.

It moves toward me and flutters its creepy wings for a second.

I don't know what it is, but it isn't a dog.

The demon pauses for a second and stares right through me. For a moment I think it might not attack, but that moment passes in a hurry. It snarls and the muscles in its legs tense.

I shout, "Troy" and run. My body feels electric as I bolt forward. I'm moving fast, but the demon's snarls grow louder and the rancid smell stronger. I need a place to hide, but I've run away from the mausoleums and the cemetery is nothing but open space and tombstones. I pump my legs, but the demon's breath, hot and nasty, burns my neck.

I turn to look at the thing over my shoulder. It's only two paces away, and although its short front legs makes its gait look weird, the damn thing moves like a greyhound. I can't outrun it. When I face forward again, my leg trips on a tombstone, and I face plant onto the dirt.

Great. I spin and the demon stands over me. It rises on its two back legs and spreads its wings out from its body. Its sharp front claws are sure to rip my throat out. It snaps its jaws and foam bubbles from its mouth.

I chuck the piece of petrified wood in my hand at it, and the demon catches it in its jaws. Two bites later, the beast reduces the stone to dust.

I shrink away from the monster, and my shoulder bumps into something hard—a tombstone.

The demon pounces and I grab the stone and yank. It comes free from the ground, and I swing it into the monster's face. It connects hard and knocks the demon to the side. I drop the marker and scramble to my feet.

The demon is out cold.

Troy shouts, "Juliet," as he runs toward me. He stops a step away and looks confused. "Are you okay? I heard you shout my name."

"I'm fine, but it's not every day I get chased by a demon." I turn to look at the monster and it's gone. "What the heck. It was just here."

He touches my arm. "What was here?"

I spin in a circle and feel foolish. "The demon from the river yesterday. It *did* have wings and it was going to eat me. I smashed it on its nasty demon head with the tombstone and knocked it out."

"It probably ran off." Troy tries to lift the stone marker, but he can't. "This thing weighs a ton. I can't even lift it. How did you raise it?"

I dust dirt off me. "You have to believe me. It was just here." I expect him to make a joke or say I'm crazy, but he doesn't.

He looks honest and worried. "I believe you, Jules. Some things are hard to explain."

I sigh and a chill washes through me. "When I talked to Sicheii last night, he said the demon thing might be Coyote in another form. Do you think Coyote has anything to do with these murders?"

He shrugs. "It's possible, but for now, let's keep this to ourselves. There's no way Ella or Marlon would believe us."

I nod and try to lift the stone, but I can't budge it. *How did I clobber the demon with that?*

While I'm close to the ground I notice something odd on the old tombstone and hesitate. It looks like a circle is carved into the stone. Dirt has crusted over it, so I wipe off the brown bits of earth and stare at the marker for a moment and wonder if my eyes are playing tricks on me, but they aren't. A Steven Holden died in 1845. Next to his name is a carving of two twisted arrows in a circle. The carving looks the same as Roundtree and Sicheii's tattoo — exactly the same.

My chest tightens and goose bumps run up my arms. I stare at the symbol and wonder what it means. Steven Holder doesn't sound like a Native American name, but there was a time when young Native Americans were taken to "American" schools to change them into "Americans," including changing their names. Maybe he was one of those people.

"Did you find something?" asks Troy.

"No," I answer, reluctant to share the symbol with Troy or anyone else. The twisted arrows worry me. It's connected to Sicheii and the more often it shows up, the more likely he's in the middle of a storm.

My phone pings. "It's from Ella."

He slides over. "Let's see what she found."

I click on the text. It contains a photograph of a tombstone. I enlarge the photo, and the writing is clearly visible: "John Dent, Born April 15, 1961 – Died July 26, 1986."

My heart races. "John Dent died the day after his article was published."

But that's not the worst part. Next to his name is a carving of two twisted arrows in a circle.

CHAPTER 16

We regroup in the parking lot near Ella's Ford. Troy and I have been arguing the entire trip back to the car. He's being stubborn. "There has to be a connection between John Dent's death and the article. It can't be a coincidence that he died the day after he published the story, Troy," I say.

He just stares ahead, a blank expression on his face. I've seen that look dozens of times. He's lost in thought. The gears spinning in his head are almost visible. Usually he'd have no problem believing in a conspiracy, but since this one involves Native Americans, he's struggling with it. He doesn't *want* it to be true, but I don't *want* my grandfather involved in this mystery and the evidence is starting to stack up. Sometimes things happen you can't control.

"I think you're right," Ella says, "and did you see that weird symbol after John Dent's name on his gravestone? I've seen it before, but I can't place it."

My heart skips. I was hoping to keep the twisted arrows a secret, but if Ella has already noticed it, I don't have a choice. She deserves to know everything. I swallow the lump in my throat and say, "Roundtree had the same symbol tattooed on his chest, and I saw the same thing on another tombstone in the cemetery, an old one."

"That's why you asked us if Brooks had a tat," Marlon says, "to see if he had the same one?"

"But why didn't you tell us about the symbol right away?" Ella's eyes sharpen and her hands fly to her hips.

I sigh. "My grandfather has the same tattoo on his chest. I don't know what it means, but I'm sure he's mixed up in this mess somehow."

"The symbol was probably just a popular design thirty years ago. I've never seen it before," Troy says.

"Perhaps it has something to do with this secret society Dent wrote about." Ella purses her lips. "We need to visit Joe Hunter. He's in the photograph. He should know something."

Hunter owns a general store near the Reservation that makes the best flavored ices. He used to work in the store all the time, but now his nephew usually sits behind the counter, which only makes the store more popular among teenagers because his nephew will sell beer to almost anyone.

"Hunter lives in Red Rock Commons," Marlon says.

We all shoot him a look.

"*What?* My grandmother's dating him."

"Your grandmother's a hundred years old," Troy jokes, which is more like his usual self.

Marlon shrugs one of his beefy shoulders. "You know what they say. One hundred is really the new seventy-five." Marlon leads us to the car.

Troy lingers a step behind, so I playfully shove him. "Come on. Maybe we'll interrupt Marlon's grandmother and Hunter on a hot date."

Troy moans as we file into Ella's car. "Great. That's a picture I don't want to see."

Ella floors it and swerves the car onto Route 100, barely sneaking in front of a blue BMW. Red Rock Commons is a senior community made up of townhouses not far from the cemetery. It takes less than ten minutes for us to enter the complex.

"Hunter's unit is number 127," Marlon says.

I point out the sign for Unit 125, which means we're close, so Ella swings the Ford into a parking space on the right side of the street next to a plain white van. After we pile out of the car, we plod our way to 127.

"What are you going to say to him?" Troy asks.

"Beats me. I guess I'll have to wing it." When we turn a corner, we see Unit 127 and a gray sedan in the driveway. As we reach the curb, the front door to the townhouse opens. Joe Hunter steps through and slams it shut. He's wearing khakis, a blue cotton shirt, and clutches a green and red-checked Samsonite in his right hand.

He sees us and speeds his pace toward the car. I move to intercept him, and we reach his car at the same time. Hunter's eyes touch on us, but mostly they dance down both sides of the street.

"I'm in a rush, kids." He presses a button on his key and pops open the trunk. Sweat runs down both sides of his face, and his shirt sticks to his body. The day is still hot, but not *that* hot.

I jump right in. "Does your trip have anything to do with Roundtree and Brook's murders?"

Hunter hoists his bag with a grunt, his arms shaking against the weight as he drops the Samsonite in the trunk. He looks inside the trunk as he talks. "I knew them both. They were good men." He slams down the trunk with a thud.

I step between him and the driver's-side door. Marlon and Ella flank me and we create a sort of human wall between him and the door. "Tell us about this secret society you're all part of."

He frowns at us, but his attention is still elsewhere. His head swivels from side to side. Fear drips off him as if he's just taken a dip in a pool.

He speaks fast, too fast. "I don't know what you're talking about. I need to go."

When he moves toward us, I stand my ground. "Do these murders have anything to do with the two twisted arrows in a circle?"

He freezes, touches the collar of his shirt, and stares at me wide-eyed. "Juliet Stone, you of all people should not be asking these questions. These are dangerous times."

"I don't understand what's happening. Is my grandfather mixed up in all this?" My heart is thumping.

He smiles at me with moist eyes, grabs my hand, and kisses the back of it. "You are a remarkable young woman. For the answers you seek, you'll need to ask Jake. I wish I could be there when he tells you what you need to know, but I must go. It's for everyone's protection." He sweeps his eyes across all of us, but they linger on Troy. "You shouldn't be here. You need to be careful."

"Careful about what?" Ella asks, her hands on her hips again.

He pulls me close to him and whispers in my ear. "You're special, Juliet. You've been *chosen*."

CHAPTER

"Holy cow! That was creepy," Ella says as she turns to watch Hunter drive away. "He sure seemed scared."

I can still feel his lips pressed against my skin as his car zips out of sight, so I wipe the back of my hand on my jeans. "Let's go." I start walking toward Ella's car.

"What did he tell you? Why did he whisper something in your ear? Was it some type of secret? Why couldn't he tell *all* of us? Did it have anything to do with your grandfather?" Ella asks all five questions in one quick burst as if they're all just one question.

"He said I was special." I shrug one shoulder.

"We already know you're *special*," chuckles Troy, which causes both Marlon and Ella to laugh.

I glare at him. He's smiling, but his eyes look nervous.

When we cram in the Ford, Ella says, "Things are getting weird super fast. There must be some connection between Dent's article, the twisted arrows, and these murders."

Marlon adds his opinion from the front seat. "I'm sorry Jules, but it seems as if Jake is in the middle of this. I mean, Hunter said to ask *him* about it. He wouldn't mention Jake if he wasn't connected."

Everyone stares at me. I sense their thoughts and don't like it. "If Sicheii's involved in these murders, then why would Hunter tell me to talk to him? He should have warned me to stay away or go to the police."

"And he said he wished he could be there when you speak to Jake, which is odd, too. He wouldn't say that if he suspected him of murder," Ella adds as she starts the car.

"Maybe we should just ask Jake what's going on," Troy suggests for the millionth time. "He could be in danger, and we can help."

"Not yet. I need more to wrestle a straight answer out of him." If my grandfather is in trouble or mixed up in these murders, then I need to help him. The only way I can do that is to force real answers from him. Stories about spirits or rocks and rivers won't do me any good, and that's what he'll tell me if I haven't put the puzzle together before confronting him.

The air conditioning kicks in and the overworked blowers rattle in protest. The car is oven-hot even though the sun melts into the horizon.

"We need to find out what Dent wrote." Ella taps the steering wheel. "We need to read that article."

An idea buzzes into my mind like a bee on a flower. "I'll call Katie. She's a first-class hacker. If there's something on the web, she'll find it." Katie hacks as a release from her strict rule-following world. Masked by an alias, the computer gives her freedom, freedom she uses to uncover other people's secrets.

Troy fires me a look, his eyes cutting. "Can we trust her? I mean, if Jake is somehow involved, we need to be careful who knows what, at least until we understand what's going on and what we should do about it."

"She *is* part of that *Bartens* crowd," Ella adds. "Her dad used to be one of the biggest fish until he got caught stealing from everyone."

I feel the Bartens wedge between us. "I trust Katie as much as anyone else, even you guys." My voice sounds abrupt and defensive. As far as I'm concerned, the matter is settled, so I hit Katie's speed dial number, and she answers on the first ring.

Katie sputters words in one long, breathless burst that slows at the end. "Are you okay? Why haven't you returned any of my messages? Are you mad at me?"

Heat flashes across my face. I had almost forgotten my fight with Tiffany, but now the whole incident comes rushing back to me—the anger and Katie's betrayal. "Why didn't you tell them what Tiffany called me?"

"I don't know what you're talking about! Tiffany didn't say anything. You ripped down something from your locker and raced at her. It all happened so fast. I didn't hear anything."

Her answer comes in a speedy *whoosh*. I take a deep breath. She sounds truthful; her voice cracks at the end, close to tears. At least she didn't realize Tiffany had hung the cartoon on *her* locker or that the cartoon was really of her dad. Sicheii is right about that—I should tell her the truth, but I'm not ready to deal with that now and definitely not over the phone. I'll need to be face to face with her for that conversation, or I'll mess it up and only hurt her.

"I'm sorry, Katie. Tiffany called me Indian trash. I thought she shouted it, but you were farther away. I guess you didn't hear her." My anger deflates like air leaking from a balloon. I feel bad accusing Katie. Besides, two people are dead, my grandfather could be next, a weird demon almost ate me, and this strange symbol keeps popping up everywhere. A little name calling from Tiffany can't compare to all that.

"Did you get suspended? What did she put on your locker? Did—"

I feel like a prisoner facing a firing squad, so I interrupt her before she shoots more questions at me. "Katie, can you do me a favor?"

"Sure."

"Don't worry. The favor has nothing to do with school or Tiffany. I found an old photograph online from *The Sentinel*. It's part of an article written by John Dent on July 25, 1986. Can you retrieve it?"

I hear Katie typing as her fingers fly over her keyboard. In a few seconds, she says, "I've got the photograph up. It's not much of a picture."

"I can't find the article connected to the photograph. Do you think you can find the piece?"

"All *The Sentinel*'s old issues are online in an archives section on their website."

I guess everyone else knows that but me. She types in staccato fashion.

"Strange, this issue is missing. The issues before and after are online."

"Exactly. Can you find it?"

Katie pauses for a second. "Why do you want it?"

I'm not ready to explain everything to her. I trust her, but I don't want to spook her, and I'm not sure what we're looking for anyway. "I'll tell you everything later," which is probably true. "You'll just have to trust me for now."

She sighs. "I can try to hack into *The Sentinel*'s server. If the newspaper was originally put on the system and then deleted, the old paper should leave a shadow. If I find the shadow, I can download the article. It might take a while."

"Thanks, Katie. Just do your best. I'll talk to you later."

"I'm not sure what we do next," Ella says as she swerves around a bus. "We could go back and talk to Jane Dent. Maybe we can find out why she lied to us."

"Let's wait and see if Katie can find the article," Troy says. "It might prove to be nothing."

"Troy's right," I say. "I'd like to question Jane Dent after we read what her son wrote. Something tells me she won't be happy to see us again. We'll be lucky to have one more crack at her."

"I wonder why Hunter kissed your hand and whispered to you," Ella says as she drives back toward my house.

I'm thinking the same thing. I know Hunter like all the other kids in the area, but we've never been close. I doubt I've had more than a two-minute conversation with him, and every one of those conversations ended with me paying for a flavored ice.

As we pass the Diary Freeze, fear pricks the back of my neck, so I glance out the back window. A plain white van drives a few car lengths behind us. It looks like the same van we parked next to by Hunter's townhouse. The driver has black, slicked backed hair and broad shoulders. I don't like the look of him—his eyes look dangerous.

Ella slows, turns right, and stops at the security gate. The white van speeds past while the driver focuses solely on the road ahead.

I'm being silly, seeing bogeymen who aren't there.

CHAPTER 18

My mind spins when Troy and I step out of Ella's Ford and she motors off. Is Sicheii's life in danger, or is he involved in these murders in a more sinister way?

He's closer to me than the average grandfather. He's played a big role in raising me, almost like a father. Even though I didn't want him to stay over, that was more about me than him. He's always been the same, always been a rock for Mom and me—a weird rock with lots of dents and cracks, but still a rock. I can't believe he'd kill anyone, but a whisper of doubt floats through my mind and that makes me feel like a traitor. He did lie to the Sheriff yesterday about where he spent the day. He went fishing. He didn't spend the day at the gallery, and he had two antique hatchets at his store.

I hesitate as we reach the garage, nervous Sicheii might be home. I glimpse through the window before starting for the door—the Porsche is gone. I take a deep breath and some anxiety drains from me. I still need more puzzle pieces before confronting him. I only have edge pieces that form the beginning of the picture. Like any puzzle, the most challenging parts are yet to come.

I turn the key, the lock clicks, and the front door opens. My head throbs as I make my way to the kitchen and drop down in a chair next to the table. Troy's face is lined with concern—his eyebrows pressed together, his deep brown eyes wide and sparkling. The expression changes his handsome face into something more, something better, but I would never tell him that. That would open up too many doors I don't want open right now. Besides, he's all too aware of his good looks.

"Are you okay?" His voice is soft like velvet. "Your face looks flushed like you have a fever." He touches me on my shoulder, and I sense his warmth through the fabric.

"It's just hot. Why is everyone always asking how I'm feeling? Ask me again, and I'll knock your block off!" I even shift in my seat to lunge at him if need be.

He removes his hand from my shoulder and frowns. He knows me well enough to realize I'm serious. He shrugs and swings open the refrigerator door, finds a pitcher of lemonade and grabs two glasses. A moment later, he sits across from me and we both gulp down full glasses and feel better as our bodies absorb the cold liquid. The air conditioning in Ella's Ford was almost useless.

My mind sticks on the twisted arrows symbol and grinds like gears in need of oil. What do the twisted arrows mean, and why is the symbol popping up everywhere? How come I never noticed it before?

My phone rings. It's Mom, so I stuff the phone in my pocket and glance at Troy sheepishly.

"Aren't you going to answer your phone?"

"No way!" I drain the last of the lemonade from my glass. "Mom is the last person I want to talk to now. She'll suspect something is wrong just by the sound of my voice and catch the next flight back. I'll never figure out what's going on with her watching me."

"Maybe she'll remember something about John Dent." He refills my glass. "She might recall his article. She would've been a teenager back in 1986."

Troy is right, but I have a difficult time imagining Mom as a teenager. The Mom I know has always been a responsible lawyer and mother. It's hard to think of her as anything else. The only blemish on her perfect record is her brief relationship with my father, and that topic is off limits. I doubt she had even met my father by 1986.

My father.

Once my mind turns to him, it tumbles down a waterfall. I've fallen down this slide so many times before. Questions, anger, and guilt churn in the water after the free fall. Still....

"What's going on, Jules? You look like you're a million miles away."

I grip my glass harder. "I was thinking about my father. He was released from prison four months ago." He was convicted of manslaughter not long after I was born. I search his name on the first day of each month since I got my own computer. It's my ritual. I'm not sure why. Maybe a part of me wonders what he's up to, whether there's any news to report about him.

"Did he call?"

I shake my head. "Nothing. He's never called or written or sent me an email or text." I've never met him and have only seen his face once, in an old photograph with Mom at Slippery River that was hidden in her room. I needed to borrow some socks and found it stuffed under a dozen pairs in her dresser drawer. I never asked her about it. What would be the point? He obviously wants nothing to do with me or us. Why she's kept that picture this entire time totally confuses me. I would have ripped it up long ago.

Troy narrows his eyes. We've talked about my biological father more than a few times and he's made his feeling clear. "You understand it isn't personal, right? The jerk has never even met you?"

"It sure feels personal." I chug the rest of the lemonade. *Could I be so bad, such a disappointment, he doesn't even want to meet me?*

I glance at Troy. He so wants to make this better for me. I see it in his eyes and the lines that drip from both ends of his lips. When he got his license, he offered to take me to see my father in prison, so I could meet him, tell him what an ass he is in person. When I said no, he suggested he go alone, but I forbid it. He'd find him for me if I asked him. He would do anything for me.

Heat flushes my face, my throat burns, and tears well in my eyes. I glance away so he won't notice.

I look at the clock on the wall and change the subject before the specter of my absentee father swallows us whole. "Do you really think my mom could help us?"

Troy swirls the lemonade in his glass. "Anything is possible."

The doorbell rings. I jump and knock my glass over. Luckily, it doesn't break, but a new thin line spreads around its base as if it is about to shatter at any moment.

Troy chuckles, so I manufacture a fierce scowl, but I'm not really angry with him. I'm more interested in who rang the bell.

He strolls cautiously toward the door, and I follow in his wake, feeling better and safer that he's here. Dusk has already settled in as the sun drifts below the horizon.

Sheriff Daniel presses his face against the glass. He isn't alone. Deputies Johnson and Jackson are with him. I swerve around Troy and open the door.

Daniels looks edgy. His eyes shift beyond me toward the rest of the house. "Good evening, Juliet," he says as he tips his cowboy hat. "Is your grandpa home? We're looking for Jake."

I glance at Troy, whose expression is stoic. Returning to face Daniels, I say, "No, Sheriff, he's out. Is something wrong?"

Daniels steps inside the doorway. "You don't mind if we come in and check, do you?" His voice is tight, and he doesn't give me a chance to object. He and the two deputies are already inside the house before I can say anything.

"It will only take a second, Juliet. We just want to ask him some questions." As if he gave a silent command, the two deputies leave the foyer and start to search the house, calling out "Jake" as they go. Deputy Jackson brushes his hand against his revolver, and my legs go weak. I remembered the words from the newspaper article—*Sheriff Daniels expects to make an arrest imminently.*

Daniels smiles thinly. "I'd sure like a glass of water. It's been a hot one today."

"Of course," I say, and Troy leads us toward the kitchen. I grab a glass from the cabinet and fill it with cold water from a water cooler. My hand trembles as I hand the glass to the Sheriff.

He tries to sound casual, but a seriousness underlies his voice. "When was the last time you saw Jake?"

"This morning. He picked me up from school."

"Around what time was that?" He questions me in a tone that makes it sound like he's just making conversation, but his eyes lock on mine, and I can tell he wants the information for other reasons.

124

"Around 9:30 or so." Daniels's eyebrows lift, so I add, "I wasn't feeling well, so he picked me up early." Another lie. This one flows easily.

"I'm sorry to hear that, Juliet." Both deputies return to the kitchen, and Deputy Johnson frowns and shakes his head.

"Where is your mother?"

"She's at work."

He glances at Troy suspiciously, as if he shouldn't be with me unattended, but he lets it pass. "Tell her to call me when she gets home, and if you hear from Jake, tell him to contact me right away." Daniels's tone of voice is deadly serious and his eyes bear down on me to make a point.

I nod, and then my heart skips a beat. An origami swan sits perched on a white plate next to the sink on the kitchen counter. How did *that* get there?

Sicheii used to make them for me. He wrote messages on the paper meant only for me. It was our secret code. Two years have passed since he last left me one.

My jaw must have dropped because the Sheriff asks if I am all right and glances in the direction of the sink.

I bite my lip. "I'm... fine. I'm just... under the weather."

The Sheriff gently places his glass on the kitchen table, tips his hat, and shoots me another piercing gaze. "Juliet, it's important Jake call me. It'll be better for him if he does. Let me know if you hear from him. You too, Troy Buckhorn." He glares at Troy for a second, but Troy stays mute, and the Sheriff saunters out of the house. His shoulders sway from side to side while both deputies follow a step behind.

Troy shuts the door after them. When the two police cruisers leave the driveway, I march back to the kitchen.

"They looked serious," Troy says.

"Did you see the way Deputy Jackson touched his gun? They must suspect Sicheii has something to do with these murders."

He rubs his hands over his face. "That's just crazy."

I walk to the sink and stare down at the paper swan in the porcelain dish. Coiled around the bird is the pendant and necklace Sicheii gave me when I turned seven. The pendant is made from turquoise and shaped as a slanted rectangle on its side, with a smaller silver rectangle etched inside the larger one. The slanted rectangle is my tribe's symbol for the Wind Spirit. Sicheii called the pendant a Wind Catcher. When I wore it, the Wind Spirit would help me, protect me, guide me.

I lift the necklace by the buffalo skinned strap. I used to wear it every day until I started school at Bartens. The leather strap chafed against the collar of my uniform, so I left it behind. At least that's what I told myself.

"Read the inscription on the back and tell me what you find." I hand the necklace to Troy.

"'You are Chosen. Love, Sicheii.' There's a circle and two twisted arrows after his name. The symbol looks the same as the one after Dent's name on his tombstone."

I had forgotten about the inscription and the symbol, having not looked at it in years. I take the Wind Catcher from Troy and loop it over my head. I'm not sure why. It just seems like the right thing to do.

The paper swan beckons me, so I lift it with shaky fingers and unfold the paper to find the message Sicheii has left for me in his flamboyant cursive.

Little Bird:
Events are moving fast. We are running out of time. I can't come home tonight without putting you in danger.

Meet me at Slippery River on the South End where you and Troy enter the park tomorrow at noon. I'll explain everything then. Keep Troy close. It's time for you to become the swan you are meant to be.

Love,
Sicheii

After his name, he draws a circle with what looks like two twisted vines in the center. He always adds the circle next to his name when he writes messages for me. I had forgotten about it. I assumed the symbol was some weird Native American thing and never asked him what it meant. Now I look at it more closely. It *could* be a simple version of the two twisted arrows. I hand the note to Troy.

While he reads it, I remove my iPhone from my pocket and stare at it.

"Who're you calling?"

"I've got to call Mom. If Sicheii's in danger, she's got to know. And from the look on the Sheriff's face, he might need a lawyer soon." I press the speed dial button and wait. Worries swirl through my mind. Am I betraying my grandfather? For some reason I'm holding my breath. By calling Mom, everything becomes real, like clay turning into brick in the hot Arizona sun.

Could he really be swept up in these murders? If so, how?

Mom's phone turns to voicemail. I groan and leave her a message to call me.

"I guess we wait until tomorrow," Troy says, his face long as worry clouds his eyes. His phone rings and he hesitates to answer it.

"You better get that." I shoot him a look. "Maybe Ella's found a new clue."

Troy retrieves his phone from his front pocket and glances at the screen. My eyes beat him to it. A full screen picture of a blonde-haired girl from school named Candy smiles at him. Candy has a certain unsavory reputation for boy hopping. He shuts off the phone and stuffs it back into his pocket.

"Aren't you going to answer that?" All of a sudden, I cross my arms against my chest and start tapping my foot. "Candy is probably wondering where you are. You must have a hot date planned tonight."

"Candy is just a friend."

"Right, just another one of your *friends*. You have so many of them." I'm not sure where this comes from, but it gushes right out of me. I see red, and all I can think of is Candy and Troy alone—his lips on hers, her hands in his hair. "I bet she's a lot of fun to hang out with."

Troy's left eye twitches, his brow furrows, and his face turns crimson. He starts to say something but stops. I wish he would just say whatever he really feels. There are some things you just can't change. I don't have blonde hair and don't look like a model. With my pointy nose and eyes that are not quite wide enough, I'll never be able to compete with the blonde-haired Candys of the world.

Instead, he waits a few seconds and mutters, "I'll call her later," through a clenched jaw.

I open a closet and toss two jackets on the floor until I grab the light one I'm looking for. I've got to find more puzzle pieces before tomorrow. I don't want to stay here in this house or this kitchen knowing Troy should be on a date with Candy. I need to move.

"What're you doing?" Troy's hands are up. "Aren't we going to hang out here?"

"You can go on your hot date with Candy if you want. You don't *need* to stay with me. I'm sure you wouldn't want to disappoint her. I want some more answers before I meet with my grandfather."

I turn toward the door.

My answers are out there.

CHAPTER

Troy blocks my path like a boulder. I think about steamrolling him but hesitate and take a deep breath instead. Candy's perfect cheerleader face flashes in my mind. She's the *last* person he should be with, but that's *his* mistake.

Why should I care anyway?

I take in more oxygen. He's free to date anyone he wants, just as I am.

I breathe again. It's just that I *choose* not to date anyone.

Another breath, and steam releases from me like a teakettle.

He must have noticed because he asks me, "What do you have in mind?"

"I want to go back to Roundtree's house and check it out."

His eyebrows bunch together, and he looks at me as if I have two heads.

"Maybe he hid something in his house that'll give us a clue about what's going on. Roundtree has to be the key. He had the twisted arrows tattoo, he was the first in the secret society to be killed, and he stood at the center of that photo."

"What would we look for?"

I'm not sure why, but I feel a little better when he says *we*, so my voice slows and the jagged edge in my tone smooths out. "The twisted arrows must be important. I know it sounds strange, but everything with my grandfather is weird. Maybe we can find the symbol in Roundtree's house somewhere and it'll lead to a clue that might tell us what's going on."

"But whoever killed Roundtree probably searched his house. They'd have found anything worth finding."

I pull open the drawer underneath the toaster and retrieve a flashlight. "Maybe, but maybe they didn't know about the twisted arrows. Perhaps Roundtree has a hiding spot with that symbol on it. He was tortured before he died. He might not have given away his secrets." I shrug. "It's worth a try. It's better than sitting here and doing nothing all night. I need to move, do something productive. Otherwise, I'll go crazy."

I step toward the door, but he grabs my arm and stops me cold in the foyer. He slides inches from me, and we breathe the same air. A bolt of electricity flows through me and I forget all about Candy and her blonde hair and small nose and floozy reputation. Well, not completely, but I shove those thoughts to the back of my mind when his face moves so close to mine.

"I'll go," he whispers, his words feathery soft and eyes wide, bright, and caring. "You stay here. It might be dangerous. That demon might show up again, and whoever killed Roundtree and Brooks is still out there. I'm sure the killer won't want us to search for secret messages. I'll tell you if I find anything."

I can't let him go without me, even if a small cowardly part of me does. Sicheii is caught in the middle of this mystery, which means it's my mystery to solve. "This isn't a movie. Killers don't always go back to the scene of the crime." I pull my arm free from his grasp. "I'm going with you or without you." I add as much determination in my voice as I can manage even though it's all bluster. Without him, I'd lose my nerve. Whenever I shut my eyes, images of Roundtree's bloodied body still float in my mind, and every time they appear, I shudder. He doesn't need to know that, so I act bold, bolder than I am.

"How are you going to get to Roundtree's house without me?" He smiles.

"I'll hitch. I've done it before."

He smirks. "Okay, we both go."

He peeks through the glass at the front door. "I don't see anyone, but if the Sheriff thinks Jake is involved in these murders, he'll probably have someone watching us. We're not going to be able to cruise to Roundtree's house without a deputy tagging along."

"I don't see anyone." Darkness has fallen outside. "I bet they have a deputy stationed by the security gate at the main entrance, but everyone forgets about the service road. If we take the bike through the dirt road, we can escape unseen."

Troy groans. "I hate the service entrance. That road is nothing more than a dirt trail. We'll kick up rocks that'll wreck the bike's paint job."

I open the front door. "Don't worry about scratching the paint. I'll help you fix the bike." I'm pretty sure the paint job is going to be the least of our problems.

I take the smelly helmet without complaint. He starts the bike with a roar, and we drive to the service road. A metal gate blocks the path with a chain secured by a padlock. The gate is meant for cars, not bikes, so we find an opening in the side and pass around it, working our way onto the dirt road behind the gate. When we reach the trail, he opens up the throttle, and in no time we leave the dirt road behind and find ourselves back on Route 100, headed to Roundtree's house. An uneasy sensation settles over me, so I tighten my grip around Troy's waist to chase it away.

The quiet Reservation unsettles me as Troy stops the bike where we parked yesterday. Yellow police tape stretches across the front door and a yellow sign in front of the house reads, "Police Crime Scene - No Unauthorized Admittance."

We jump from the bike. "Are you sure you want to go in?" he asks, his eyes jumpy as he scans the empty street.

"You're not afraid of ghosts, are you?" I tease him with feigned confidence and stroll toward the side of the house. "We'll have better luck going in the back way." Today, it's my turn to tug him along with an invisible chain forged by our friendship.

Troy lopes behind me. An eerie quiet blankets us. We move swiftly, guided by slippery moonlight. When we scoot to the back of the house, soft river sounds fill the night air as water splashes against the riverbank. Random thoughts occupy my mind and crowd out the dread I feel when returning to the crime scene.

I flip on the flashlight and sweep the light across the back of Roundtree's house. The beams catch more yellow tape around the maple tree where he was murdered. The cool night air turns frosty when the light from the flashlight sweeps over crimson streaks in the dirt at the tree's base.

Troy points toward an old glass door with an antique brass lock and studies it for a second, unsure what to do. He hands me a small screwdriver as he twists the tiny Allen Wrench free from his keychain. Before he goes to work, I grab the doorknob, twist, and push. The door opens without much resistance, so I pocket the screwdriver, smile at him, and shrug one shoulder as we step into the house. Sometimes you just have to try.

The floor creaks under my feet and my breath catches in my throat. The place is a mess—upturned furniture, books and papers strewn around, bits of wood and stone artifacts, broken pieces of Roundtree's life tossed about haphazardly. It takes the wind out of me. I feel the violence and rage of the attacker, as if a two year old had thrown a temper tantrum, only this tantrum lasted hours and way more intense than anything a two year old could muster.

Troy whistles and scratches his head as he steps over smashed objects. "Someone certainly trashed the place."

"Either that or Roundtree could have used a housekeeper." I smirk, trying unsuccessfully to lighten the mood. "Let's check out the living room. That's the oldest room in the house." Sicheii had brought me here once to show Roundtree a new artifact he had purchased for the gallery.

I step carefully around debris, trying not to smash anymore of Roundtree's stuff. The living room is more of the same. We don't live in tornado alley, but this is what I imagine his house would look like after one hit.

One item sticks out from the rest and I pick it up. "This *is* weird."

"What is it?" Troy asks.

"Well, this is the only thing that's burned, but you can still make out the picture. Sicheii gave it to Roundtree a few years ago. It's an ancient piece of buffalo hide with an odd painting on it of a white ghost with purple eyes. It looked like rays were shooting from the ghost's eyes. I once asked Sicheii about it and he told me it had something to do with Coyote, but I've never seen Coyote drawn that way. Why do you think they burned it?"

Troy shrugs and looks away. "Who knows? I guess it wasn't that important or they would have taken it with them. Where do we start looking?"

I drop the hide and run my hands through my hair. "Let's take a look along the walls. Maybe there's a safe." Dark wood paneling covers the walls. We start at the nearest one and swipe the light from the flashlight against the wall in a slow arc. Troy follows the path brightened by the beams and brushes his hand against the wood in places. He disturbs dust as he searches for the smallest sign of a safe or a hiding spot, or the twisted arrows symbol. We work quietly, but his breathing speeds up. Mine starts to match his.

We inch our way along the wall when a lightning bolt threatens to split my head in two. I bend at the waist. A vision of a white van, the same one from earlier in the day, flashes in my head. It's pulling up to Roundtree's house.

My hand trembles, and the light from the flashlight dances unsteadily around the room. "We have to go, Troy. Someone's here.... They've pulled up in a van."

He glances at me oddly. I can't blame him, but he has to start moving, so I grab his t-shirt to push him toward the back door. But before we go back the way we came in, the front door crashes open.

Bang! Wood splinters.

Troy shoves me toward the back door. "Run," he whispers.

I'm not going to leave him. We're in this together. I shut off the flashlight and hope the darkness might hide us.

I should have known better.

CHAPTER

Events slow. Air freezes in my throat. A silhouette moves into the doorway, sweeping a beam from a flashlight across the room before it lands on us. The intruder's slicked black hair glistens in the darkness. A dark golf shirt stretches taut against a well-muscled chest and arms, and he moves with the athletic grace of a dancer or a martial arts expert.

A sinister smile twists his lips. "Gotcha!" he says.

"Run!" Troy shouts as he leaps toward Slicked Back Hair. I try to grab his arm to stop him. This is no drunken college student, but I'm a second too late and he darts ahead.

Slicked Back Hair sidesteps him and swings the heavy flashlight forward in a short chop. It crashes hard into Troy's face.

He goes down in a thud. Bone breaks and blood spurts from his nose.

My chest squeezes and my vision tunnels around Slicked Back Hair. I tense to take a run at him, but strong hands grab my hair from behind. A second intruder must have snuck in through the back door. He swings me in a painful circle and flings me to the hardwood floor. The flashlight tumbles from my grasp, switching on as it leaves my fingers.

My forehead collides with the floor. I rise to my knees when the beam from the flashlight catches my attention. The light finds a speck of silver on the wall, a twisted arrows symbol carved into the corner of the room. It's so small we would probably have missed it.

I stand on shaky legs.

Troy struggles to get up when Slicked Back Hair plays soccer with his head.

Thud!

His neck snaps back, he crumples, and lies still on the floor.

I'm so angry my whole body shakes. My hands ball up into fists when Slicked Back Hair pulls a revolver from the small of his back and aims the gun at Troy. "Make another move and I plug your boyfriend." He speaks calmly and measured and is more terrifying because of the control in his voice. "We're supposed to take you alive. Him," he nods toward Troy, "we don't need."

My hands shoot up. I take him at his word. From the look on his face, I figure he'll enjoy killing Troy if given an excuse. The second guy who grabbed my hair glides in front of me and stops no more than a foot from my face. He smells like peppermint. He's shorter than Slicked Back Hair, wider in the chest, and clumsier looking.

He smiles at me and reveals a gold front tooth. "She's the one we're looking for mate," he says with a slight English accent. "She's the medicine man's granddaughter."

What has Sicheii gotten us into?

I stare at Troy and my heart tightens as if someone twists it with a tourniquet. He's breathing, but he's still out cold, blood splashed on his face and his shirt. *How badly is he hurt?*

"Don't worry about him, love," Gold Tooth says. "We won't kill him *if* you come with us peacefully."

"Try to run for it, and I'll gladly put a bullet in his skull." The sneer on Slicked Back Hair's face ominous and unmistakable.

Gold Tooth shoves me toward the front door. "We're going for a ride. If your grandfather behaves, you'll be fine."

When was the last time Sicheii behaved?

Panic swells inside me. I fight the urge to check on Troy. I need him to be safe. This is my fault.

"Come on now. We don't have all night." Slicked Back Hair points the revolver back at Troy.

I have to go. The faster I leave with them, the safer he'll be. If I give Slicked Back Hair an excuse, he'll shoot him for sure, so I go quietly with them, shuffling my feet in short quick steps, just short of a run. I need to leave Troy behind to get Slicked Back Hair and his gun away from him.

I exhale when we leave the house. I didn't realize I was holding my breath, but at least they've left without shooting Troy. Maybe he'll be safe. I cling to that thought like a life preserver.

Slicked Back Hair grabs my arm, pulls me toward the back of the van, and his fingers dig in my flesh. Gold Tooth opens the double doors and removes steel handcuffs from a hook, while grinning at me. It is a wicked grin, a sadistic grin, a scary grin. His eyes are alive with dark possibilities.

I stare at the handcuffs fearfully. I don't want them circling my wrists. I don't want to go in the back of the van. "There must be some mistake. I haven't done anything. I'm sure my grandfather will tell you whatever you want to know, if we just call him."

Gold Tooth grabs me from behind and wraps his thick hands around my shoulders. I struggle, but he's bear strong, and I can't budge.

Slicked Back Hair clasps the cuffs tight on my wrists, takes my iPhone from my back pocket, and tosses me into the back of the van. He connects a two-foot chain to the cuffs and locks it into an iron ring in the floor with a heavy padlock. The ring looks worn.

How many other people have they captured this way?

A new level of fear ripples through me. Panic rushes to my head with the sound of my beating heart. I want to cry, but I stuff the tears down my throat and yank on the chains with both hands. They hold.

"My, she is a feisty one. Usually they start begging by now." Gold Tooth laughs at me. "Pulling on those chains won't help you. Be good and we'll try not to hurt you."

"What about the boy?" Slicked Back Hair asks. A certain amount of eagerness animates his voice. He's a predator and senses an easy kill. My heart sinks and my hands turn clammy. In my mind I shout, *No! Don't kill Troy! Please. Anything but that!* But no words slip past my lips. I can't breathe.

Gold Tooth glances back at the house. "Piss off. The Seeker wants as little mess as possible, mate. Let's deliver the girl first. We can always kill him later if he wants. He won't be hard to find."

The doors slam shut, plunging my world into darkness. I can breathe again. At least Troy is safe for now. I try to survey the inside of the van, but it takes a full minute for my eyes to adjust to the darkness. Cardboard covers the back windows. Only a slight trace of light escapes from the small, round window separating the back of the van from the front.

The van starts with a healthy rumble, and we lurch away from the curb. My heart races in my chest like a scared rabbit. I don't know who these people are, but they're serious, and I'm in trouble.

I yank hard on the chains. They hold, but the iron ring gives a tiny bit. I try again and get the same result. I'm not strong enough to yank the ring loose, so I inch close to it on hands and knees to inspect the clasp.

The van takes a left turn, probably onto Route 100. Left is toward town. Two heavy screws connect the metal ring to the van. I clumsily reach into my front pocket and pull out the small screwdriver Troy gave me.

A whisper of hope flutters through me. I go to work on the right screw and hope they won't look back and see what I'm up to. I sneak a glance at the small window. They think I'm nothing but a helpless teenage girl. I need to be more.

The van moves slowly. They probably don't want to attract any attention. Still, I only have a few minutes. Once they clear town or they arrive where they're going, I'll have no chance. I twist the screwdriver using all my strength. My hand aches as the small tool digs into my palm. Sweat pours down my face as the screw gives—slowly at first, and then more easily. The van stops, and I jump away from the ring.

I glare at the small window and see Gold Tooth smiling back at me. When the van starts again, he blows me a kiss and turns away. I tug on the chains. Only one screw secures the ring this time. It lifts more than it did before, but the screw holds and so does the ring. I scoot over and try the screwdriver on the left screw, but this one is fastened too tightly for the small tool to loosen. The screwdriver bends in my hand and snaps. Terror rips through me. I'm more scared than I've ever been, but I can't give in to the fear.

The van stops again. We're at the center of town. One more stoplight and they will probably head for the highway. I need a new plan. Time is running out.

When I scramble to the side of the van, the two-foot chain pulls tight. There's an indent in the van's sidewall where the back wheel sits. It's large enough for my feet to wedge against. When we start moving, I jam both my feet against the nook, focus all my attention on my legs and push.

The ring loosens. I concentrate harder, first on the muscles in my feet, then legs, arms and hands. Strength I have never felt before flows through me. It's as if the muscles hear the desperate plea from my brain and oblige. I push with my legs and pull with my arms and strain every ounce of energy in my body. I focus on nothing but yanking the chain loose.

A soft groan escapes my lips. The ring springs free with a clank. My back bangs hard against the side of the van. I glance at the window toward the cab—nothing. Heavy Metal music reverberates back from the front.

Good, listen to the music. Don't worry about me. I'm just a helpless little girl.

Only one stoplight remains. I slide for the back doors, waiting, hoping for a red light, hoping for a chance. If the van doesn't slow, we'll speed out of town and it'll be too late. I've been stuck at this light more times than I can count. I just need a little bit of luck.

The van slows, the brakes squeak, and my hand clutches the latch. I count to three and turn. The door flies opens, and I jump out. My shoulder hits the pavement hard.

The car behind us blasts his horn, slams on the brakes, and locks his tires, burning rubber in the process. I roll toward the sidewalk, jump to my feet and run.

The pavement pounds hard against my feet, and my shoulder stings with jarring pain. A few faceless people float past me on the street. The cuffs still bind my hands, but the two-foot chain falls away behind me.

I look over my shoulder toward the van. The passenger door flings open. As I turn back in front of me, I crash right into the chest of Mr. Cordingly of all people. He catches me before I fall. He frowns and is about to say something nasty when he looks me over and notices the cuffs, my ripped shirt, and bloody shoulder. He looks behind me and sees the van, and a steely look settles into his eyes that I've never seen before.

"Run! They have guns!"

Cordingly pushes me behind him. "I will not. You are a student under my care." He slides between the van and me. "Go. I will stop them."

For an instant, I don't know what to do. What chance does he have against Gold Tooth? But he makes my decision for me when he steps forward to meet Gold Tooth who's sprinting toward us. I turn and run, pumping my legs as fast as possible. The street blurs past me when a gunshot rings out. I stumble for a step before I regain my balance and keep going. I don't look back. There's no need. Tears spring to my eyes when I take a hard left down a side street. My lungs ache.

My vision blurs and my legs start to burn when a dark sedan pulls to the side of the road next to me. The door opens, and a face jumps out of the car.

"Here, Juliet!"

The voice is new, but I know that face. It's the same face from Mom's photograph. I dive into the sedan and slam the door shut.

The back windshield explodes. My father stomps on the gas and tires screech as the car bolts forward. He jerks the car hard to the right, and the backend fishtails, but we're in the clear.

"We have to go back for Troy."

"Who's Troy?"

"He's my best friend." My entire body feels as if flesh and bone have been replaced by led and bolts. I can't move my arms or lift my head. "He's at Roundtree's house."

My head explodes in white light. I fight hard, but my eyes close, and when they do I see nothing but blackness.

CHAPTER

21

I hear garbled voices that sound as if they're whispered outside on a windy day. "You should have shown her the letters, Summer... she doesn't even know...."

I try to hear the rest of the conversation, knowing it's important and about me, but the wind picks up and blackness returns.

Mom talks to a doctor. "When will she come around? It's been two days." She sounds scared. I want to tell her I'm okay, that she doesn't have to worry about me, so I try to pry open my eyes, but the lids are impossibly heavy.

"It is up to her," a soft voice says. "She still has a high fever."

I fall into all-consuming blackness again. I don't know how long, but eventually the darkness turns to color. Troy sits with me on the cliff high above Slippery River. The sun is bright and the colors vivid. He frowns.

"What's wrong?"

"You need to embrace your inner swan," he says casually, as if he's making sense.

"What do swans have to do with anything?" Before he answers, a red-shouldered hawk calls from high above. The red feathers on its wings turn into flames that glisten in the sun. The colors twist together, and suddenly I am the hawk—well, not really. I'm still me, but I can see what the hawk sees.

He circles above Devil's Peak. There's a ledge high up toward the summit. The hawk circles lower again, and the sunlight glitters off the twisted arrows symbol carved into the stone.

The hawk squawks, and the world twists back to the way it was—Troy sits beside me again. I reach for his hand, but he pulls his out of reach. "You can't be ashamed of who you are. You're part of the Tribe."

My face flushes with heat. "I know, but Bartens is different. How can I fit in? I can't..."

His eyes narrow and his face pinches together. "You want to be just like Tiffany and Morgan, don't you?"

"No, that's not it!" I shout, but part of me *is* jealous of them, wants to be accepted by them, wants to belong in their world. I despise myself for feeling that way. I hate them, but they have everything I'm supposed to want. My emotions jumble together. It's impossible to know what's real and what's imaginary.

"When you reject the Tribe, you reject me."

"You don't understand. I just want a future." My shoulders fold down, and I lean back against the cliff face. Tears moisten my eyes. I look away, not wanting to see him so cross.

"I understand, Little Bird," he says, but his voice sounds old and weathered like my grandfather's voice. When I glance up, Sicheii sits with me.

I try to slide away, but there isn't enough room on the ledge to go more than a few feet. "What have you done? Those men wanted to take me. They were going to kill me. They said they need something from you."

"It is not what I've done, but what you haven't done. The fault lies with you." He stands. There isn't much room on the ledge. His toes dangle over the edge.

My heart leaps. Sicheii's gray eyes look dark and disappointed. He switches his gaze to the river below.

Worry whips through me. "Don't jump. I'll do better. Tell me what to do." The wind picks up, and his straw hat blows off his head and floats toward the river.

He frowns. "It might be too late. I warned you." He jumps without uttering another word. I lean over the edge and stare down toward the river, but he's gone. I see the hawk again. This time, he beats his wings, just one powerful stroke and flies off into the distance.

A cold breeze brushes against my face, and I feel an urge to jump. My feet inch close to the ledge. A small stone careens toward the canyon below. The wind gusts. The pull to jump is too strong. He *wants* me to leap. I'm certain of it, so I bend my legs and spring forward. The river rushes toward me. I scream and open my eyes.

Mom holds my hand. She looks old. Her hair, pulled back in a low ponytail, appears dull and listless. Her face is colorless, with wrinkles forming at the corners of her eyes. When she notices my eyes have opened, she smiles, and her face transforms like the sun breaking through clouds on an overcast day. Some of her youth and beauty return, and she squeezes my hand tighter.

"Welcome back, sweetie," she whispers as if she's concerned she might chase me away if she speaks too loudly. "How do you feel?'

Where am I?

I glance around and find myself in a private hospital room. An intravenous line is plugged into my right arm, my shoulder aches, and my mind feels sluggish as if I'm wading through a marsh. Rain darts against a dark window. The staccato pelting sharpens my thoughts.

"I'm okay. Just a little tired. What happened?" I attempt to sit up, but my body feels heavy and lethargic. I only manage a half-shuffle to shift partway up when the pain in my shoulder barks. The lines in Mom's face deepen.

"Don't worry, Mom."

She squeezes my hand. "Don't try to sit up so fast."

I shake my head as memories return and bolt upright as if someone has thrown a bucket of ice water in my face. "Where's Troy? Is he okay? We've got to find him."

"He's fine, Jules." She stands and leans in close, gently stroking my cheek. "He has a broken nose, but it will heal."

"What about Mr. Cordingly? Is he all right?" I remember the protective look in his eyes and the gunshot. Mom's expression and her ghostlike color tell me the answer even before she says anything.

She shakes her head. "He didn't make it."

The air is knocked out of me, and I gasp for breath. Mr. Cordingly saved my life. He traded his life for mine.

"Does he have a family?" The words sound lame. He sacrificed his life for mine, and I don't even know if he has a family.

"He has a brother back in England, but other than him, he had no one." Mom tenderly brushes some loose strands of hair from my face. "Don't blame yourself, honey." She tears up and her voice cracks. "If it wasn't for your father... I don't want to think what would have happened."

I breathe deeply, the air filling my lungs. My father saved me. He must have gone back for Troy.

My father?

When I look up, I see him standing behind Mom with his hand on her shoulder, Mom's fingers circling on top of his.

What in the world is happening?

"Jules, this is your father." She squeezes his hand again as he slides around her to the side of the bed. His long, thin fingers grab the guardrail, and his pale complexion contrasts with Mom's dark skin.

"Hello, Juliet." His voice is soft and sweet, which is not at all like I imagined it. He stands a full head taller than Mom and wears a t-shirt that fits comfortably over his lanky frame. His bright sapphire eyes sparkle, and he has the same longish, pointy nose as mine. He smiles at me and my mind careens in circles. The clatter in my head grows louder, as if a child just received a drum set on Christmas and is pounding away in my head.

I fight through the racket. "What are you doing here?" The anger in my voice surprises me. *After all, didn't he just save me?* I should be thankful, but sixteen years of anger bullies any other feelings out of the way.

"When I heard about the murders, I came right way," he says. "I knew Jake was mixed up in it just like before. I was worried about you. I needed to protect you."

The drumming in my head starts to sound like voices, but I can't hear what they are saying. "Just like before?" I fight through the clamor, but it's maddening. "What are you talking about? What's Sicheii involved in?"

The door opens. Sheriff Daniels and Deputy Johnson step into the room, each holding a hat by their waists. They have solemn expressions on their faces and move slowly, as if they are inching toward me with bad news. Mom gives them a cautionary glance, and they stop. Worry darkens her eyes.

She says, "Sheriff Daniels believes that grandfather might be involved with these recent deaths in some way. They are looking for him and want to ask you some questions, if you are up to it."

But I'm not up to it. Acid churns in my stomach, bile rises in my throat, and the voices practically scream in my head! I jam both of my hands against my ears to drown them out, but it doesn't help. Pain rips through me. I screech.

Mom jumps back.

A doctor races into the room.

"What's wrong, Jules?" Mom sounds just like another one of the voices in my head.

"The voices are so loud!" Tears flow down my cheeks freely. A dam has broken that I'm not sure will ever stop.

"What voices?"

"The ones in my head. They keep coming back. I just want them to go away." They're so deafening, I jam a pillow against my ears, but that does nothing to quiet the noise. The sound comes from inside my head.

How can I quiet that?

Her face turns white and the next face I see, a man's, is unfamiliar. He says something to a nurse who enters the room, but the voices are too loud for me to hear them.

I'm afraid of what might happen next, so I shut my eyes tight, and the blackness returns. This time, I welcome it.

CHAPTER 22

I wake to find Mom staring out the window, her shoulders stooped, her hands pressed against the wall. My head throbs dully, but the voices are soft like water gently lapping on the sides of a small creek, so I shift in the bed and hope they don't get louder.

She must have noticed that I'm awake because she turns, a forced smile stuck to her face as she twists her hair. "Are you feeling better?" She's worried about me. Strain shows in her eyes, the thin tight line made by her lips, and her fingertips that twirl the ends of her long hair. She really wants to ask me about those voices I've been hearing, but she's anxious about bringing up the topic. That's okay with me. I want to know what's happening with Sicheii before we talk about me.

"I'm feeling better."

Mom visibly relaxes. Some of the tension leaves her shoulders and neck as she strides to my bedside.

Before she asks me any follow-up questions, I strike first. This is my window of opportunity, so I need to take advantage of it. "What's going on with Sicheii, and why does the Sheriff think he's mixed up in these murders?"

She looks away and rests her eyes on the doorway. It looks like she's hoping a doctor or nurse will rescue her.

I *need* to know what's happening. Sicheii's in trouble and it has something to do with those two thugs who grabbed me, so heat starts to flush my face. "Tell me what's going on!" The words come out in a low growl.

"Don't get worked-up, Jules." Mom sighs. "I'll tell you everything I know. Do you want something to drink first?"

My throat is desert dry, so I nod. Mom hands me a plastic cup of water with a straw. My eyes lock on her until she starts to talk. It takes a full minute, but she buckles. I knew she would.

"I don't know how much you've heard about these... deaths." She doesn't want to call them murders because she's worried it might upset me. Since I don't burst out in tears or pull my hair out of my head, she continues. "Old Man Roundtree, Samuel Brooks, and Stuart Baker have all died in the past week."

"Judge Baker was murdered?" Stuart Baker was a long-time local judge and as white as snow. As far as I can tell, he didn't have a drop of Native American blood. *How does he fit in with the twisted arrows?*

"Yes, sweetie. He was killed three days ago." She squeezes my hand. "Sheriff Daniels believes your grandfather may be involved."

"Why?" There's a difference between lying and keeping secrets. At least I think there is. I decide to keep the twisted arrows secret because I don't want to give anything away that might implicate Sicheii—not even to my mom. "They should be looking for those guys who attacked me and Troy. They're probably the killers."

"The Sheriff and the other deputies are searching for them, sweetie, but they don't think those two are involved in the slayings. A team of burglars has been targeting houses after someone's died or gone on vacation. The Sheriff believes you and Troy just interrupted a burglary."

"He's an *idiot.*" I sip water through the straw. I'm not going to tell Mom or the Sheriff that Slicked Back Hair wanted Sicheii. That will have to be a secret for now because it means he's in the middle of these crimes in some way. I need to talk to him before I make him seem more suspicious than he is already. "What evidence do they have against Sicheii?"

Mom frowns, but I fire a hard stare at her, count to ten in my head, and she cracks. "They found an antique hatchet in Grandfather's apartment with blood on it."

"Anyone could've put that hatchet in his apartment," I blurt out, immediately suspecting Lisa. "Why would he keep something like that?"

"I don't know, sweetie, but they found some other evidence at Baker's house."

"Like what?" The skin on my face is on fire, and the plastic cup bends under my grip.

"They found strands of long white hair. The results of the DNA test aren't back yet but they think it's your grandfather's hair."

"What does Sicheii say? Have you talked to him?"

She shakes her head and squeezes my hand. "No one's heard from him. I've checked with everyone, and I can't find him."

I don't like the defeatist sound in her voice. She sounds like she believes the worst, which is not like her. A hatchet and a hair shouldn't be enough to convince her that her father murdered three people. I study her for a second, and she starts twirling her hair again. "What else aren't you telling me?" Then I go with a hunch. "What does this have to do with my father?"

Her face freezes.

Bingo.

Her eyes twitch toward the door. "I'd better find him so we can explain together."

My father's name is Ayden Connors. That's the one thing I've known about him my entire life. Just a name. Everything else is a mystery, like the bottom of a deep well. Anything could be down there because it is too deep for the light to reach.

My throat tightens and my heart pounds as if it will explode as Mom leads him into my room. Ever since I was little, I dreamed of the moment when I would first meet him. I know this isn't technically the first time we've met. He saved me in Old Town, and he *was* in the hospital room the last time I woke up, but those times don't count. I never got to talk to him or really *see* him.

As a young girl, I often fantasized that he was innocent, hoping that one day the truth would be discovered, and he would rush home to be the father that everyone else had. Once, right after my fifth birthday dinner, I asked Mom a few questions about him, and she shut me down. She took hold of my hand, told me he was guilty of his crime, and I should do my best to forget him. We were better off without him. "He's bad," she said.

Of course, I couldn't forget about him. Who could forget about their father? But it was clear she'd never fill in the blanks, so I asked Sicheii a few times about him, but he always answered my questions with stories about spirits — usually the Great Wind Spirit. It didn't take long for me to be left with only my imagination, so I invented many different versions of my father. They varied from *Prince Charming* to *Jack the Ripper*.

So when he strolls into the room behind my mother, I feel this crazy nervousness mixed with part giddiness and part dread. What if he was innocent after all? What if he proved to be a greater disappointment than I already assumed? What if he doesn't like me? *What? What? What?*

He walks stiffly, his blond hair cut crew-cut short. Small thin wrinkles line his face, and a scar meanders two inches down his right cheek in a thin white line. His back is slightly bent forward as he walks. He's five inches taller than Mom, and his arms are corded with muscle underneath a simple blue t-shirt. They approach the side of my bed with him a step behind Mom.

"Juliet, this is your father, Ayden."

He moves next to her. A shy light smile brightens his face with only the edges of his lips bending upward. It's definitely not a *Jack the Ripper* type smile, but it's not a *Prince Charming* smile either. I realize he's probably somewhere in the middle of those two extremes like everyone else.

"Hi there, Juliet." He has a distinctly Irish accent, and his glacier eyes sparkle with a bit of mischief. "You are even lovelier than your mother."

Years of emotions bubble up inside of me like an active volcano. It's all too much. "Don't *hi* me! I'm almost sixteen years old and not one letter. Not one phone call. *Nothing!*" Spit flies from my mouth, the plastic cup crumples under my grip, and water splashes over the sides.

He steps backward, a shade lighter than he was a minute earlier, and Mom steps forward. "Don't become so upset, Juliet." She touches my arm. "It's not all Ayden's fault."

My jaw drops. "Don't you do that!"

"Do what, Jules?"

"Don't defend him after all these years! You're the one who said he was *bad* and that we were better off without him."

Mom shifts on her feet uncomfortably as her fingers twist the ends of her long hair. "I don't remember saying those things, and there are reasons why you never got any correspondence from Ayden."

"Reasons! It's been almost sixteen years. Did he forget how to write in jail?"

"Actually, he might have written you a few times." She averts her eyes away from mine.

"What are you talking about?" My heart sounds like a war drum. Mom's a bad liar like me. I can tell that she's upset, so I hold my breath and wait.

She bites her lip. "Ayden wrote you one letter each week. I just never gave them to you."

My mouth opens, but it takes a while for the words to spill out. I'm so furious I can barely breathe. "After all this... I can't believe you... You've been lying to me... *I hate you!*"

Ayden leans closer. "Now don't be too hard on your mom, Juliet. She was only doing what she thought was best."

"*Out!*" I point toward the door. "Both of you! *Out!*"

Mom twirls her hair.

I chuck my pillow at her, hitting her square on the face.

Ayden grabs her arm and pulls her in the direction of the door.

Mom's face goes white, but the twinkle in his eyes brightens.

CHAPTER

Befuddled. Confused. Shocked. Upset. Stupefied. Dazed. Really pissed off! I feel them all as if my emotions have become ingredients in some awful angry stew I'm forced to eat.

I've spent almost sixteen years living in a world without a father, believing he wanted nothing to do with me, that he was *bad*. But now I find out Mom kept him from me, hid his letters, and lied to me. And now she seems to like him? She holds his hand and smiles at him?

Argh!

I punch my pillow. Words, thoughts, and emotions swirl in my mind like a dust storm. Everything I thought was solid crumbles beneath me. One moment I'm the angriest I've ever been, and the next I'm elated with a sense of giddiness bubbling inside of me as if my heavy emotional stew has turned into a carbonated soft drink. It's ridiculous. I feel like two different people. I'm more comfortable being angry, but the giddy Juliet keeps nudging her way into the picture.

My father wrote me letters.

What should I do? I have a father, and he wants to be part of my life. Was he innocent of his crime? Perhaps he isn't bad at all. If Mom could have hidden all those letters from me, she could have easily lied to me about him.

But he *did* spend fifteen years in prison for manslaughter. He *was* convicted. Someone died. And what does all this have to do with Sicheii? The dust storm rages on.

My thoughts settle on Sicheii. *What's he mixed up in?* I can't believe he tortured Roundtree. But I hesitate, caught by a whisper of doubt that trips me up. Could he do something so extreme? He's always been mysterious. His beliefs are rock hard. What if they were challenged? What if he had to kill to keep the world in some type of balance only he could see? Would he murder to do that? Sicheii's core is strong. I've never seen him waver from doing what he thought was right. He never even hesitates. But torture is a totally different extreme from murder. I can't imagine him torturing anyone.

I am lost in the middle of the dust and debris of my own thoughts when the door opens. I expect my mother to step through the doorway with an explanation I don't want to hear, but Ayden stands at the threshold instead. I raise my pillow threateningly, and he tosses both of his arms up in surrender.

"I'm unarmed. I come in peace. Don't fire." He smiles at me. "Can I come in?"

I lower the pillow but keep it close just in case.

He ambles to my bedside. "I've waited so long to meet you. I'm sorry it has to be here in this place. But we can't make our own world. We have to live in the one we're given."

"I can't believe you wrote me letters and that *woman* hid them from me. I could strangle her!" I look down and my hands are indeed strangling the pillow.

Ayden's face softens, and he rests his hand lightly on the side guard. "Don't be too hard on your mother, Juliet." The short sleeve on his t-shirt rolls back an inch, revealing the edge of a tattoo. It looks like a skull. "She had her reasons to keep me away from you."

"There's no reason for lying to me! I deserved to see those letters. I thought you wanted nothing to do with me. Do you know how hard that was?" My face burns and probably turns red. With the color comes voices, mumbled, jumbled voices, which grow more numerous and louder. "I thought you hated me, that you wished I was never born. You have to be angry with her, too."

"At first, sure, I was angry with Summer, but I could never stay angry with her. Not when we were kids and not now."

Not when they were kids?

I assumed Ayden was a one-night stand, a momentary lapse of judgment, but now it's obvious there's a more substantial connection between them. A thousand questions threaten to spill out of my mouth all at the same time when he lifts his hands up, palms out.

"I know you must have questions. Let me tell you the truth, and you can decide for yourself."

I nod, do my best to keep my mouth shut, and quiet the voices in my head. If I try hard, sometimes they grow weaker.

"I met your mother in elementary school. We hit it off instantly. I can't say it was love at first sight, but we were close from the beginning. We were so different, it was easy to see why your grandfather disliked me from the first."

"Why would Sicheii dislike you?"

"Oh, he had his reasons. My brother was six years older than me, and by the time I was in sixth grade, he led a gang that dealt drugs. I helped him. At first, it was no big deal. I'd just deliver a package, collect some money. But that was only at the beginning. By tenth grade, I had a clientele of my own. The money was easy."

I sit up higher. "My mom was dealing drugs?" The idea is so foreign it might as well have come from a different planet.

"No, Summer never dealt drugs." Ayden jabs with his pointer finger to make the case. "She was always better than that, better than me. She kept a distance from that side of my life."

"But she knew what you were doing?"

"We were in love." He shrugs. "When you're in love, you overlook the other person's faults, especially when you're young. And I had many faults. Still do." A sly smile slips across his face.

"Sicheii must have known about you."

"Your grandfather has a way of knowing everything. He warned me to stay away from Summer, but it would have taken a bullet to keep me away from her. Summer felt the same way."

"But how—"

He lifts his hand to silence me. "My brother got busted when I was sixteen. He got caught dealing and had to go to the pen for five years. I took over the gang."

A faraway look clouds his eyes. "I didn't know what else to do. My brother needed me to run things. I couldn't let it all break apart on him." He pauses for a second. "Oh hell, I'd be lying if I didn't say I wanted to be the *man*. The money was good and the power was, well, I got a bigger high from being the boss man than from anything we were selling."

He clutches the side guard with both hands, and his knuckles turn white. "I did bad things those years. I'm not going to lie to you. I hurt people. Your mother didn't know what I was doing."

"She must have known some of it."

"She never knew any of the details, but I guess she didn't ask that many questions either. For a few years, it all worked, and then Summer got pregnant with you."

He smiles, and this time it's such a full, genuine smile I return it with one of my own.

"You changed everything for me. I wanted out. I wanted to open a bar, have Summer work the books. I would be the bartender. We could have a happy ending, even a white picket fence."

"What happened?"

"I needed one last score to make enough seed money to start the bar. I even had the place picked out on the edge of Old Town. We decided on a name: *Second Chances Saloon*. I planned to sell a mountain of blow to some college kids. I cut a deal for everything we had left."

"So you would've had enough money to buy the bar and come totally clean?"

He shrugs. "Well, not totally. My brother was going to lend me some of the dough. I'd stop dealing drugs, but in return for the loan, we'd launder some of his cash through the place. Just enough to pay him back."

"Mom knew about that?"

"Yes. Summer wasn't happy with it, but it would get me out of dealing and it would only be temporary. But we never got that far. Before I sold the coke to the college kids, rumors started circulating—rumors about your grandfather and Roundtree."

"Rumors about what?"

"This was a long time ago." He twists the side guard, and the cords in his arms and neck stiffen. "There was a rumor that Roundtree had developed a new super drug with your grandfather's help. This new drug was going to make everything else obsolete. I was in the business and had a reputation at that point, so it interested me.

"I probably wouldn't have paid the gossip any attention, but these dodgy guys from out of town show up asking questions about Roundtree. They wore suits. They looked like they had money."

"You confronted Sicheii with this rumor?" I can't imagine Sicheii involved in drugs — Roundtree maybe; Sicheii never.

"No. I didn't. Things might have turned out differently if I had, but I talked to Summer instead. *That was a mistake*. She got really cross with me. She thought I was making it all up, that I wasn't serious about getting out of the business. We fought hard. It was quite the dust up. We had never fought before that, but she stormed out on me. I was so bloody angry. She should have believed me. She was four months pregnant."

His face twists and his nose flares. He's reliving the argument he had with Mom at that moment, the emotion still raw even after all these years.

"Later that night I was working Old Town, killing time. It wasn't such a ritzy place back then, and there were many shadows and hiding places. I was waiting to meet the college kids for the final score when your grandfather shows up heading to his gallery. He moved in a hurry, but his strides were off. He stumbled as he walked, so I followed him.

"When he reached the front door, the light from the gallery brushed against him. Dried blood crusted on his hands and splashed against his shirt. This was none of my business. I wouldn't have said anything, but a second later, one of those guys from out of town appeared on the street, hustling toward the gallery. I'm not sure why I jumped in his way. I was young and acted without thinking.

"Maybe I thought if I helped your grandfather, he would cut me some slack and make things easier for us. Anyway, this guy barreled into me. We both tumbled to the ground. The wanker got up and started berating me! I've got a temper, just like you. No one is going to yell at me like I'm some punk. We started to tussle. He had a gun. I had a knife. I got to him first. The police found me standing over him. He was dead and I was still... kicking him." Ayden stops, his jaw clenched tight. He looks me in the eyes, and his face trembles a little.

"I later found out that two of the outsiders were killed in Roundtree's house. Roundtree claimed he killed them when they tried to rob him." Ayden shakes his head. "Roundtree was old even then, so I can't imagine him getting the drop on those two by himself. They looked like pros to me. So you see! When I heard about Roundtree's murder and then Brooks, I knew it had to involve your grandfather. The outsiders had asked about him also."

"How did you find me?"

"Your Mom gave me the information to track your cell phone. I followed the signal to Old Town."

One part of his story jumps out at me like a bronco. "You killed that man in self-defense. You were innocent of manslaughter!"

He frowns and releases the side guard. "Don't start making me out to be something I wasn't now. I was a bad kid. He might have had a gun, but I wanted to kill him." He glares at me. "I *wanted* to kill him. Besides, it was only a matter of time. I should have been thrown in jail long before then."

"Didn't Sicheii say anything in your defense?"

He laughs, his voice frigid. "Your grandfather testified against me. He said he saw the fight and there was no gun. The police never found the weapon. He turned Summer against me. She had to choose between us, so she chose him."

He runs his hand through his short hair.

I must have made a face because he says, "Now don't get like that with your mother. I was a bad kid. She made the right choice. She did what was best for you both."

He doesn't blame Mom, but I sure can.

How could she turn on the man she loved?

CHAPTER

I lie on my hospital bed alone, happy for the solitude. After Ayden finished his story, I told him I needed some time, some space to sort things out. I'm sure he wanted a different reaction from me, but everything feels so new and raw. I need time to sort through my feelings — time to think. He wasn't the horrible villain I sometimes imagined, but he was a drug dealer and a killer. Even if he killed that man in self-defense, he still confessed he wanted to do it.

I wrestle with my new reality when a doctor strolls into the room with Mom a step behind him. His gray curly hair, short wiry beard and mustache look as if they are made from wool. He's shorter than Mom and waddles as he walks, probably because he carries a few extra pounds around the middle. His white lab coat flops open and hangs at his sides. He couldn't button it if he tried. He looks oddly familiar, but I doubt I've ever seen him before.

He smiles as he approaches the bed. He has a friendly, reassuring smile, if such a thing is truly possible. It makes me like him before he utters a word. He holds a clipboard in his hands, but he doesn't look at it. "Hello, Ms. Stone. Is it okay if I call you Juliet?"

I shoot icicles at Mom, who maintains her distance, a step behind the doctor, a stony expression carved on her face.

I look back at the doctor. "Juliet is fine."

"Good. You can call me Doctor Dan, if that is okay."

"Sure."

"Now tell me about these sounds you have been hearing. Your mom says you described them as voices?" His voice rises as he finishes, which transforms the assertion into a question.

My self-preservation instinct kicks in. He isn't an ordinary doctor. The badge hanging from his lab coat reads *Dan Epstein - Psychiatrist*. I don't like where this is heading.

I hesitate before answering. "I don't think... I said anything about voices." I glance toward the door. "I just had a headache, that's all." I don't like the way he said *voices*. I certainly don't want to be the kid who talks to voices in her head. Visions of a straight jacket and padded walls darken my imagination. Bartens sucks, but it's a lot better than a psychiatric hospital.

Doctor Dan doesn't say anything. He just waits. After a long moment, I look back at him and his small, moss colored eyes.

He sighs and smiles at the same time. "I can't help unless you're honest with me. Are you hearing them right now?"

I really wish I were a better liar! Even with all the experience I've had lately, he still sees through me in a second, so I sigh. "Yes. I don't hear them all the time, but recently they've been louder." My skin turns clammy.

"Do these sounds talk to you? Do you understand what they are saying?"

My voice is husky and coarse like sandpaper. I do my best to keep tears from my eyes. "No. I never understand them."

He touches my arm. "Don't worry, Juliet. We'll find out what's causing your condition. Hearing noises is a common problem, especially when someone has been through a lot." He squeezes my arm.

I feel better. I hadn't realized how much the voices have been bothering me until now. I can't hold back the tears any longer, so they start to fall.

Mom bites her lip and looks at her feet.

"Is it always the same sound you hear or different ones?" Doctor Dan reaches into his lab coat, pulls out a wad of tissues and hands them to me.

"I think they change." I wipe my eyes with the tissues. "I usually feel emotions when I hear them, like anger or fear or excitement."

"That's good. How long have you been hearing them?"

I think for a second. "I don't remember exactly. Maybe they started two months ago. At first, the sounds were like white noise. I figured it was no big deal, but it's been getting worse. Now they sound like voices, but I still can't understand them. They're starting to make me crazy."

"You've been hearing voices for two months and you haven't mentioned it to me, Jules?" Mom squeaks. "Why not? We could have done a strategy session."

"I don't want a *stupid* strategy session. I want them to go away. Besides, you're always too busy. Working. Hiding letters. And let's not forget all the lies you've been telling me!"

My dinner sits uneaten on the bedside table. Mom left with Doctor Dan and then returns right away with worry etched on her face. She sits at the edge of my bed. "Since when do you keep secrets from me?"

I roll my eyes. "Really, Mom? You've kept the letters from Ayden secret from me for sixteen years."

"That's not the same thing, Jules." She twirls her hair. "I thought I was protecting you. At first, you were too young to understand. With time, it became too hard to change. The lie was easier than the truth. I've saved the letters." Tears glisten in her eyes. "You can have them when we go back home."

"So that makes it all better? I've thought my father wanted nothing to do with me for my whole life, that he hated me, and now I can just have the letters and all is forgiven. You're kidding me, right?" I'm about to really launch into it, but the noises in my head start to thunder, and I feel an overriding sense of melancholy, which tempers my anger and saps my energy.

"I'm sorry. I made a mistake, but we can't have any more secrets. I need to know everything that's going on with you to help with these *voices* you're hearing."

She keeps chattering for a while, but I tune her out and turn my energy to quieting the noise in my head. When it seems like she has finished, I smile weakly at her and tell her I want to take a nap.

Doctor Dan returns an hour later without her. He's carrying a chocolate glazed donut in his hand, which he gives to me.

"How did you know this is my favorite kind?" I ask. Mom believes sugar is poison, so she never lets me buy donuts or other sweets. The only exception is ice cream and flavored ices. It would be impossible to live in Arizona without them. Sicheii, on the other hand, has no problem with desserts. We used to sneak around Old Town without Mom knowing. It was our secret. Sicheii's always been good at keeping secrets.

Doctor Dan grins as I take a healthy bite into the pastry. "Us psychiatrists never reveal our secrets."

We talk for a while. He asks general questions, like "How is life at home? Do you have many friends? How is school?" It seems stupid to lie to him, so I answer his questions truthfully.

I ask him some questions of my own. "What the heck is wrong with me? When will the voices go away? Why's this happening to me?" He doesn't really answer any of my questions. I don't think he can, so it's a test of sorts. He is honest at least.

He takes three vials of blood and promises to come back and see me tonight. He gives me two pills to quiet the noises in my head so I can sleep. He doesn't call the noises *voices*. I notice that right away. He always refers to them as sounds or noises. Who knows what that means, but it seems important.

When he leaves, Troy, Ella, and Marlon stroll into my room, and my heart skips a beat when I see Troy. Fresh white tape stretches over his swollen nose, and black circles darken both of his eyes.

"Troy, I'm so sorry! I should never have made you go to Roundtree's. This is all my fault."

"You're not the one who hit me with that flashlight." He shrugs. "I could have ducked."

"Besides, he looks cuter with a crooked nose," Ella says. "It gives him character. How are you doing?" Her eyes quickly scan my body and linger on the discarded IV bag by the side of the bed.

"I'm fine, really." There's no way I'm telling them about the voices. "I should be out of here soon."

I notice Marlon eyeing my unfinished dinner. "Are you going to eat that Jell-O? Red is my favorite flavor."

Some things don't change, even in hospital rooms. "Go ahead."

Ella and Troy step to the side of the bed while Marlon dawdles behind with the cup of Jell-O in his hand. He looks for a spoon, doesn't find one, and sucks the Jell-O out of the plastic cup in one noisy gulp. Finished, he smiles at us. "Did you know there were only four original flavors: lemon, orange, strawberry, and raspberry?"

"Where'd you learn that?" Troy asks.

Marlon shrugs. "Snapple cap."

Ella ignores him. "Did you hear about Judge Baker?"

I nod. "It's odd. I don't think he has any Native American blood, and the twisted arrows thing seems to be all about the Tribe. Are there any rumors about who killed him? It has to be connected somehow."

"Nothing new," Troy says as his eyes dance around the room. "I gave the Sheriff a description of the guy who clobbered me at Roundtree's house, but it was dark and I couldn't really remember what he looked like. I just remembered that he had oily hair."

"I gave descriptions of both guys to the Sheriff this afternoon, but I doubt they were much better. One of them had a gold tooth."

"I don't remember two guys."

"You were flattened by the time Gold Tooth showed up behind me." I sit up high in the bed and smooth the cotton blanket over top of me. It's rough against my fingers, nothing like the blankets at home, but I'm happy to have something to do with my hands. "I got to meet my father," I say, dropping the bombshell.

Ella's mouth makes an O shape. Troy crosses his arms against his chest, and Marlon munches on a cold roll leftover from my dinner.

"He's not really what I imagined." I tell them everything Ayden told me, and I toss in the hatchet and Sicheii's hair the Sheriff found at Judge Baker's place.

"They must suspect the two guys that kidnapped you for the murders," Marlon says. "They were at Roundtree's house and they're dangerous."

"Yes, but just because they were at Roundtree's house after Troy and Juliet got there doesn't mean they're the ones that killed Roundtree," Ella says. "It doesn't necessarily connect them to the other two."

"The idiot Sheriff thinks we interrupted a burglary and they're unrelated to the murders," I say.

"He could be right." Ella crosses her arms against her chest. "The hair and the hatchet don't look good for your grandfather. Still, what's his motive and what's this secret society all about? They're just some old guys, as far as I can tell. I don't see the connection, although Marlon found another one of those twisted arrows symbols."

Marlon mumbles with his mouth full of roll. "I saw it in Joe Hunter's general store right by the cash register."

"Did you see Hunter reach for his shirt collar when we confronted him? He must have wanted to make sure we didn't see his tattoo," I add.

Ella whispers, "Do you think your grandfather has something to do with these murders?"

"I don't know what to think." I lean toward them and speak quietly. "But the guys at Roundtree's house said they wanted to use me to capture Sicheii. I haven't told that to the Sheriff or even my mom. Sicheii's wrapped up in these murders somehow."

"That doesn't mean your grandfather killed anyone." Ella touches my arm. "I haven't found out anything new about Dent's article, although *The Sentinel* ran a story that said Dent died in a car crash. His car flipped off Eagle Ridge Road and burst into flames when it hit the gully."

"That's always been a dangerous road. They probably didn't have the guard rails in back then," Troy says. "What do we know about this Ayden character? He seems suspicious."

"Only that he saved us!" I shout surprised at how quickly I became angry. "If he didn't go back for you, who knows what would have happened?"

"It sounds like someone's framing Jake to me. This Ayden guy might be holding a grudge. I mean, he obviously has a beef with Jake and Roundtree from way back. I'll bet Judge Baker was the one who sent him up the river. He's already admitted killing one guy. He could be behind these new ones."

"Troy!" snaps Ella. "That's Juliet's *father!*"

"He's a drug dealer, Ella. It seems very coincidental that he shows up in town just when all these murders are going down. I'm just saying, he seems very suspicious to me."

"Stop it, Troy!" I yell.

"How could you take this guy's side over your grandfather's?" Troy's eyes narrow. "Jake's been there for you and your mom your whole life. This other guy just showed up a couple days ago. We don't know anything about him."

Ella glares at him.

"I'm not taking anyone's side, Troy. Sicheii's caught up in this somehow. We need to figure out how."

Troy huffs and turns his back on me.

I want to strangle him. He's being pigheaded.

"We can check out part of Ayden's story," Ella offers. "I'll search the Internet and see if anyone else was killed when your father was arrested."

"That won't tell us much," Troy says, his back still turned to us.

Before I can say anything else, Ayden appears in the doorway, hesitates when he sees my friends, and looks at me. "I didn't realize you had visitors. I could come back later."

"No, come in. I'd like to introduce you to my friends."

Troy turns to face him, his expression cross. Lines that don't normally crease around his eyes and mouth develop. Deep rivers dig into his forehead.

"Guys, this is my father, Ayden." I can't believe those words came out of my mouth – *my father.*

Ayden thrusts his hand out. Marlon and Ella shake it. Troy looks at it as if he's contagious with the plague or something. Ayden keeps it outstretched for a few uncomfortable seconds. When it's clear Troy won't shake it, he brings his hand down to his side and smiles. "I understand, Troy. I have some work to do to earn your trust."

"You certainly do," he grumbles.

"I'll leave you to your friends, Juliet." Ayden turns and leaves.

"I wonder how he got that scar," Marlon says.

Ella stomps down hard on his foot.

"Ouch," he says and hops on one foot. "Why'd you do that?"

"I imagine he got that scar in prison," I say.

"Well, he seems nice to me. It's great that he's back and wants to connect." Ella shoots Marlon a dangerous look, and he retreats a step back. "When are you going to be sprung?"

"I don't know. I still have a little fever. And you know *my mom.* She quarantined me last year, thinking I had the chicken pox when a few freckles showed up."

I'd probably be leaving tonight if it weren't for the voices.

How long do they lock you up for hearing voices?

Locked up might be a little dramatic, but that's what it feels like.

We chat for a few minutes, but Ella gets antsy, shifting her weight on her feet and looking around. I can't blame her. I hate hospitals too, so I take pity on her and fake a yawn. "I'm getting a little tired. The doctor gave me some sleeping pills a little while ago, and they seem to be kicking in."

Ella jumps at the bait. "We'd better roll." She leans toward me and rubs my arm. "Besides, you don't have any more food left for Marlon. If we stay much longer, he'll be forced to eat the tray."

Marlon waves and they rush from the room.

After Ella and Marlon leave, Troy slides to my bedside. "I'm sorry I jumped on Ayden. He helped us, but that's not enough for me to trust him." Troy frowns and looks at me with wide, soft eyes. "Some guys just aren't meant to be dads."

He's talking about his own father. "Is your dad still hassling you?" I don't know when we agreed *hassling* was our code word for *beating*, but I can't say *beating* and I thought things had improved between them.

Troy shakes his head. "He hasn't touched me since my fourteenth birthday. You remember the rock climbing accident when I broke my arm."

I nod. I'm the only one besides Troy who knows the truth.

"Birthdays were always the worst for me. I don't know why. Maybe they remind him that I was born. He thinks I'm just a leech that sucks away his money and his life. I've heard him argue with my mom enough times about it when he's drunk. I'll leave that house soon, maybe live above my uncle's garage. I'd have left already if it wasn't for my mom. She's begged me to stay."

He shrugs. "Jake spoke to my dad the day after my fourteenth birthday. They sat close together in my living room, and since then he hasn't hit me once. I don't know what he said or did, but that was the last time my father's *hassled* me or my mom."

My heart swells. I had no idea Sicheii spoke to Troy's dad. He does many things as a medicine man, but that's his world, not mine. "I wonder what he told him."

"Maybe he threatened him with an antique hatchet?" Troy shoots me a half smile. "Just go slow with Ayden. Not all dads are good."

Troy is only being protective, and I love him for it. "Ayden was a drug dealer and has a slippery past. I'll take it snail like slow with him. He has to earn my trust also."

His eyes widen and moisten, and a thick silence separates us for a long moment. "I should have done a better job of protecting you. I don't want to think about what could've happened." He reaches over and sweeps a strand of hair from my eyes. When his fingers brush against my forehead, a jolt of electricity pricks me.

Does he feel the same thing?

"I can't believe that guy flattened me with one swing of the flashlight. I'm such a loser."

"He hit you on your weak spot. You've always had a glass nose." I smile and suddenly wish I looked better and straighten the blanket again. "Did you meet Sicheii at Slippery River like he said in the note?"

He shakes his head. "When they released me from the hospital, they were worried I might have had a concussion. Mom went all smothery on me. She wouldn't let me leave her sight until my uncle grabbed me at two to work in his garage. He promised to keep an eye on me for the rest of the day. By the time I got to the garage, it was too late to go to the river."

"I don't know, Troy. The evidence is starting to pile up against Sicheii. The twisted arrows seem like trouble to me. Whatever secrets they're hiding, someone's willing to kill to protect them."

A nurse walks past the empty doorway.

"I hope he hasn't done something we'll all regret."

CHAPTER 25

The time on the television reads nine forty-five. I chased Mom and Ayden from the hospital for the night a few minutes earlier. She wanted to stay, but I threw her out. I really don't need her hovering over me, fussing about what I've eaten or haven't eaten, and she could use the rest. Besides, every time I look at her, I think about those letters she hid from me and my blood heats up.

"Let's talk about these noises you've been hearing, Juliet." Doctor Dan sits with his back toward the window, his clipboard flat on his lap. A brown crumb probably left over from his dinner is tangled in his beard, hanging precariously on the left side of his mouth.

"When are the noises loudest?" He slides his chair next to my bed by shuffling his feet forward, and the chair scratches against the floor.

"Usually when I'm angry."

He scribbles on his clipboard. "Good. That should narrow it down."

I smile. "Not so much. I'm angry a lot."

"Oh." He frowns and the sudden downturn of his lips frees the crumb. "Are they louder when you're near other people or when you're alone?"

I hesitate for a second, having never thought about that before. "Always when other people are around. Usually the more people, the louder they get." They were blood spurting from my eardrums loud the other day when plenty of people crowded around me.

I want to ask him why he calls these sounds noises instead of voices, but I'm uncertain what rules govern our relationship. He must have recognized the expression on my face because he pauses and leans back in his chair. His green eyes are flecked with gray. They seem intelligent and earnest at the same time. "This *is* a two-way conversation. You are allowed to ask questions."

"I notice you don't refer to these sounds as voices. You call them noises. Why?"

He tugs on his beard. "That's because I don't know what they are yet. Usually when people hear voices, the voices are their subconscious telling them to do something, like some course of action they really want to take, but are afraid to. In your case, the sounds are not decipherable. Therefore your subconscious isn't suggesting you *do* anything. Your situation doesn't fit the normal scenario. These noises might not be voices at all. I'm not quite sure what they are yet."

"Is that really bad?"

"It is neither bad nor good at this point. We will have to discover what's going on together."

"Argh. I just want to fit in and be normal."

"Normal *how?*" He fiddles with his beard. "Bartens normal, or the normal life you had *before* you went to the private school?"

That's a great question. I wish I knew. "Beats me. I just want the noises to go away and for me to be normal like everyone else."

"There is no such thing as normal, Juliet. It's a fallacy, a fiction created by Hollywood or school or church or whatever. I'm sure a normal teenaged girl would never have escaped that van. Let's do away with normal as our goal, shall we. We are all unique. It's important we embrace our uniqueness and understand who we are."

Funny, but I could imagine Sicheii saying the same thing.

He leans forward. "Let's try something different. Accept the noises in your head. Don't try to make them into voices, but listen closely and tell me if any ideas form in your mind."

I nod, although my skin turns clammy. It seems strange to make the noises louder. I want them to disappear, and this feels like we're headed the wrong way on a one-way street. Still, I follow his instructions and concentrate on the sounds in my mind. The noise is not particularly loud, so I attempt to turn up the volume. It feels weird trying to understand the sounds as opposed to stifling them. The harder I concentrate, the louder the noise gets. I pinch my forehead tight and start sweating. The sounds lie just outside of my comprehension. It's maddening.

"Don't try to make the sounds into a voice, Juliet. Envelop them and embrace them."

I do just that. I stop turning up the volume and start sculpting the sounds in my head as if they're made of clay. I mold them, playing with them, probing them, twisting them. The number eight flashes in my mind, and I open my eyes. I didn't even realize I had shut them.

"Yes, Juliet?" One of his bushy eyebrows arches upward.

"I don't know, Doctor Dan, it's probably nothing."

"Tell me what you saw. There's no wrong answer."

"The number eight flashed in my mind." I shake my head, confident I sound foolish. "I must have imagined it."

Doctor Dan's eyes twinkle brighter. He slowly reaches into his lab coat and pulls out an origami swan matching the one Sicheii had left for me at home the other day and holds the paper steady in the palm of his hand.

"This is for you."

I look at the paper bird and back at him. "Where'd you get the swan?"

"An old friend gave it to me. It's for you. Take it." He slides his hand closer to me.

I don't want it. "How do you know Sicheii?"

"That's not important." He nods at the swan and encourages me to grab it.

I reach out and take the paper bird softly between my fingers.

He immediately rises. "I'll see you tomorrow." He turns and leaves me alone without waiting for me to open the message and without giving me a chance to ask any more questions.

I stare hard at the figure in my hand. I'm not sure what to expect. Part of me imagines that the stupid thing will start moving on its own, but the laws of nature still hold. There's no magic at work here. The bird just sits uncomfortably in my hand, unreasonably heavy.

I start to feel foolish. It's just a note from my grandfather. It cannot harm me. Perhaps it will offer some new evidence or explanation about the murders. Maybe the message proves his innocence.

Just staring at the thing isn't an option, so I unfold it and find Sicheii's fine handwriting on the inside of the white paper.

Little Bird:

The Great Wind Spirit has blown. It is up to us to understand what she wants and to do her bidding. Our time has come.

The correct answer is eight.

Love,

Sicheii

The correct answer is eight.

How did he know the number eight would flash in my mind? What is he talking about with the Great Wind Spirit? He looks to many spirits as guides. The one he thinks is most powerful is the Wind Spirit. But what does that particular spirit have to do with these murders and me?

I read the note again and my gaze sticks on the dime-sized circle with twisted lines after his name. I move the paper close to my eyes., and now I'm certain it's meant to be the twisted arrows. What type of weird society did Sicheii join, and why am I in the middle of it?

I crumple up the swan in my hand. I had expected, even hoped for some answers, and all I get are more questions.

The time for questions runs short. Whether Sicheii likes it or not, I'm going to find some answers.

CHAPTER 26

Dreams scare me. Not like clowns for some people or spiders or close spaces or heights, but they still scare me. The idea that my subconscious lives a separate life while I sleep freaks me out. It's hard enough to manage one life. Do I really need another?

Hospital rooms are a fertile ground for dreams. The same nightmare keeps replaying in my mind in a freakish loop.

I'm late for class. When I enter the classroom, everyone is sitting at his desk. Ms. Arnold points to a seat up front, her face angry and tight. She hands me a test. I forgot about the exam and didn't study. Morgan and Tiffany snicker from the back row. I slouch and glance at the paper. The words are written in an ancient Native American language I don't understand. Katie sits next to me and she's busy filling in the bubbles. I don't know what to do. That's when I wake in a sweat, feeling unprepared for upcoming events.

When I open my eyes, Katie is standing by my bed. She stares at me, holding the string for a Mylar *Dora the Explorer Get Well* balloon. For a second, I think I'm still dreaming, but she waves at me with a stiff shake of her hand, looking painfully nervous. The balloon bobs up and down with each flick of her hand. Her Bartens uniform fits snugly, as if she's gained a few pounds since I last saw her.

I sit up. "I guess they let anybody in here."

She smiles shyly and ties the balloon to the foot of the bed.

"You brought me a Dora balloon?"

"I remembered those pictures of you with a Dora backpack when you were a kid. When I saw it at the gift shop, it seemed perfect." She beams at me.

"You're the best!" I smile. "It *is* perfect!"

"They almost didn't let me in." She places her hands to her hips. "One nurse wasn't too happy about me visiting you."

"Tough. I'm happy you're here."

She tentatively walks to the side of the bed, her eyes curious. She's studying me, wondering if anything is seriously wrong. You can't see voices from the outside, so I figure I'll pass her inspection.

"How are you feeling?" she asks, her voice quiet.

"I'm fine." I shrug. "I should be released in no time."

"Did someone really try to kidnap you?" Her eyes widen and her skin turns pale. When they first suspected her father of fraud, many people levied death threats against her family. They hired the best private security team, but the money ran dry. Now only one bodyguard follows her dad around all day.

I nod and tell her about the murders, the ill-advised trip to Roundtree's house, Ayden's rescue, the letters, and even my conversation with Ayden about his drug dealing past.

Her skin becomes paler as the story goes on. When I finish, she's turned ghost white. "I can't believe your mom hid those letters from you. That's awful."

I eagerly agree with her. After a series of questions about my father, most of which I can't answer, she says, "At school, they told us Mr. Cordingly died during a robbery attempt. They're having a memorial for him today. They didn't say it was connected to what happened to you."

"That's a shame. I wish I could go. He died protecting me.... He was a true hero."

"I guess you never really know about people. Sometimes they do surprising things." A faraway look settles in her eyes. She could be talking about Mr. Cordingly or my mother, but she's thinking about her father.

She starts gnawing on her nails. "You know how I tell everyone that my dad is innocent?" She glances at me and I nod my head. "Truth is, I don't know. Lots of evidence is piling up against him, and I overheard him talking to his lawyer last week."

She looks up at me. Her hands shake, and I grab them. They're ice cold. "And he said—"

She bites her lip. "They were talking about countries without extradition treaties." She pulls her hands from mine and wrings them together. "My dad's thinking about running to Croatia."

I want to say something to lessen the hurt, but my mind is a blank. After all, what do I know about fathers? I just stare at her quietly instead and wait. Sometimes just being there is all you can do. I hope it's enough.

It takes a minute for her to return to the present when she wipes the tears from her eyes with the back of her hands and refocuses on me. "I found the article you wanted." She removes a folded piece of paper from her pocket and hands it to me. "Someone deleted it from *The Sentinel's* server after it was posted in the archives. I hacked into their system and retrieved the original article. It's not long."

I had forgotten she was going to dig it up and unfold the sheet of paper.

"A secret society among the local Native American population has long been rumored to exist. The above photograph was taken at one of their secret meetings. The leader of the society is apparently Charles Roundtree or "Old Man Roundtree," as he is called among his followers. The existence of the society is not surprising, as rumors go back for decades about their organization, but their purpose is truly shocking. They call themselves the Order of the Twisted Arrows. Stay tuned to my column as I detail their history and their dark purpose in the days ahead."

The article is nothing more than a teaser, but my eyes focus on the words "their purpose is truly shocking." Cold sweat breaks out on my face.

What did Dent uncover, and did the secret kill him?

I glance at Katie. "It looks like there was more to this story. Did you find anything else?"

She shakes her head. "Nothing else shows up on their server about this society or on the Internet. Apparently, only this article was ever reported."

"I'm not surprised. The reporter died in a car crash the day after it was published."

Katie's mouth momentarily flutters open. "You don't think this secret society really exists, do you?"

I consider telling her about the tattoos and the twisted arrows symbol that keeps popping up, but I don't want to involve her so directly in this mess. Besides, I have no idea what the symbol means, and she has so many other things to worry about with her dad. I simply say, "I'm not sure. With Sicheii anything is possible."

"You don't think your grandfather has anything to do with these murders, do you? He owns the most successful gallery in

Old Town." She's always very conscious of what people *do*. She still has a hard time believing successful people can be criminals. I'm sure it's her upbringing. Mine is very different. Sicheii taught me to look past appearances and focus on the person underneath.

She points to the date at the top of the page. "This article was written almost thirty years ago. I know your grandfather is in the photo, but he would never be involved in murder."

"I don't know what to believe." I tell her about the hair and the hatchet and Sheriff Daniel's suspicions. The picture isn't a good one.

"Those can all be explained, and I don't trust the Sheriff or the authorities one bit." Katie glances at her watch and her lips turn downward. "I have to go."

I check the clock next to the bed. "You have an hour before school starts. That's plenty of time."

"I know, but the angry nurse said I could only stay fifteen minutes. He wasn't happy I came to visit in the first place."

"What angry nurse?" I sit up straighter and my chest tightens. "The one with the English accent and the gold tooth."

CHAPTER 27

Doctor Dan bursts into the room with quick purposeful strides, his lab coat flapping in his wake, kinetic energy spinning from him. He waves his arms as he speaks and looks a little like a ruffled penguin that's trying to take off. "Good morning, Juliet. I'm happy you're up. We have an appointment in my office. You'll need to put on your street clothes." He looks like an unmade bed dressed in the same clothes he wore yesterday, only now his shirt and pants are more wrinkled and his beard more unruly.

The urgency in his voice propels me into action. This must have something to do with Gold Tooth.

He glances at Katie. "I'm sorry young woman, but visiting time is over for this morning. You'll have to go." He points to the door with a stern expression pinching his face.

She frowns at him and flings her arms around me, which temporarily squishes the breath out of my lungs. "I'll be back later," she whispers before she spins and walks out of the room. I have the feeling I won't be here when she returns.

I grab my bundle of clothes from the closet and hustle to the bathroom.

"You need to hurry, Juliet. You have some visitors we would like to avoid." The playfulness from yesterday has vanished from Doctor Dan's voice, which has hardened into steel.

I fumble with my jeans in the tiny bathroom but manage to slip them on straight. My heart pounds. I can't go back to the van.

When I open the bathroom door, Doctor Dan is peering out of my room and down both sides of the hallway. His head swivels back and forth as if he's watching a tennis match.

"Katie said she spoke with a nurse with a gold tooth. One of the guys who tried to kidnap me has a gold tooth. I'm guessing it's not a coincidence."

Doctor Dan glances at me. The corners of his eyes are webbed, and tight creases form at the end of his lips. "I'm afraid you are correct, Juliet. We have to go to my office on the second floor right away. They'll be looking for you here." He surveys me up and down. "You'll need to put on some shoes first."

Stupid! I had forgotten about my sneakers. Luckily, they're in the closet.

"Why don't we call the Sheriff?" I finish slipping on my sneakers and tie the laces.

"There's no time. The hallway looks clear. Walk right behind me. Don't look directly at anyone. Our destination is the elevator at the end of the hallway to our left."

He shuffles from the room at a brisk pace. I follow close behind and focus on the back of his flowing lab coat. I wonder whether Gold Tooth or Slicked Back Hair will pounce from one of the doorways. Neither of the two nurses on duty lifts their heads.

When we reach the end of the hallway, he jabs the elevator call button three times and shifts nervously on his feet in front of the shiny stainless steel doors.

No one notices us. Once the elevator door opens, we squeeze on. He presses two, and I turn to face the doors and the hallway.

I gasp. The air freezes in my throat. Gold Tooth saunters through the doorway at the opposite end of the floor. His right hand is tucked inside his white nurse's coat where I imagine he's hiding a gun. The doors close, and the elevator drops.

I don't think he saw me, but it takes forever until the elevator door opens on the second floor. When it does, the hospital has been transformed into an office building with a narrow hallway, white wooden doors on both sides, and yellow walls.

Doctor Dan leads me off the elevator, moving at a more measured, confident pace than he did when we raced from my room. The hallway is empty at this early hour, and he stops at the third door on the left side of the hall, removes a roll of keys from his lab coat, unlocks the office, and holds the door open for me.

His office is small and exceptionally neat for the wrinkled doctor. A simple oak desk sits at one end by two windows. A computer screen is perched toward the left side of the desk. The rest is smooth wood without papers or files of any kind. A black pine bookshelf blocks most of the other wall with an assortment of hard covered books stacked neatly on it. They're all psychiatric textbooks that I can't imagine anyone reading.

"Take a seat, Juliet." Doctor Dan waves at one of two leather high-backed chairs in the corner of the office.

I have no intention of sitting. Instead, I grab him by his coat. "Tell me what's going on. Why did my grandfather give you that note, and how did he know I was going to guess eight?"

He smiles. "You are going to have to ask him."

"Is... he... coming here?" The words catch in the back of my throat, and I release his lab coat.

"Not exactly." He glances at his wristwatch. "Wait here." Without warning he leaves and shuts the door behind him. The lock twists and the deadbolt latches in place.

Click.

Really? I try to turn the doorknob but the door is locked and there's no way for me to unlock it from the inside, which is really strange. *What do I know about the doctor? Why did he lock me in the office? Was it for my protection or to keep me here?*

I turn and survey the sparsely decorated room. Something odd starts nagging me, like a stick poking me in the side. *What's missing?* I stroll toward the windows and turn in a tight circle. There are no personal effects of any kind: no pictures of the doctor or his family, no mementos or stupid desk toys, no diplomas hang on the walls — *no diplomas.* My heart quickens. I've never been in a doctor's office without diplomas.

I step behind the desk and open the drawers — nothing, no files or office supplies. When the light streams through the windows, I notice the outline of half a dozen rectangles on the walls where frames have recently been removed. A frost inches up my spine. This isn't Doctor Dan's office. This is an empty office waiting for a new doctor.

Who is Doctor Dan? Where did he come from, and whose side is he on?

My pulse accelerates into a rapid drumroll. Strange sounds fill my head, anxious sounds. I spin and examine the windows. They're standard white vinyl windows with plain glass.

The noises grow louder. The walls start closing in on me. I'm trapped. I yank on the windowsill and it's locked. If Sicheii wanted to meet me, why didn't he just come to the office? I glance at the door, certain that Gold Tooth or Slicked Back Hair is about to burst into the room.

Panic starts to overwhelm me. My feet turn numb. All I see is the inside of the van and the metal ring. I tug and the ring won't let go of the chain.

I shake my head to clear it. I need something sturdy, so I grab a stainless steel trashcan underneath the desk. It feels heavy. The voices grow louder. They almost scream at me. They can't take me again. There's an alley below the window that's only ten feet down.

Screw it! I'm tired of other people being in charge!

I heave the trashcan against the glass with all my strength and it shatters. Shards rain down onto the empty street below.

I hear footsteps. Someone is in the hallway, just outside the door. Sweat stings my eyes. I need to act. There's now way they're locking me back in that van.

The doorknob turns. I wiggle my way out of the window feet first and hold onto the sill, suspended in midair. The plastic edge of the windowsill digs into my fingers and my shoulders ache.

When the door swings open, Lisa is standing there with Doctor Dan right behind her.

"Juliet!" she shouts.

I hold my breath and let go. A second later, I land on my feet in the alley, and race toward the main street.

When I reach the corner, I notice the palm of my hand is bleeding. I reach for my phone to call Troy, but it's not with me.

I peek over my shoulder.

Lisa jumped from the window, and she's sprinting after me.

CHAPTER 28

Wild thoughts race through my mind.

Who can I trust?

How do I find Troy?

I pump my legs and make a quick right in front of the hospital. I almost barrel into an old woman with a cane and wide brimmed straw hat, but swerve at the last second to avoid her. Breathing heavily, I start to gather up some real speed when a crack on the sidewalk trips me up. I lose my footing and stumble forward. About to face plant onto the concrete, I slam into a mailbox, which knocks the wind out of me. I stagger back a step and suck in air. Stars circle in front of my eyes. My injured shoulder screams at me.

Lisa has to be gaining ground on me, but I can't get enough air to start running again. Panic creeps into my thoughts as does images of the inside of that van. I'll never be able to escape from that van again.

A white Toyota pulls up beside me.

"Get in, Juliet." Ms. Arnold waves for me to hurry.

I glance over my shoulder. Lisa has reached the main street with Doctor Dan red faced and huffing behind her. There's no sign of Slicked Back Hair or Gold Tooth or the white van. But how far behind can they be?

I yank open the back passenger door, jump in, and slam it shut. Ms. Arnold stomps on the gas and the tires screech. Lisa stops running and angrily places her hands on her hips. Bent at the waist, Doctor Dan gasps for air. I exhale deeply in one long gust. They won't capture me, at least not yet.

"What's going on, Juliet?" Ms. Arnold's eyes, dark and small, flicker to the rearview mirror.

"I needed to leave the hospital in a hurry."

"Why?" She takes a hard right and the tires protest, but she keeps the car from skidding into oncoming traffic. "Does this have anything to do with your kidnapping?"

"I thought the school was keeping that quiet." I assumed everyone at Bartens believed I got hurt as part of a failed robbery attempt.

She takes a quick left and slows the car. "Some of us know better than the school's story." She shoots me a meaningful look. "Does your mom know you left the hospital?"

"No... no one knows."

"Okay, Juliet. Let's go to my place so we can check out your hand. That cut looks nasty." She tosses me a hand towel with little green tennis balls embroidered on it. "Use the towel to put pressure on it."

A shard of glass has sliced into my palm. The glass is gone, and the wound is already clotting, but I push the towel against the blood anyway. "What were you doing at the hospital?"

"I was on my way to visit you before school starts." She smiles with only the corners of her mouth. "Good thing I saw you."

A few minutes later, she parks in front of a small brick apartment building on the outskirts of Old Town in a neighborhood locals call *Yuppyville*. She bounces out of the car and holds the door open for me, a concerned look in her eyes. "How's that cut?" She peeks at the towel.

"The bleeding's stopped. It's no big deal. It doesn't hurt."

"Great, let's go." She shuts the door behind me, checks both sides of the street, and opens the glass door to a high-class apartment building.

My sneakers squeak against marble tile, and my fingers brush against mahogany walls. Ms. Arnold hustles us toward the elevator with one arm around my shoulders, presses the call button and waits impatiently for the elevator to arrive. When the door opens, she pushes me in and jabs the button for the top floor.

The shiny steel doors act like a mirror. She's dressed casually in a t-shirt, shorts, and sneakers. She bounces nervously on her toes, her eyes never meeting mine. When the bell rings, the door opens and she unlocks a cherry wood door with a shiny brass placard that says "PH-1" on it toward the top. When I step inside, she bolts the door behind us.

"There's a bathroom on the right." She takes brisk steps and points to a white door. "Clean the cut and I'll find a bandage."

The cold water feels good against my hand. My breathing steadies. Why would Doctor Dan and Lisa work with Gold Tooth and Slicked Back Hair? What do they want with me? Nothing makes sense. Sicheii's led me down a sinkhole where I can't find my footing. I'm going to strangle him when I see him next!

Ms. Arnold returns a moment later with a large Band-Aid and some antibacterial cream. She clicks her tongue as she bandages the wound. "Do you know where your grandfather is? Everyone wants to talk to him."

I shake my head as she leads me into the living room. The blinds are drawn even though light streamed through the windows just a minute ago.

"I'll make you some tea and then you'll tell me everything." She disappears into the kitchen.

I pace the living room in small steps. Questions pop into my mind quickly like I'm playing *Whack a Mole*. The only problem is I don't have any answers to bash the mole in the head, so questions keep jumping up all over the place and crowding around me. In the end, all my thoughts return to Sicheii.

What has he gotten us into?

Almost by osmosis, I start to notice the apartment around me. The place is gorgeous. The duplex has floor to ceiling windows, hardwood floors, a gourmet kitchen, and a giant sized living room. It looks like a model apartment from one of the design magazines my mom reads. How can Ms. Arnold pay for an apartment like this at what Bartens pays her? The teachers all complain about the awful pay. Never directly to the students, but you would have to be deaf and clueless not to overhear the conversations.

She appears at my side, holding a cup with steam swirling above it. She smiles as she hands it to me. "Drink it. The tea will make you feel better."

I take the cup and sip. "Thanks. This is a really cool apartment."

Ms. Arnold glances around the place as if she's looking at it for the first time. "I'm just house sitting for a friend. Take another sip."

Feeling like a student in her class, I comply. The tea tastes sweet, as if she added a tablespoon of honey, but it doesn't taste like honey exactly. It leaves a bitter aftertaste on my tongue.

"Come sit on the couch." She pats a black leather sofa and we sit close together. I get the feeling that something is off. I can't put my finger on it. A sensation creeps along my body that starts at my toes until my head starts to swim.

I notice her t-shirt and shorts, and they strike me as odd. "You're not dressed to teach."

"I was taking the day off."

"I thought you were going to teach after you visited me." I don't like the expression on her face. Her eyes look calculating and detached. Noise starts to flood my head. "Maybe I should call my mom." My tongue feels thick and fat and my words come out slow and slurred.

She takes the cup from my hand. "That's not a good idea, Juliet." Her voice starts to twist towards me as if floating through a tornado.

I notice a sketchpad on the coffee table. She's quite a good artist, but that's not what steals my breath away. She's drawn a picture of the demon that chased me at Slippery River and the cemetery. I point at the drawing. "You've seen... this before?"

"Sure. It's my friend's pet."

A pet? This is bad. I try to get up, but my body feels heavy, and she pushes me back down and leans in close to my face, her lips only inches from my ear. "Do you know what you are?"

"What're you talking about? I'm not anyone special." My head spins groggily. Her face turns fuzzy and then refocuses.

"You really don't know, do you?" She chuckles. The sound grates against my nerves. Her face turns fuzzy again, and this time, it doesn't clear. "They haven't told you." She strokes my cheek with her fingers.

I look at the cup and three stare back at me. I try to yell but can only sputter, "What... have... done," and that takes an eternity. My body folds back into the couch, my breathing labored. I'm a fool for trusting the wrong person.

She sits up straighter. "I wasn't at the hospital to visit you. I was watching for your grandfather. They think he is the one we need. They believe he holds the key the Seeker is after. I don't think they're right."

I open my mouth, but the drugs in the tea have stolen my voice and my tongue flops out, leaving me voiceless.

Her face twists and turns as if her features are reflected in one of those oddly shaped mirrors they use at carnivals. "You are the key," she says and leans close to me. Her fingers lift my chin. "You are the Alpha." Her hot breath brushes against my cheek. I want to pull back, but I've lost all control over my body.

My mind staggers in drunken circles. *What's she talking about?* I'm just a normal teenager. All I've ever wanted to be was normal, but my eyelids start to close on their own, and it takes all my will to keep them open.

"I've been observing you. You're special. You moved so fast you were a blur when you attacked Tiffany the other day. No one moves that fast, and the ring from the van was bent. It would take two hulking guys to bend that ring.

"They think the Alpha has to be a boy. Ha! *You're* the one we need. You contain the secret. The Seeker will be so pleased. He will reward me generously. This apartment will only be the beginning. I'll be wealthy beyond your imagination. You *must* be the Alpha."

I smell her perfume—roses with a slight hint of tobacco. The smell makes me ill. Bile fills my throat. I try so hard to stay awake, but my eyes close and won't open. Just when all turns gray, I hear splintered wood. Ms. Arnold screams and jumps off the couch. I try to twist, to see what's going on, but my body is too heavy and my eyes stay closed.

Strong arms lift me. Familiar arms, and I smell incense. Gray turns black.

CHAPTER 29

I can see, yet I'm not awake. I'm dreaming, but it feels more real than my usual dreams, almost like I am reliving a vivid memory. Two suns light a cloudless blue sky with a bright red hue. Beams of light beat down hot on my face.

I stand on a cliff of bluish rocky soil. Below me a battle erupts. Short, wide people with bushels of curly black hair on their heads and faces wield wooden spears. Leather skins cover only a small portion of their bodies. Thick-knotted muscle bunches on their arms and legs and backs. At least a thousand adults brandish spears. They look angry, nervous, scared even.

They're not human. They have bent backs and only a few teeth, which they've filed to sharp points. Their eyes burn blood red. Both men and women have curly black beards. Only the small ones – the children - do not. The adults form a ragged line six deep in front of round, blue, clay huts that I guess are their homes, while the children stand fifty feet behind them, bows and arrows with shiny metal tips clutched in their little hands.

The second group is tall and thin and hairless. Their features are fine and handsome, and their eyes shine an electric shade of violet. Dressed in light, almost translucent tunics that hang to their knees, they could pass as extraordinarily beautiful humans, but they're different. Marching forward in perfect formation of neat squares five rows deep, each warrior holds what resembles a glass sword with light glimmering off the sharp edges. They show no fear. They move as if conducting a harmless training exercise. All the fear emanates from the short brutish people even though they outnumber their opponents two to one. Nothing separates the two forces except flat, bluish rock.

The children shoot a wave of arrows that take flight like a flock of birds that whistle through the air.

The oncoming army never slows their gait. When the arrows start their downward plunge, they fall harmlessly to the ground five feet in front of the approaching soldiers as if all their momentum was somehow stolen away before they could do any harm.

One of the short, brutish warriors jumps in the air and waves his spear in looping circles over his head. He must be the leader of his people. He wears a long leather cape and stark white horns protrude from the curly hair on his head. I can't be sure, but the horns probably come from an animal—a decoration or a symbol that he's in charge. He turns to face his people, screams a high-pitched battle cry that echoes in the rocky canyon, and his army surges forward. The ground shakes from their sandals and anger and fear.

The taller soldiers never break formation or change their pace. When the two forces collide, it's no contest. The glass swords carve through spears and into flesh. They cleave away muscle and bone as easily as the arrows had flown through the air. The horned leader is the first to fall. Blood splashes the ground. Screams echo and death spoils the air.

Within minutes, piles of dead, brutish warriors litter the battleground—hundreds dead. I want to scream for the battle to stop, but I have no voice. I can do nothing as the remaining brutish people turn to retreat. Parents frantically wave at their children to flee. The attackers race forward. Their long legs carry them past the brutish people in a blur as they swing their glimmering swords of death.

A horrifying scene of carnage plays out below me. I hope the children will be spared, or can escape, but they are neither fast enough nor shown any mercy. Most run and are struck in the back. A few try to fight, swinging their small bows as clubs. They are no match for the beautiful soldiers. I try to look away, but I cannot turn. In a few minutes, the entire village is massacred. Not one member of their tribe stands.

I search for the dead among the taller warriors. Surely a few have been killed, but only one man appears injured. A spear has pierced his side. He wobbles on his knees. Four compatriots stalk toward him. The tallest of the four swings his glass sword; the injured man's head topples from his shoulders. I wince at the brutality of the scene and wake.

Scorching air roasts my flesh. When I open my eyes, I see nothing but darkness. Not normal darkness, but disorienting total darkness, as if all light has been sucked out of the world. *Am I awake? I can't tell.*

I push away the horrible images from the battle, and memories of Ms. Arnold and the apartment shove their way into my mind. I sit up fully awake now. I'm on a rough mattress and hear a nearby shuffling sound in the darkness.

I'm not alone.

My heart skips a beat and my mouth goes dry.

"Who's there?" My voice sounds timid and my eyes strain against the darkness. I expect Gold Tooth or Slicked Back Hair to answer or grab me. I'd run if I could see where to go.

A shadow strikes a match and tosses it on a small stack of dry wood, which instantly bursts into flames. The sudden flash burns my eyes. The flickering firelight provides enough light for me to see. I'm sitting at one end of a small oblong structure made totally of clay.

The shadow moves and I look into gray eyes framed by long white hair. The flickering firelight plays games with his eyes, turning them wild.

My heart jumps. "What's going on, Sicheii? Where are we?"

He moves close beside me. "We are at my sweat lodge, as the Great Wind Spirit has commanded." He speaks matter-of-factly as if he's merely reporting the weather. I know he has a secret sweat lodge. All medicine men have one where they ask the spirits to cure people or speak to them or whatever weirdness they do in private. I've never asked to visit his or even seen one before.

"Who are these people that are after us?"

Sweat glistens off his chest and the twisted arrows tattoo over his heart. "That's a very complicated question." He lifts the back of his hand to my brow and frowns with his lips and eyes. "You have the fever. We don't have much time to talk."

"Tell me what's going on!" The words escape fast as I ball up my hands into fists. He's so infuriating.

"You are a very special young woman. You are not ill as your mother suspects." His face twists sourly; his displeasure at Mom reflects in his eyes. "These voices you hear are a gift from the Great Wind Spirit. You can understand the thoughts of those around you, human and animal. You must embrace this gift and learn to control it to break the fever. It's your first test before you receive your other gifts."

"What do you mean gifts?" I huff. "I don't want any gifts. What's wrong with everyone?"

"The time for childish games is over, Juliet." Sicheii touches me on the arm. His fingers feel cool to the touch, and the simple gesture steadies me. "You know differently. You can't deny your uniqueness any longer. You must be a rock."

"How did you know I would see the number eight when I was with Doctor Dan last night?" I have so many questions, I'm not sure why this one jumps to my lips. Still it did, and it spilled out.

He smiles. "I told him to clear his mind and think only of that number. I knew you would read his thoughts."

I slump my shoulders and sit heavily on the mattress. "You've gone insane." Still, as crazy as he sounds, he does make some sense. How else would he have known I was going to say eight? Eight isn't even my favorite number. My favorite number is six.

A mischievous smile springs to his face. "You know the truth. You just have to let yourself believe."

Could I have gifts? I've never been special—just an average student, a good lacrosse player but not great, an average looking girl—nothing special.

"What do I have to do?" I sound mousy and small, as far away from special as imaginable.

Sicheii glances back at the flames for a moment before his eyes meet mine. "Every animal has the spark of life given to it by the spirits. That spark is unique to the creature. Your mind is more finely tuned than others. You can pick up their sparks and hear the thoughts behind it." He smiles. "If you concentrate hard enough on the voices, you can understand them like a radio receives stations. People generally think in words, but animals see images."

I recall the day Troy and I found Roundtree dead behind his house. I saw those cuts on his chest. They weren't my imagination. They could've come from the goats. *Argh*! This is so weird, but there's truth underneath the weirdness. "How do I tune my brain? Do you have this *gift*?"

He shakes his head. "The Great Wind Spirit chose you. You are Chosen. No one else has these gifts." He passes me a glass of water. "As our leader, Roundtree knew more. He had the Ancient Book of Gifts, but he refused to give it to me. All I can do is help you with the old ways: through the stones, the prayers, and the ancient medicines."

"How come you didn't tell me about this earlier?" I practically growl at him. "Why does everything have to be a secret?" I feel heavy and tired like a pack animal that has carried supplies for too long.

"I am only an agent of the Wind Spirit." His face softens and his shoulders go limp. "This is how it's written. Besides, you would be in danger if others knew about your special nature before you accepted your gifts."

"Did you kill Roundtree and the others?" The words sound pillow-soft. I have to ask. I study his eyes, but the firelight dances in them, so I don't see the truth.

"There is no time for that." Tension jumps into his body, his back stiffens, and his jaw clenches. "We must concentrate on you and controlling your first gift. Later we can talk about all you need to know."

"Great."

He turns and shouts in the old language to the fire-keeper outside. Every sweat lodge has a fire-keeper. He or she keeps a fire burning, makes sure the stones smolder, keeps everyone safe, and protects the lodge from outsiders. Even though this is a secret sweat lodge, I'm not surprised he has a fire-keeper. I wish I understood what he said, but I've never tried to learn the language.

He ambles toward the opposite end of the lodge where a leather hide acts as a door and takes the handle of a long shovel and lifts three smoldering stones. Thin wisps of smoke circle above them. He meticulously places the three stones into the fire and creates a perfect triangle. The stones sizzle in the fire pit. He tosses sage, cedar, and sweet grass on top of the hot stones to purify the smoke. The heat spikes. He returns the shovel to the fire-keeper and closes the leather hide.

Before he returns, he chants an old song and shakes a leather and wooden rattle. He asks the Great Wind Spirit to guide us and protect us. The flames dance upward for a heartbeat, and I see the adobe bricks that make the sweat lodge and the grass that's been used as mortar.

As the flame burns brighter, the air turns hotter. *Why make it hotter?* The air is practically on fire as it is. I bring my hand to my mouth to thwart some of the heat. The sweltering temperature blasts me in suffocating waves. When I take in air, the heat burns my lungs, and my skin feels like it's on fire.

He returns to my side and frowns. "You have the fever. You must concentrate hard on your gifts. You cannot fail." His eyes lock onto mine; they look like diamonds, sparkling in the firelight, hard, severe, untamed.

My head swims, but I don't like the jagged edge to his face and the desperation in the tilt of his head. "What happens if I fail?"

"If you fail to control your gift, the fever will consume you, and the Great Wind Spirit will take us both."

I struggle to stand, but my arms and legs are loosely tied to a wooden post by heavy rope.

CHAPTER

"Are you crazy? Untie me!" I pull hard against the rope with both arms, but the restraints hold, and the cords dig into my wrists, so I stop. "It's hot in here, and I don't feel well." My head reels, thoughts collide against each other, none make any sense. The herbal incense and the fever burning through my bloodstream send my mind careening out of control.

Sicheii scowls at me, as if I had given him the wrong answer to an important question. "You must quell your anger to survive. There's nowhere else for you to go. White medicine can't cure you." He brushes a couple of stray hairs from his eyes. "It is written The Great Wind Spirit requires you to face this test in a sweat lodge. You must search within and embrace your gift. It's the only way to break the fever. You must control the gifts the Wind Spirit has given you."

"Help!" I shout at the gate, hoping to reach the fire-keeper. "Help me!" I repeat the cry four times. Each time, my voice loses more steam.

He glances from the leather door to me. "You will find no help from outside, Little Bird. You must look within. You must ask the Wind Spirit to guide you." He moves toward the gate where he takes another handful of herbs from his leather pouch.

"Please, Sicheii, let me go!"

He ignores me, begins chanting again, and tosses more herbs on the flames.

The fragrance fills the lodge, and makes the air heavy. *Is he crazy? Could he be right?* My thoughts spin and spin and spin. I see the photograph of the secret society from the article, Roundtree's dead body, the twisted arrows tattoo, the look on Ms. Arnold's face after she drugged me. The heat rises and the smell of incense fills my lungs. I sag down on the mattress, my body a led weight. He circles the fire, round and round, and ignores me as if he's alone. My anger bursts into all-consuming rage like a wildfire. I need to let it go, but I can't.

I collapse on the mattress and slip in and out of consciousness. Dreams twist and torque through my mind. One moment, Troy sits next to me. He seems sad, with moist eyes and a deep frown. The next moment, a hatchet slices open my chest.

Morgan and Tiffany show up in one of my visions. They laugh at me and call me *Indian trash*. They tell me I'll never be welcome in their clubs.

Ella tries to explain something important about the murders while she drives her Ford recklessly, and Katie is crying. I can't console her. I fail her.

Lucid times mingle with the visions. Sicheii hands me water from a glass. The visions and reality twist together so neither is recognizable. Anger is my only constant companion, consuming me, sucking away my energy.

I must have fallen into a deep sleep because I find myself in a vast city made of crystal. I feel different, lighter. It's serene and otherworldly. The anger has finally vanished, a weight lifted from my body.

I twirl in a lazy, looping circle. Tall structures soar upward in all directions. Paved roads sparkle with silver and crushed stone, and small circles of sapphire colored grass appear randomly. Crystal structures stretch off into the distance as far as I can see. The city should teem with life, but I find none. No vehicles nor people nor noise of any kind.

I wander down the widest of the ghost streets and pass buildings of increasing size and elaborateness. They're completely foreign looking. Some curve with vast arches, while others point with jagged edges. Most are translucent, but a few are opaque and block out the light. A sun, larger but dimmer than ours, floats high in a greenish sky with three small moons that circle close to it in the distance.

Where am I, and how did I get here?

As I travel down the wide avenue, the buildings become spaced farther apart until a circular stadium shines in the distance. The first traces of life sprout as I move closer to the stadium—signs appear. Not paper signs, but screens with fixed images. Most have a purple triangle with a yellow circle in the center. An "X" drawn in red crosses out the entire symbol. A few have an image of a beautiful looking man. He's hairless with fine features. Purple islands float in the otherwise blue ocean of his eyes. They seem to glow dangerously. The same red "X" crosses through his face. He isn't human. He's one of those warriors from my prior dream who ravaged the short, brutish people.

I feel as if I'm floating above the street as I go. Before realizing it, I cross the arched entranceway into the stadium. It's vast, much larger than any stadium I have ever seen. The sides stretch as tall as the tallest building in Phoenix. Energy, anxious and angry, buffets against me as I push open gray crystal doors and enter the main floor of the arena.

Inside the crystal coliseum is a field of knee high, wispy, blue-green grass surrounding a wide stage six stories tall. On the stage sit three tall, hairless, almost human looking people. Two are men and the third a woman. They wear white and silver tunics that shimmer with the symbol of the triangle and the circle on their chests.

Six others sit on glass thrones that tower over those with the symbols — three men and three women. Their tunics glisten with golden specks and each has a red crystal pendant shaped like a disc hanging from their neck. I cannot tell their age. Their lack of hair and fine features disguise them, but the man and woman in the center throne chairs are clearly well aged, with lines around the eyes and stooped backs.

The oldest woman shouts, her face red as spit flies from her mouth. Her hands clutch the side of her throne chair, the muscles on her forearms tense. I tear my eyes from her and glance up into the stadium, where I see thousands and thousands of these people. I can't tell one from the other, but a quarter of the stands are full with those who wear tunics with the triangle and circle symbol in one section. Separated from the rest, they're guarded by others who hold clear crystal swords. The sun reflects off the weapons and makes it appear almost as if the guards hold staffs of light.

When I return my gaze to the stage, the old woman stops yelling and glances at her comrades who sit on thrones beside her. A sly, confident smile graces her face. A decision must be reached. Her chair is a few feet taller than the rest. Each of her comrades nods his head and beats his chest with a fist. They are all in agreement.

When the last one does the same, the old woman faces the three sitting before her, her expression severe. She grabs the crystal pendant around her neck and it turns blood red. She waves her other hand and the tunics of all three are ripped. A red slice appears across their foreheads as if she has cut them with an invisible knife.

The stands roar. Not a cheer or shout or cry, but the sound of thousands and thousands of people beating their fists against their chests and stomping their feet. A wave of energy, like a current, races through my body. Those in the stands with the symbols on their chests stand stoically. I squint and see their tunics rip. Blood splashes across their foreheads.

The ground beneath me sways. I open my eyes.

Sicheii gently shakes me. "You cannot sleep now, Little Bird." I sit up and he says, "You must concentrate on the voices."

My head whirls, and Sicheii's face changes into that of Doctor Dan. "Turn your attention to the sounds. Embrace them, Juliet. Feel them intensify, shape them."

Is this reality or another dream?

"What do I do?" My voice sounds weak and pathetic, and I despise it. My right heel stings, and I remember the story Sicheii told me of my birth. I feel the connection between that story and the voices as if tied together by a silk cord.

"You don't have much time left," Doctor Dan says. "Concentrate on the voices, embrace them, fine tune them with your mind like you did the other night. It's the only way."

I close my eyes, my body wobbles, and I reach into my mind for the voices. Determination replaces my fear. *I will not die here.* I focus on the loudest voice. It sounds like a radio station that isn't quite tuned in, full of static and gibberish.

My skin burns. I refuse to open my eyes for fear I might see flames engulfing my body. The sounds grow louder but no more comprehensible. My body rocks. I almost topple over and have to put my hands down on the mattress to steady myself. If I fall, I will never rise again, but I will not fall. My eyes stay clenched shut.

I play with the noises and mold them, twist them. They start to come into focus. The unintelligible words begin to sound like Sicheii's voice. My lungs are on fire. I gasp for breath and open my eyes.

Sicheii's face leans close to mine. He takes shallow desperate breaths.

"Déélgai," I say. "Déélgai, you crazy old man."

He bends backward at the waist and lets out a full-bodied "WHOOP." A smile beams brightly across his face. "What does déélgai mean, Little Bird?"

Déélgai is an ancient word, but I understand its meaning. I not only hear the word but see the image from his mind. "Swan... Sicheii. It means swan."

"Yes it does." He lifts the back of his hand to my head. "The fever has broken. You've passed your first test." He feathers his fingertips against my cheek.

"Great, now get me out of here." Other words and images flash in my head. They all come from Sicheii's mind. His relief and love wrap tightly around my body like a wool blanket. I so want to be angry with him, but how can I?

He cuts the ropes from my wrists. I try to stand, but my legs wobble, so he lifts me. "How long have I been here?"

"Almost three days." He carries me through the sweat lodge and into the cool night air.

A shadow hovers close to the campfire—the fire-keeper in the distance. I don't need to see him to know who he is.

CHAPTER

31

Sicheii carries me to a rusted 1970s RV. He kicks open the screen door and gently places me on a plastic kitchen chair. The camper smells old and musty and acrid as if the vehicle is displeased we are using it and hopes to drive us away with its foul stench. The Formica kitchen tabletop peels in long, curved strips. Age yellows the once white kitchen cabinets, which hang crookedly on rusted hinges. Thankfully, the light is dim.

"Let me find you something cool to drink. You need to hydrate." Sicheii swings open the door to the mini-fridge, pours two glasses of iced tea, places one in front of me and downs the other in three noisy gulps.

I stare at the condensation that clings to the outside of the glass. My throat is scorching dry and the tea's amber color inviting. My fingers wrap around the glass, and I peer inside. What else is in the iced tea? Another drug, maybe? What new test does he have in store for me? A fire burns through me, so I toss the cold liquid in his face.

He smiles in return. "The anger is never far from the surface with you, is it?" His long, white hair and bushy eyebrows resemble a wet mop as iced tea drips from his face in little streams.

"What have you done to me? I could have died!"

He sighs. "I've let you fulfill your destiny." He takes the empty glass from my hand. "If I refill this glass, will you drink the tea?" He stares at me, eyes boring into mine, making no effort to dry his face. One drop of tea clings to his eyebrow until it gives up and falls to the kitchen table below.

Despite my anger, I fight hard not to grin. "Yes, Sicheii, I'll drink the tea."

He moves slowly, shoulders slumped, and dries his face on an old green towel. I wonder if he has spent the entire three days in the sweat lodge with me, worrying and praying to the Great Wind Spirit. He looks much older than he did a few days ago.

He returns, and this time, he brings the pitcher with him. He hands me another glass of iced tea and places the half-full pitcher on the cracked kitchen table. I can't recall ever being so thirsty before, so I eagerly take the glass and chug. The cold liquid flows down my parched throat, refreshing and reviving me. I don't even mind the little splash that sloshes down the side of my face.

I refill the glass. "Everything started the day I was born, right? You did something weird to me in the hospital. These voices are connected with that story you told me on my thirteenth birthday."

He shakes his head. "That is only the middle of your story. Your destiny goes back over 200 years. The Wind Spirit spoke to our ancestors and described what had to be done. They recorded the encounter in the Book of Knowledge. Only a few of us were allowed to be secret keepers. Only a few knew and understood what was required. Only those who could be trusted."

"Only those with the twisted arrows tattoos," I say, interrupting him, and the light in his eyes burns brighter. "Yes, I know all about the tattoos and your little club."

"The Order of the Twisted Arrows is no little club, Juliet. We are sworn to carry out the Wind Spirit's wishes." He pours himself another glass from the pitcher.

"So I'm the secret you've been trying to keep." I hunch back in my chair. "The entire mystery this whole time is about *me*. All these people, sworn to keep *me* a secret."

"The Order goes back over two hundred years, Juliet. This secret has been carefully guarded and only entrusted to a few select individuals. But yes, it all culminates in you. This is the only way our people can survive."

"What does any of this have to do with the survival of our people?"

"The Wind Spirit demanded that we inject her essence into the Chosen to let the spirit bind with the Chosen's spirit. This way, the two spirits can twist together and the Wind Spirit can empower the Chosen with gifts you will need to save our people from death."

"So that needle you stuck me with was filled with the Wind Spirit's essence?" I shake my head. "You injected something *weird* into my blood."

"Yes, but it was not some drug. It came from the Wind Spirit and was handed down to us over two centuries."

I drink the second glass of tea. This time, I take my time. I need a little space to wrap my mind around what he is telling me. "Why did you choose me? Someone else must have been more worthy. I'm not special."

"I didn't choose you. If there were any other way, I would have found someone else. I know this is a big responsibility, but the Wind Spirit was specific. She told us the exact star configuration when the Chosen would be born and instructed us that the Chosen had to be one of our descendants." He shrugs. "You were born at exactly the right time and were the only eligible candidate."

He opens his hands on the table palm out. "You see, the Wind Spirit chose you over two hundred years ago. There was nothing I could do but accept your destiny."

I groan. "You could have told me. You didn't need to lie to me my whole life. First Mom, and now you. Why is everyone lying to *me*!"

"It's not my place to question the Wind Spirit, Juliet. We are bound to keep your role secret until you face your first challenge. There was no other way." He clenches his right hand into a fist and taps the table. "Besides, secrecy is critical. Others seek to destroy you. They will kill you if they have the opportunity."

"Great. The story only gets better. Does Mom know about this?"

"No. She would never have understood."

"You said reading thoughts was only one of my gifts." I push my glass to one side. Intrigued, I wonder if there's some benefit for being the Chosen whatever. "What other gifts are you talking about? Anything useful?"

He frowns. It is a full-face frown; the many lines in his face turn downward together. "I don't know. Roundtree had the Book of Gifts. I tried to persuade him to give it to me, but he said he had hidden it in a safe place." His hands smooth back his hair. "I warned him, but he would not yield or relinquish the book to me."

"What does it say? You must have read it."

He shakes his head. "It is not for any of *us* to read. The Book of Gifts can only be read by the *Chosen*."

215

"Did you kill Roundtree?"

Sicheii's face turns red. "Don't ask questions you already know the answer to!"

He rarely gets angry, so the outburst surprises me and the force of his words makes me lean back in the chair. I stare hard at him and try to fine-tune my brain like a receiver to read his thoughts. Words and images come, but they come so quickly they jumble together. I sense sadness and guilt, but I can't tell what it all means. A flame behind his eyes scares me, and for the first time, I really wonder whether he was involved in the murders.

I snap from my trance, tired and weary. The effort to manipulate his thoughts and images sap the rest of my waning strength. I feel as if I'm made of stone and lean on the table with my head hung low. "What do we do next?"

He smiles, and his face returns to his old self, confident, happy. "We eat. I'm starving." He looks through the RV's rusted window. "The fire should be perfect for a barbecue."

CHAPTER 32

Alone, I close my eyes. I'm not sure how much time passes, but it seems to cease. Weariness has seeped into my body beyond flesh and blood and bone and into my soul like a slow trickle of water has seeped into a sponge until it can't absorb another drop. I would be content to sit in the plastic chair with my head resting awkwardly on the peeled table for the rest of my days.

But the smell from the barbecue triggers an animal survival instinct. Steak sizzles against stone slabs and my stomach jumps. It's the only part of me with any life. If my stomach wasn't tethered to my stone-like body, it would do cartwheels at the thought of eating freshly grilled steak.

I lift my head and find a shadow figure by the door—the vague form of the fire-keeper, nervous, anxious. He knocks softly.

I narrow my eyes. Blood rushes through my veins. "Come in, traitor!"

The door opens, and Troy skulks into the RV, his shoulders stooped with his eyes focused on his feet.

"You knew about this madness and you didn't tell me? How could you?" My mouth hangs open. I have a hard time believing Troy is complicit in Sicheii's schemes, yet he stands before me as his fire-keeper.

Troy raises his eyes, eyes I have stared into so many times before. Always, I believed in a best friend and imagined a future. Now I see a liar.

"Jake explained things to me six months ago. They needed new blood for the Order and wanted me to look after you... protect you."

"You've been lying to me for *six months!*" I shake my head and rub my hands through my hair. "I can live with my mom and even Sicheii, but not you." A hole opens in my heart. A sharp pain stabs through me that almost doubles me over with cramps, but still I grip the table hard and stay upright. Bits of Formica from the table snap in my hands.

"Once I knew the truth, I was bound to stay silent, Jules." He steps toward me and rests both his hands on a kitchen chair. "If I had told you, you would be in danger."

"You let me think I was going crazy to protect me? Lift up your shirt." I know what I'll find on his chest, but I want him to lift his shirt anyway.

He hesitates. "There's no need to do that, Jules. I've always been on your side." Guilt weighs down his voice, making it slow and lumbering like a buffalo.

I glare at him. "Lift up your shirt."

Troy frowns and lifts his t-shirt. A twisted arrows tattoo blazes on the smooth brown skin on his chest.

"No wonder you were reluctant to help me this whole time. You knew what the ink meant. You realized what was happening.

Did you kill Roundtree? Maybe help my grandfather as he tortured him?"

"No, Juliet. I had nothing to do with Roundtree's death and neither did Jake. The Seeker's people tortured Roundtree. They were looking for you." Troy waves his hands. "He knows about you now and won't stop until he gets you."

"You are a *liar*! Why should I believe anything you say?"

"I'm your best friend, Jules." Troy tries to smile, but his mouth won't budge beyond a thin grim line. "You have to trust me."

I shake my head and turn away from him. I can't look at him. "I don't know what you are, but you're not my friend. Friends don't lie to each other, not about something like this. Get out. I never want to see you again. Go be with Candy. I'm sure she misses you!"

I stare at the grimy window until I hear the screen door swing open and close a few moments later. The weariness returns, and I bang my head against the table.

Clunk.

I don't know what to think.

Clunk.

Everything is mixed up and everyone has been lying to me.

Clunk.

I feel alone. Troy anchored me, his friendship has been the cornerstone I've built my life around. I'm not sure what happens next and that scares me. I never thought I'd have to think about life without him.

Sicheii calls from outside that the food is ready. I debate whether I should get up or stay and melt into the smelly, broken kitchen table forever. My belly grumbles and makes the decision for me.

It takes considerable effort to leave my chair, but I can't stay in the dirty kitchen forever. I push on the table with my hands, find my feet, and trudge outside. The night sky is clear and the campfire flames are low and dance a slow waltz. Sicheii has changed into a blue linen shirt and his favorite straw wide-brimmed hat. He laid out a red woolen blanket a few feet away from the fire where he's placed two large, sizzling steaks on a white ceramic serving platter.

I trudge toward the blanket, dragging my feet across the ground. Dirt drifts in the still air behind me. Sicheii smiles when I sit cross-legged next to him.

Troy hasn't left. He sits near the fire watching and sulking in the darkness. I want to ask him to leave, but I don't have the energy, and part of me wants him to stay.

Sicheii prays to the Great Wind Spirit for delivering me out of the darkness. I tune him out. I should wait for him to finish, but I don't care about hurting his feelings at the moment, or the Great Wind Spirit, or any of this mess, so I grab the plate, a fork and knife, and dive in.

My grandfather has many shortcomings, but he's a magician around a fire-pit. The meat bursts with flavor. It's been a lifetime since I last ate. A little energy returns to my body, and I sit up straighter and glare at him. "So who decided to kill John Dent? Was it Roundtree? Did you need to kill him to keep your secrets?"

He chuckles and wipes grease from his mouth with a white cotton towel. "You are so quick to believe the worst in me that you refuse to see the obvious in front of you."

"What does that mean?" I am tired of his riddles. "Just tell me the truth this time."

"We didn't kill John Dent." He smiles. "When he broke his story about the Order, we took him in and told him the truth. He was in danger and saw the grievous error he had made and decided it was best to disappear."

"Sure... I saw his grave."

"He's not dead. He changed his name and went back to school. You met him as Doctor Dan Epstein."

I slice off another piece of steak and slip it into my mouth. So *that's* why Doctor Dan looked so familiar. He was the grown up person from the picture on his mother's mantel. I add him to the long list of people who seem to have no problem lying to me.

"What about Ayden? You knew he killed that man in self-defense. You could have prevented him from going to jail."

Sicheii places his fork on the serving dish. He hesitates for a couple of seconds as he thinks about what to tell me.

"I'll know if you're being honest. I'm the Chosen, remember?" I have no idea if I can tell whether he speaks the truth through my gift, but a good threat works even if it only has the illusion of being carried out.

"Yes, you are," he replies. "Ayden was a dangerous drug dealer. He was no good for you and Summer. You could never be safe around him, and we needed to keep you safe."

"So you let him go to jail?" I clench my hands closed.

"It's not as simple as that. The Seeker was on to us. He had sent three men to investigate our town. They made a connection between the Order and Roundtree. The only way we could cover up the situation was to have those deaths appear like a drug deal gone bad. We planted enough evidence and covered our tracks well enough that we fooled him, at least temporarily. Your father had to pay that price to keep you safe."

"But he was innocent." I toss my fork onto the plate with a loud clang. "He spent fifteen years in jail. I could have grown up with a father!"

Sicheii touches my leg, and his eyes convey real sorrow. "I'm sorry you didn't have a father growing up, Juliet. I did my best to fill the void, but Ayden was not an innocent man. He had committed many crimes for which he had not been punished. Life has a way of catching up to you, and this time, it caught up with him."

I swipe Sicheii's hand from my knee and eat in silence. Frogs call out in the distance. An owl hoots and ruffles the leaves in a nearby tree.

Troy shivers when he hears the owl. He believes that owls warn us about upcoming death, and his eyes scan the nearby trees as he looks for the bird.

"We need to make plans, Juliet," Sicheii says. "I don't know what your teacher told the Seeker, but we have to assume he knows you are here or will figure out how important you are soon. He won't stop until he captures you. Besides, the rest of your gifts will come quickly, and I don't know what they are or how to help."

"Gifts," I snort. "I don't want any more gifts."

"You are Chosen," he says, his voice low, deep, and full of concern. "You don't have any choice. If we knew where Roundtree kept the second book, we would know more."

"What happened to Ms. Arnold?" She was my favorite teacher, the only person other than Katie I trusted at Bartens and another one who lied to me.

"She is being held in a safe place. She can't hurt us now." He stares hard at me. "We need to focus on you and your gifts. They are the key to fulfilling your destiny. You must embrace them before the Seeker finds you."

"Who is this Seeker you keep talking about?"

"I don't know exactly." He sighs. "He's sent here by Coyote to find you and harm you. We need to keep you secret until you are ready to face him."

"What about that demon that keeps showing up?"

He shrugs. "I can't tell for certain. Coyote visits other worlds. He might have brought it back with him to help the Seeker. Either way, we need to keep the demon away from you until you're prepared."

"I don't care about the Wind Spirit or these gifts or the Seeker or this demon." I stand. "I want nothing to do with any of this. I'm done. I'll run away if there's no other way."

"Jules, you can't ignore your responsibility," Troy says from the darkness, his voice soft like a summer breeze. "Without you, we'll all perish."

"I guess you'll have to think of something else." I turn my back on them and stalk toward the RV. I'm so tired. The only thing I want is a bed with sheets. It doesn't matter what type of bed.

I'm sure of only one thing though. I don't want to be the Chosen.

CHAPTER

Light fights through a dirt-encrusted window and tap dances across my eyes. I jam the pillow on top of my face in hopes that the past few days were nothing more than a nightmare, hoping that when I wake, Mom will hover over me as she did before, anxious to start her trip.

Of course, Mom doesn't appear, and there's no redo. The world doesn't work that way. We have to live in the imperfect and face our faults and mistakes and those of others.

I growl and toss the pillow aside. The bedroom is tiny, just large enough for one twin-sized bed, a small table, and an elfin-sized closet, which I refuse to open. Who knows what Sicheii has stuffed in there? I don't want to find out. The more I learn about my grandfather, the weirder he gets. I can only take so much and have reached my limit.

I know I'll never fall back to sleep now. My mind is awake, even if the rest of my body wants a few more hours of rest. If I try to sleep, I will just lie in bed and become angrier with each minute that passes. I refuse to buy a ticket for that Ferris Wheel. I hop from the bed and catch a glimpse of myself in a dusty mirror. I'm still wearing the same jeans and t-shirt from when I left the hospital. Dirt and grime blot my face, and my hair is a greasy, stringy mess. I look like a wild child, raised by wolves. A sly smile crosses my face as I wonder what Tiffany and her pack of sharks would think if they saw me now.

I brush hair away from my face and move stiffly to a small bathroom, eyes half closed. I let my dirty clothes drop to the floor, swing the shower curtain open, and work the controls. The hot water feels good as it bounces off my head and forms little rivers down my body. My eyes close and my mind roams. The voices are there, just under the surface. Now that I understand how to manipulate them, I play with them. Two distinct voices bounce inside of my head, one from Sicheii and the other from Troy. I ignore Sicheii and dial down the volume much like the control on my iPhone, and focus on Troy's instead. I listen intently, increase the volume, and shape the sounds until words form.

He worries about me, worries this Seeker is dangerous, worries I might run off. He wants to protect me.

I pull back and quiet his internal voice. It doesn't feel right to listen to his private thoughts. It's like I'm reading his diary without his permission. And in truth, part of me is afraid to know what he thinks about me anyway. My feelings for him have always been complicated, always deeper than friendship alone, but he's never shown any sign that he shares those feelings. Now his betrayal looms so large it crowds out my affection as if it's a roadblock I can't pass—not yet anyway.

I breathe deeply and push Troy from my mind with a mental shove. Other concerns are more pressing at the moment. I must sift through lies and truth and find my way. The water turns cool as I wash the rest of the grime from my body. A neat stack of clothes waits for me on the sink. On top is the *Beatles* t-shirt Troy bought me as a Christmas gift. The local radio station ran a *Beatles* weekend in the beginning of December, and I got hooked. Troy bought me an *Abbey Road* t-shirt a few weeks later for the holiday. He can be thoughtful that way.

I smile despite myself and lift the shirt to my face. It smells fresh, like the detergent Mom uses. I forget for a moment I'm angry at Troy and Mom and Sicheii. I dress in the fresh clothes, swing open the screen, and enter the hot Arizona morning to face two people whom I love, but who felt it perfectly fine to lie to me about the most important aspects of my life. My anger returns and my face flushes.

Both Sicheii and Troy turn to face me. They stand near a small campsite with two sleeping bags neatly folded behind them. They both slept outside with the bugs while I snoozed in the bed in the RV. They would sacrifice everything for me if they have to, but I've never asked them to and I don't want it. I just want to go back to an ordinary life.

When I trudge toward them, they both stand, bodies rigid as if they are waiting for bad news. I nod toward a plate of scrambled eggs, which looks cold with a slight film on top, but I'm hungry. "Is that for me?"

"Yes, it is." Sicheii waves at a blanket not far from the fire. "Take a seat."

I sit cross-legged at the edge of the blanket. Sicheii hands me the plate with the eggs, and Troy places a glass of orange juice next to me. They stand near me as if I'm their queen and they my subjects. It weirds me out a little.

"Sit down." I look only at Sicheii. I can't look at Troy, not just yet. "And if you lie to me again, I'm gone."

They sit on the far end of the blanket as I eat my breakfast. When the eggs are gone, I glance at Sicheii. "So tell me about this Seeker. Who is he and what does he want from me?"

His lips curve downward and the lines on his forehead bunch together. "He is Coyote's pawn. You are the Chosen who will defeat the Seeker, using the gifts the Great Wind Spirit has given you."

"You have no idea who or where he is?"

"No, except for the description from the Book of Knowledge. The Wind Spirit tells us he will be cloaked in beautiful clothing, tall and fine featured with eyes that could melt ice."

"That's not a lot to go on. I hoped for something like a jagged scar across his forehead or a skull tattoo on his arm." I pause for a second. "You said I need to prevent the extermination of our people. What do you mean?" I have so many questions, but extermination sounds bad so I start there.

"Coyote and the Great Wind Spirit are locked in a battle over our fate. Coyote believes we have treated Mother Earth poorly. He wants to end our time on Earth and return her to nature, to a time before the First Man. Coyote is using the Seeker for his purposes. You must kill him. If you fail, he will lead an army of demons who will destroy us."

"Seriously, an army of demons?" Intense pressure squeezes my chest, and I resist the urge escape. "Where is this Book of Knowledge you two seem so enamored with? I need to see some proof of this Great Wind Spirit thing—something tangible."

Sicheii nods toward Troy who jogs to the RV. As my eyes linger on his back, Sicheii says, "Don't be so hard on him, Juliet. He's only living up to his oath. All he wants is to keep you safe."

"He's supposed to be on *my* side!" I am shouting now, the veins on my neck pulsing. "He's been lying to me for months!

227

He's supposed to be my best friend, the one person I can always rely upon." Unwanted tears brim my eyes.

Sicheii touches my leg. "Blame me then. I shouldn't have involved him, but I needed the right person, someone the Order could trust."

I jerk back my leg. "Don't think I'm not mad at you either! I'm your granddaughter. You could have trusted me." I wipe away tears that have not yet fallen.

"This has nothing to do with trust." He lifts his hands palm upward and the wind gusts as if he caused it to blow. "I did what was best for you and our people."

I huff and watch Troy return from the RV. He holds two bundles covered in black velvet. He refuses to lock eyes with me, keeping them on the ground until he stands over us and hands the bundles to Sicheii.

He unwraps a small package and removes a leather notebook. The tattered journal is no larger than a child's diary. He hands it to me with both hands.

I look at it suspiciously and remember the dream with ancient Native Americans, jewels, and the campfire from only a few days ago. This could be the same book the old man had at that meeting. The leather is old and dry and cracking. Inscribed on the cover is a simple golden square slanted on its side—the Tribe's symbol for the Wind Spirit. I open the journal and find neat looking symbols written in black ink, the pages yellow and brittle.

I laugh a full body laugh. "What in the world is this?" Tears roll down my face. "I've never seen anything like it. Who could understand this?"

Sicheii frowns. "The book was written over two hundred years ago by an esteemed medicine man chosen by the Wind

Spirit. The symbols are an early version of our language. Only those in the Order can discern its meaning now."

I carefully flip through the yellowed paper. "Six pages? *The Book of Knowledge* is only six pages long! You have to be kidding me. I wrote a history paper that was longer than this last week!" I study the first page. "I thought the Chosen was supposed to be able to read it. I have no idea what these symbols mean. The journal could be a cookbook for all I know."

Sicheii smiles as he reclaims the leather journal. Nothing fazes him. "I said only the Chosen can read the Book of Gifts. The Book of Knowledge is for the Order to understand."

"Well, if the Book of Gifts is written with those symbols, I'll never understand it." There's more. I stare at the second bundle. Anxiety ripples through me.

What do I want? Do I want proof that this crazy story is true? Something more solid than my ability with these voices, or do I want something easily dismissible? Something that makes me laugh and means that I am not special or Chosen and everything is a big mistake.

"I see you are interested in the second bundle." Sicheii lifts it with the tips of his fingers and folds away the black velvet cloth. "We call this the Seeker Slayer. The Wind Spirit gave it to us. The Seeker Slayer has helped convince Troy about the truth behind our Order." Sicheii smiles. "It has convinced many people of our truthfulness."

He removes a crystal object from the velvet wrappings. The crystal is shaped like a capital T. The long part of the T is the size of my palm. Light sparkles off the antiquity, ricocheting within the internal structure much like a diamond—only this is no diamond. Slight traces of teal and emerald reflect from inside the crystal. The twisted arrows symbol blazes on the long portion of the T in shining silver.

I know Sicheii wants me to take the relic, but my hand hovers in the air. "What's it made from?"

He shrugs. "The Seeker Slayer is not from this world but comes from the land of spirits." He smashes the end of the crystal on the slab of stone he used for cooking, and the stone splits. The crystal stays whole without chipping or cracking. "The structure is harder than a diamond."

"They had it tested at the University and it doesn't match anything in their database," Troy says as he leans forward. His eyes plead with me. He wants me to believe this tale, that he was right to side with my grandfather.

I ignore him and focus on my grandfather. "Why do you call it the Seeker Slayer?"

"Only the Chosen can wield this weapon. You will use it to kill the Seeker." Sicheii pushes the crystal closer toward me.

"I don't want to touch it." I shrink away from him. I don't know why. Maybe I fear what the relic represents, its weirdness, and its otherworldliness. If I take it, I suspect there's no going back. "It doesn't look like a weapon to me."

Sicheii's voice is patient and strong. "You've passed the first test, Juliet. You have accepted the first gift. You must accept this weapon. It's the only way."

I glance at him and then at Troy. I wish I had a plan, a way to go back to a normal life. "I've never asked for this."

"I know, Jules," Troy says. "None of us asked for this, but what if it's all real? What if this is the only way? Those guys at Roundtree's house were real enough." Troy manages a half-grin. The skin under both of his eyes is still dark and his nose swollen.

I inch my hand toward the relic. It pulses with energy as I move closer. I steel my nerves and grab the crystal in my right hand. A soft shock and a vibration run through my body as if invisible fingers tickle me and grab hold of me. The air above the crystal shimmers and reforms into a three-foot blade made from the same material as the hilt. Etchings glimmer down its center.

I have seen swords like this one before: in my dreams.

CHAPTER

I drop the crystal sword, and the blade disappears before the hilt touches the ground. Sicheii smiles, and Troy's face turns ashen. I want to run, to leave this place and the sword and Sicheii and even Troy behind, but my eyes are locked on the crystal hilt. My breathing is shallow and raspy as air sticks in my lungs.

I am *not* special. I am not the smartest or the strongest or the fastest or the richest person. I'm an average girl born between two worlds—one rich and the other Native American. I'm the victim of a cosmic mistake.

Still, I close my eyes, and visions of Gold Tooth and Slicked Back Hair and Ms. Arnold darken my thoughts. They think I'm special, and as long as they do, everyone I care about remains in danger.

I push bile back down my throat. I must be more than a scared teenaged girl if I'm going to survive and confront this Seeker, this menace, this future I don't want but has been thrust upon me.

"What was that?" I hope Sicheii has more insights and will share the deeper meanings behind what's happening than he has thus far. I search his lined face for answers and realize his knowledge is limited. He has no more secrets to reveal.

"The sword is called the Seeker Slayer," Sicheii answers. "The weapon is blessed by the Wind Spirit. You must use the sword to destroy Coyote's pawn."

"Does it come with an instruction manual?"

He shakes his head.

I stare at the crystal hilt as if the relic is a living thing. *What does all this have to do with my dreams? How is the Wind Spirit connected to the tall and beautiful looking people with the crystal swords who come from another planet?* Sicheii's description of the Seeker fits one of the tall warriors from my dreams, but that's crazy. They were just stupid dreams, crazy images from my imagination.

They weren't real, or were they?

I remember to breathe, and with air, resolve slowly nudges aside some of my fear. I can't ignore the people looking for me, the crazy sword that only appears when I touch the hilt, or the voices and images I hear and see. Even if this whole thing is a big mistake, I'm not going to make it easy for this Seeker to harm me or anyone else I care about. I have to find a way to protect them. I need to be this Chosen. Special. Fearless.

My legs start to bounce. "Let's go. We can't sit around here all day." I jump to my feet. "We had better find that Book of Gifts before the Seeker finds me."

"I tried to force Roundtree to divulge its hiding place to me, Juliet, but he refused. I don't know where to search. I've prayed to the Wind Spirit for guidance, but she won't answer."

"I know where Roundtree hid the second book." At least, *I think* I have a good idea. I smile and turn my back on them. For once I know something they don't, which feels good. "And you had better bring that crystal thing with us. You never know who we might run into. A magic sword could come in handy."

I head toward the RV and wonder where my grandfather parked his car. There's no way they took the RV into the desert; both front tires are flat. I cross the front of the rusted metal house and find an old green SUV.

"Where's the Porsche?"

"The desert is no place for the Porsche. I may be odd, but I'm not crazy." Sicheii chuckles. "Besides, don't you think the SUV is a little less conspicuous?"

"Maybe just a little." At least we won't have to cram into the sports car.

I slide into the passenger seat, and Troy hops in back with a backpack slung over his shoulder. He doesn't need to tell me the Seeker Slayer is in the bag. I feel its presence.

Sicheii settles behind the wheel and turns the key in the ignition, starting the SUV with a slight wheeze and a sputter. "Where to?"

"Roundtree's house. The Wind Spirit showed me a sign."

Who knows?

Maybe the Wind Spirit caused that flashlight to shine on the tiny twisted arrows symbol in Roundtree's living room.

The drive to Roundtree's house is uneventful and quiet, so I have time to wrestle with my thoughts. I don't believe in fate, that our destinies are predetermined in the stars. Troy doesn't have to stay in this sleepy town to work for his uncle. He can forge his own future. Still, I find myself written into an ancient story I cannot escape.

I am the Chosen, whether by mistake or not. The Seeker is real. I don't believe in demons but I've seen one and events are happening that have no other explanation. I am the mystery behind the Order of the Twisted Arrows. People have died to learn that mystery and others have died to keep it secret. Whether I want it or not, those deaths force a certain grim responsibility onto me.

Sicheii parks in front of Roundtree's house, where this story started for me and ended for Roundtree. We amble out of the SUV. With no one in sight, I lead us around the side of the house toward the back door.

Most of Roundtree's blood has washed away, but crimson stains darken the dirt at the base of the maple tree. The stains cause me to shiver and remind me of the seriousness of our situation. This isn't some adventure for children. These people won't hesitate to kill us, so I'll have to kill them.

I turn the handle to the back door, and it opens with a creak.

Light flows through the windows in little streams and dust particles swirl in the air.

"What are we looking for?" Troy asks.

I ignore him. He hates the silent treatment, and I'm not prepared to let him off the hook so easily, so I creep toward the living room in silence. Sicheii follows behind, a thin smile stuck on his face.

The last time I was here, Troy almost died. I sneak a glance at him and shudder. For a second, I expect the van to pull up, but shove that thought from my mind. I have to be stronger than the van.

I lift the charred hide I noticed the last time we were here and show it to Sicheii. "This was more than just an old painting. This had a picture of a Seeker on it, right?"

He nods. "It was made around the time the Order was established. I have others. I'm not sure what they mean. Roundtree and I prayed on it and even spent a couple of days in the sweat lodge, but the Wind Spirit failed to give us a vision."

"So that's why they burned it. They didn't want any evidence of a Seeker around."

At least I've solved one small mystery. Still, it won't help us find the Book of Gifts, so I move to the center of the room where Gold Tooth threw me to the floor and glance in the direction where I saw the twisted arrows symbol, but nothing unusual glimmers against the wall.

Blood rushes to my head. I didn't imagine the symbol. It was here! The room looks the same as it did the other day. No one else has been here. No one could have removed it.

Maybe I'm just not looking in the right place. What was I doing when I saw the symbol?

I close my eyes and remember. Gold Tooth had tossed me to the floor, so I stoop low and bend at the knees. The light reflects off a speck of silver in the corner of the wall. I smile and point. "Look over there, Sicheii. You'll find the twisted arrows."

He glides toward the wall and swivels his head toward me.

"Look close to the ground, right in the corner."

He stiffly squats and, after a few seconds, his fingers brush against the silver twisted arrows symbol. "Well done, Juliet. The Wind Spirit has spoken true."

Troy and I join him.

Sicheii tries to pry open the wood paneling with his hands, but his fingernails slip against the smooth wood. "Get something hard, Troy. We need to break through the paneling."

Troy finds a heavy metal bookend on the floor shaped like a bison. He returns and bashes the bison against the cherry wood three times before the wood splits. Sicheii touches his arm to stop him, brushes away the splinters, and finds a small leather notebook hidden within a hidey-hole in the darkness.

He smiles and lifts the leather notebook toward me. I hesitate for a second and sigh. The small notebook looms large. It's real, and if it's real, everything else is. I need to find the rest of the puzzle pieces, some of which are in this notebook, so I grudgingly take it from him. The cover has the same silver rectangle symbol for the Wind Spirit etched on it as the Book of Knowledge.

I try to flip open the book, but it's sealed with wax.

"The Book of Gifts is only to be read by the Chosen. It has been sealed for over two hundred years," Sicheii explains.

"Terrific." I use my thumbnail to cut through the wax and open the notebook. I expect to find pages with the unreadable symbols like those in the Book of Knowledge. Instead, the book is really a box, which holds a small crystal vial the size of my palm. I shift the box and a clear liquid sloshes to one side.

"What's this?" I ask Sicheii.

The liquid inside the vial turns red and starts pulsing.

My heart skips a beat and so does the red fluid.

CHAPTER

Each pulse of light from the vial coincides with my heartbeat. When my heart quickens, so do the pulses.

"What should I do with it?" I ask Sicheii.

He bends his neck back, closes his eyes and hums, softly at first, and then progressively louder. After two minutes, he makes a loud popping sound, opens his eyes, turns toward me and shrugs. "I got nothing. What do you think you should do? You are Chosen."

"Thanks." I frown. "I think I'm supposed to drink the fluid. The pulsing light seems connected to me." I lift the box with the tiny bottle close to my face. No design graces the surface, just the smooth edges of the vial and the pulsing light from the liquid. There's no top, so how am I supposed to pour the liquid out to drink it?

"Let me try the potion first," Troy offers. "It might be dangerous. Coyote is a trickster. This might be a trap." He sticks his right hand out, palm up.

I swing the box away from him. "You had your chance to protect me. You should have considered that before you lied to me."

I reach into the box and lift the vial with the tips of my fingers. When my fingers touch the glass, the pulsing stops, the fluid turns blood red, and the top of the bottle disappears.

Everyone makes life-changing decisions. Sometimes you don't realize how important the decision is when you make it, like when my mom slept with Ayden. She didn't know she would become pregnant, yet it happened anyway, and her life was forever changed. Other times, you know the importance of the decision before you make it, like when Sicheii injected me on the day of my birth. This is one of those times. I decide to be bold and bring the edge of the vial to my face, feel the smooth surface against my lips, and tip it upward.

The liquid is thick and syrupy and tastes like roses. Upon contact, my tongue, the roof of my mouth, and the back of my throat all freeze. I swallow and the frigid sensation spreads throughout my body.

I start to shiver. The cold threatens to overwhelm me and I crumple to the ground. A million tiny bees sting my insides at the same time, and I squeal.

Everything changes.

I have only been in the ocean once, when I was eight. Mom and I stopped in Santa Monica before going to Disneyland. I wore a pink two-piece with Little Mermaid characters on the bottom and seashells on the top. The air smelled of salt water, suntan lotion, and fun. People laughed, music played from a nearby portable radio, and a man sold ice cream from a box he had strapped over his shoulders.

I stared out at the waves, lost in the beauty of the ocean when the man called out, "Ice Cream!" I turned and saw a boy my age race toward him with money squeezed tightly in his fist. He stumbled on the sand and face planted. I looked at my mom, who was frantically pointing toward the ocean. I turned and a wave blasted me in the face. I flew backward, tumbling along with the wave and sand and seashells, drinking in the ocean water in gulps. As suddenly as the wave hit me, it receded, taking water and sand and shells with it. A moment later, Mom grabbed me. I'll never forget those two feelings — the first, a sudden explosion of energy and the second, a draining sensation as the wave retreated.

The same thing happens now, only way more intense. A million thoughts and images flash through my mind, flooding me with energy much like that wave. Then the energy leaves me just as suddenly as it came. The crystal vial drops from my hand and rolls toward Troy along its side until it clunks against his sneaker.

The bottle has turned black and has cracked.

I close my eyes and my world turns black as well.

CHAPTER

I wake and find myself in a well-worn leather chair, Roundtree's ravaged living room scattered around me. Troy stands close, his arms crossed over his chest, eyes full of worry. He shifts his weight from leg to leg.

"I'm all right," I say, my voice husky as I rub my aching head. Stars float in front of me, and my mind feels sluggish as if it's working with a few seconds delay.

"What happened? Are you hurt?" Troy's voice sounds as if it passes through a tunnel.

"It's obvious what happened." Sicheii grins. "The Wind Sprit blessed Juliet. She is the Chosen and will deliver us." His voice is wrapped tight with confidence bolstered by years of certainty.

A weird sensation rifles through me like someone is tickling my brain with a feather. I shake my head, clear my vision, and chase the stars away. "I'm not sure what happened. One minute, I was freezing cold, the next - stinging pain everywhere, and then I

JEFF ALTABEF & ERYNN ALTABEF

was flooded with... thoughts." I don't know a better way to describe the rush that whipped through me.

"Thoughts?" Troy asks. "Do you remember them?"

I frown. "Some of them." I rub my eyes. The tickling stops and my mind clears.

Sicheii leans forward, his voice breathless with anticipation. "Did the Wind Spirit show you the rest of your gifts?"

"It doesn't work like that, Sicheii. It only reveals the gifts my body is ready to accept." I'm not sure how I know this but I do. Part of me is amped from the fluid, and the other part is scared like I'm a child who learns how complicated and unpredictable life really is for the first time.

I glance at Troy. I'm still angry with him, so my tone is frosty. "Toss me that bison you used to break the wood."

He retrieves the solid brass bookend from the corner of the room, dusts off a few loose splinters, and hands it to me.

I concentrate on the muscles in my hand, wrist, and arm. I feel nerve endings fire and direct the energy to my hand. When power pulses through my fingers, I wrap them around the head and bend it back as if it were made of tin.

Troy's mouth drops, and I flip the disfigured bookend back to him and beam a full-faced smile.

"How did you do that?" He tries to bend the head back, but as big and strong as he is, the head is stubborn and stiff and stays in place.

"I can direct the energy in my body to specific muscles, strengthening them. It acts like a weird energy funnel. I must have tapped into that ability back at the cemetery with the tombstone and when I bent the ring in the van to escape." I shrug, but my legs buckle, and I plop down onto the leather chair. "It must take a little getting used to."

"What about the Seeker? What are we to do about him?" Sicheii asks.

"Avoid him. He is extremely dangerous. He will be tall and beautiful and will have gifts also—strength, speed, the ability to read people, and the power to move objects with his mind. I'm warned to avoid him until I retrieve the Book of Wisdom. He won't hesitate to kill me."

"What's the Book of Wisdom?" Troy asks.

I glance at Sicheii, and his body goes rigid. "I don't know, Juliet. I've never heard of another Book."

"It is the third and final Book. It completes the story and tells me everything I need to know."

"Why didn't the Order know of this book? Where is this book hidden?" Sicheii scowls, his eyes narrow, and the muscles in his jaw clench. Indignation flows from him.

I sense emotions faster than reading thoughts. The stronger the emotion, the easier for me to read, and Sicheii is pissed. He feels betrayed.

"The Wind Spirit meant no slight against you or the Twisted Arrows Order by keeping the third book secret, Sicheii." With strength now returned to my legs, I rise from the chair and step close to him. I take his large, calloused hands in mine. "You are most trusted by the Wind Spirit."

I make this up because he needs to hear me say it. I just now realize how much he has sacrificed to keep the Order's secrets. His entire life has revolved around those secrets. He could have had a different life, one far from here. He has kept things from me, important secrets, but he did it to protect me, to keep me safe, to let me satisfy the destiny he believes I must fulfill. Unlike Mom, he acted out of pure love and obligation. He deserves to believe he has done the right thing. I can't change the past, so I forgive him and give him the present.

"Only I can find the third book. When I'm ready, its location will be revealed to me."

He nods, the tension releases from his jaw, and his body uncoils.

I feel someone approaching like a psychic radar system. Every living animal casts off a certain spirit energy. The human spirit is different from other animals, and each individual human spirit is further distinct from other humans like fingerprints. If I concentrate hard, I can identify a person by their spirit energy. It's another gift.

I look toward the back door. "We have company." The spirit energy flows toward me like a fog rolling over a lake.

Sicheii glides toward the window and peeks out.

"It's Lisa," I say, as her face appears in my mind.

A second later, she swings open the door and bounds into the room, sweeping her eyes over Troy and me. She glares at me, but the expression lasts only a second as her eyes search out Sicheii.

"Jake, we have a problem." Dark circles smudge under her eyes, and small lines crack from the edges of her lips.

"What's wrong?" His boot crunches a broken picture frame as he steps toward her. The photo in the frame shows Roundtree sitting on a rocker with a young girl in his lap. Even though she's young, I can tell the girl is Lisa.

"It's Summer." She brushes her straight black hair from her face and pushes it behind her shoulders. "She's gone missing."

"Missing?"

"I tried her cell phone, and she didn't answer. I drove to her house to check on her, but she's gone. Ayden doesn't know where she is, and he's worried. He hasn't seen her since this morning when she went to the store."

"Maybe she's just running errands and the battery on her phone died," Troy says.

My stomach lurches and a dark feeling drapes over me, squeezing my chest and throat. "Mom always carries a back-up battery just in case work calls. Something must be wrong."

Sicheii rubs his hands through his long white hair. I have never seen him do this before. He looks uncertain.

"Do you think the Seeker has her?"

He glances at me. "It's possible. I asked her to leave town, but she refused to go without you."

My heart lumps in my throat. The last time I saw Mom, I was angry with her and tossed her from my hospital room. I still want to be angry at her a little longer for keeping those letters secret, but now I'm terrified that the Seeker might harm her, and I'll never see her again. For sixteen years, it was just us three. "What did you do with Ms. Arnold?"

"We're holding her until we decide what to do with her."

"We'd better hurry." I march toward the door. Moving makes me feel a tiny bit better. When I think of Gold Tooth and Slicked Back Hair with my mom, my hands ball into fists. I don't care what the fluid told me. I need to find this Seeker, and Ms. Arnold is the only loose thread we have.

"We've got to find Mom. I won't let them have her."

CHAPTER

Fear comes in many flavors. I seem to have experienced them all in the past few days: fear for your life, fear he won't love you back, fear you won't belong, or you will mess up, or get in trouble, or can't help a friend when she needs you. I thought the fear that raked through me in the van was the worst until now.

Now that I'm afraid for my mom, I realize there are worse fears still. Some people become paralyzed by fear, unable to think, move, act. Not me. Fear propels me. It couples with my anger and forms a turbo boost.

We split up in two cars. I drive with Sicheii, and Troy goes with Lisa. We head to Old Town where our investigation into the murders began. Sicheii parks the SUV in the back of the parking lot farthest from his gallery and we start on foot. We avoid his gallery just in case the Seeker has people watching it.

I walk beside his long, loping strides. He moves briskly, but not hurriedly. Only those who know him well would notice the tension in his jaw and the urgency in his eyes.

I study those we pass: dozens of tourists, one with a brand new cowboy hat with the tag still dangling from it, another one who's sunburnt and carries a shopping bag from the *authentic* boots store. Still, I have to wonder if any of them work for the Seeker. The voice in my head tells me to be wary. He will have resources, perhaps unlimited wealth.

We scoot down Front Street, which runs parallel to Main Street. The buildings are all made from brick just like those on Main Street. The art galleries and restaurants are similar in appearance, but not quite as upscale or large. When we pass 2nd Street, we take a left onto 3rd. The neon sign for Aunt Maye's Big and Tall Western Outfitter greets us. Sicheii presses the button to J. Dent's apartment and the buzzer rings almost immediately to let us in.

Sicheii takes the stairs one at a time. He moves stiffly as he pulls himself up by using the handrail. I don't know exactly how old he is. I guess I should, but I don't, and for the first time, he seems aged. His energy is waning. The events of the last few days have taken a toll on him. He needs rest.

Lisa stands in the doorway and holds the door half-open.

Jane Dent's apartment looks the same as I remember. Only this time, her son, Doctor Dan, slouches by the windows, peeking through the curtains. He wears blue jeans and a blue check collared shirt that balloons slightly at his midsection and falls untucked below his waist.

He turns toward me as I follow Sicheii into the apartment, and grins, but the smile looks forced. His mustache and beard are gone. "Nice to see you again, Juliet."

I glance at him and the photograph on the mantelpiece. Now that the truth is out, the resemblance is obvious. I should have realized it before. "I see you've shaved."

247

He touches his chin. "I only wear the beard and mustache when I don't want to be recognized. It's an abundance of caution after all these years, but old habits linger."

I remember the pained expression on his mother's face when we questioned her. "Does your mother know you're still alive?" I scan the room, expecting to find her.

He releases the curtains, allowing them to fall and fully block the windows. "Yes. Only a few know the truth. I don't visit with her much for obvious reasons, but we stay in touch."

For her, that must be a big loss. There's no way she faked the look of sadness that crossed her face.

Troy slides into the living room from the kitchen with a sandwich in his hand. I shoot him a dangerous look. The last time we were here, he knew the truth and stayed silent. Another lie.

Dan locks eyes with Sicheii. "Jake, I don't like this situation at all. We're too exposed here. They could find us."

"The Seeker has no way of knowing about you or this apartment. You are safe here." Sicheii settles his hand on his shoulder. "I've kept you safe all these years. You have to trust me. How is our guest?"

Dan reluctantly turns his back on the windows. "She's mildly sedated. You can question her. She should be able to answer."

"Good," Sicheii glances at me. "Shall we find out what she knows?"

I nod, and Doctor Dan returns to his pointless vigil by the window. He pulls the curtains back an inch and looks for signs of danger he probably won't recognize if he sees anyway.

Sicheii leads me to a back bedroom. Ms. Arnold is handcuffed to a brass bed, a piece of gray duct-tape stretched across her mouth. Her eyes are closed and puffy and her skin a sickly pallor. A small trace of crusted blood sticks to her temple.

The room is small. The only other furniture besides the bed is an oak nightstand. There's just enough room for Sicheii, Lisa, and myself to stand in the room, so Troy straddles the doorway.

I shake the footboard and her eyes open. When they find me, they widen and sparkle.

Sicheii slides next to her and leans close to her face. His voice is rich with malice. "I'm going to remove the tape. If you yell, it won't be good for you. Do you understand me?"

Ms. Arnold nods with a small bounce of her chin, and he rips off the duct tape with one hard pull.

She sits up and pulls her knees to her chest, ignoring everyone in the room but me. "I knew you were the one from the start. I should have told the Seeker months ago."

"Did you tell him about Juliet?" Sicheii leans toward her.

When she glances at him, her eyes flicker. He scares her. "I called him before you barged into my apartment."

I grip the footboard hard and twist my hands over the brass. "Where did they take my mother?"

She chuckles and Sicheii slaps her hard across the face. A red mark appears on her cheek where his hand struck her. She ignores him and zeroes in on me. "The Seeker will have her by now, Juliet. You are the only one who can save her."

"Tell me where he's hiding."

Her voice rises, and she sounds giddy with a crazy kinetic energy. "Who said he's hiding? You're making a mistake. All of you." She cackles. "You should join him. He will win. He is too powerful. You can't stop him!"

"Tell me where he is!"

Ms. Arnold rattles her cuffs, her voice shrill, spit flying from her mouth as her face reddens. "He's right where you would expect him to be, you stupid little girl!"

"And where is that?" My knuckles turn white. How could I have trusted her? I am such a fool.

She pauses, and the light temporarily dims behind her eyes.

I'm not going to wait, so I reach into her mind, and increase the volume on her internal voice, molding the sounds, sharpening them. I concentrate hard and feel my body shake, but her thoughts stay muddled. It must be the medication. My body feels as if it might explode with energy, but I bear down harder. Air sticks in my lungs and a flashing white light burns my eyes. A thunderclap breaks in my head, and her thoughts are revealed.

I pull back from the bed, woozy. "He's at the casino."

Ms. Arnold goes limp, her breathing shallow. She's unconscious.

I wonder if I broke her somehow.

I should feel bad, but I don't.

CHAPTER

We all make choices and decisions. Life is full of little compromises — like you want to get an A in Geometry, but your favorite TV show is on, or you want to lose weight, but that ice cream calls you from the freezer.

But there are some compromises we cannot make.

I've never considered myself a particularly brave person, but I won't let them hurt my mother — not if I can stop it.

"We have to save her," I say, my back to the fireplace in the living room.

Sicheii runs his hands through his hair again, and indecision creeps back into his eyes. "The Wind Spirit warned you to avoid the Seeker until after you've found the third book. You cannot confront him now."

I start to tap my foot, and my hands find my hips. "I don't care what the Wind Spirit said or what you say, Sicheii. I'm going to save Mom. I won't leave her for those *people*." A chill shivers through me like a late frost surprises an early blooming flower. I see the inside of the van and the sneer on Gold Tooth and Slicked Back Hair's faces and suspect that the Seeker will be worse. I don't want to imagine what they might do to Mom.

"We need a plan," Troy says. "If we act quickly, we can surprise them. The Seeker won't expect us to know where to find him."

"The Casino is a big place." Lisa steps toward me, her expression grim but eager to confront the Seeker. She looks like she wants revenge as much as I do. "We'll need to know where he is in the Casino."

"You had a special relationship with Roundtree, didn't you?" I remember the photo from Roundtree's house.

"He was my godfather, so I have good reason to find this Seeker."

"He'll be in the Villas," Doctor Dan offers, his back to us as he continues looking out the windows. "You need a special pass to gain access into that part of the Casino, and it provides the most privacy."

Troy smiles. "Ella's mom works nights at the Casino. She has an access card that gets her into the Villas. She cooks private meals for the whales."

"I forbid this." Sicheii crosses his arms against his chest. "We must honor the Wind Spirit's wishes. Juliet cannot go looking for the Seeker or Summer until she is ready. I will go alone."

"You will do no such thing. You heard what Ms. Arnold said — only I can save Mom." Heat flushes my face. I'm not a child any longer. The days when my grandfather could stop me from doing something are over.

Troy steps in between us. "I'll go with Jake. He's right. This is too dangerous."

"The Order has been keeping these secrets for over two hundred years. Others have died to honor the Wind Spirit's wishes," Sicheii argues. "You can't throw that away now that we are so close. We can save Summer without you."

I look back and forth between both of them. Each loves me in his own way. I don't need any special gift to know how they feel. It's etched across their faces, in the light behind their eyes, and in the worry lines on their foreheads.

My anger snaps like a dry twig. How can I stay vexed at those willing to sacrifice their lives to protect mine?

I take Troy's hand and relief washes over him. "I know you would go and do your best, but that won't be good enough. I have to be the one to save Mom." I squeeze his hand tight and see his expression melt like snow on a warm day. "I won't be able to live with myself if something bad happens to her, knowing that I could have saved her. I know you understand. You would save me if you had to."

I swing my eyes to Sicheii, who stares at me hard. It is the same expression he used to chastise me when I was little. It won't work now. "I'm sorry, Sicheii. I'm sorry you've sacrificed so much and have had to do things you regret. But that wasn't my decision. I'm grown now. I'm Chosen. This is my decision."

He isn't convinced, so I try to reach him on a different level. "I feel the Wind Spirit in this. It can't be a coincidence that Mom's been taken now that I have the sword. This must be what I'm supposed to do. It's a sign from the Wind Spirit that my time has come and that I have to rescue Mom." I know it's a lie, but some lies are good. Well, if not good, then necessary. If he thinks the Wind Spirit wants me to go after Mom, maybe he'll go along. I try to look sincere.

253

His arms drop to his side, and a tentative smile nudges across his face. "You believe the Wind Spirit is calling you? You can feel her with your second sight?"

I nod, worried my voice would betray the truth.

"It is written you will slay the Seeker and save our people from the army of demons. If now is the time, then we must pursue our fate. You will slay the Seeker and the demons will be defeated."

People are willing to believe crazy things if they really want them to be true. Usually he's hard to fool, but he wants me to fulfill this prophecy so badly this fib works on him. I step toward him, stand on my toes, and gently clunk my forehead against his. He used to do this to me when he wanted me to pay special attention to what he was saying. Now I do it to him.

My voice is full of tears. "I love you. You are my father and grandfather. You're my rock. It's time for you to trust me and let me fulfill my destiny. You've taught me how to be strong even if I didn't want to listen." I pull my head back and manage a smirk. "After all, I am your granddaughter."

He smiles. "Yes you are. You're much stronger than me."

I hug him, and at that moment, I've forgiven him for everything—the needle at my birth, the lies, being the Chosen, the Seeker. He's lived his life, so I can fulfill my fate. He's the one who taught me how to rock climb, he's the one who went to my lacrosse games, he's the one who spent time with me and told me stories. He made sure I knew that I was loved. He's made mistakes, but they were born from love. I know that now and wouldn't change him if I could.

We separate and he looks at me with a self-satisfied grin. "You are the Chosen."

Troy interlocks his fingers with mine. This isn't the first time we've held hands this way, but it feels different, stronger, more substantial than ever before. I feel heat where his skin touches mine. I absorb the contours of his fingers, the callouses in his palm, the strength in his hand. It's almost as if our flesh has molded together and formed one hand, stronger and better than the two.

"We will all go together," he says. "We just need a plan."

"Troy, you call Ella. Ask her to *borrow* her mom's access card and meet us here. I'll call Ayden. He needs to know what's going on."

Sicheii groans and turns his back on me.

I'm done with secrets. Ayden is my father and deserves to know the truth—at least, the truth about Mom.

CHAPTER

"What are you going to tell Ella and Ayden when they arrive?" Troy asks. We sit in the corner of the living room on the couch close together, our knees touching. He smiles. "The whole story might be a bit much for them to believe right away."

I smirk. "I could always take out the sword. That's pretty convincing."

Troy grins back, and his eyes light up the way I'm used to seeing them. "It won't be good enough for Ella. You know how her mind works—"

"It spins a mile a minute."

"Yes. She'll try to find some *rational* explanation for all of this." He rolls his eyes. "We could be stuck here for hours. Marlon will raid the kitchen and tell us more ridiculous facts he's learned from Snapple caps."

"I'll figure out something, but I'm going to tell them the truth the first chance I get." I hate the idea of lying to them, but Troy is right. We have to move fast.

The buzzer rings. When I open the door, Ayden hesitates at the doorway, his eyes silently asking if he can enter.

"Come in."

He strolls into the apartment, his shoulders swaying as he moves.

"We were so worried about you, Juliet." He inches toward me as if he wants to hug me, but he doesn't have it in him yet, so he stops in his tracks and looks down toward the floor.

"I'm fine." I smile back at him. "I'm feeling much better than before."

"Are you still hearing the voices?" He whispers as if he does not want to disturb this secret conversation I might be having.

"They're all gone, but that's not important now." This is the first lie I've told Ayden, but it's a white one. "Mom's been taken. We need to rescue her."

Sicheii enters the living room from one of the back bedrooms, and a cold frost follows him.

Ayden's eyes lock on his, laser tight. He seems to grow taller, and his chest puffs out. "What is *he* doing here?"

Sicheii stops ten feet away from us. "Where else would I be?"

Ayden turns toward me, his hands curled tight. "Juliet, I can't be here with him." His voice is low and rumbly, and his cotton t-shirt rubs tightly against his shoulders. "He's robbed me of everything."

"You did that yourself," Sicheii says. "We don't need him. He's *unreliable*."

"You didn't give me a chance!" Ayden explodes and inches toward Sicheii. I sense the aggression in the air as if two rams are about to butt heads.

"You had many chances and you couldn't change. I warned you." Sicheii's face turns red and the veins on his forehead pulse. "Don't blame me for your own faults!"

257

I step between them, separating the two bulls. "We need to work together. It's the only way."

"But—" Ayden growls.

"But nothing! I know what Sicheii did to you was wrong. He should have told the truth." I place my hand on his arm, which is tight with anger. "But you admitted you had done bad things. If you hadn't gone to jail back then, who knows what path you would have followed?" The tension relaxes in his arm.

I turn to face Sicheii. "And *you've* robbed me of a father." Tears rush to the surface of my eyes. "I need you both to get Mom back. I can't lose her." Sicheii's eyes soften, but I don't care. I rush from the room and into the main bedroom, slamming the door shut hard behind me.

I have a difficult time breathing as tears rain down my face. Mom's been missing for hours, and my imagination whirls at a breakneck speed. An unlimited number of nasty things could have happened to her by now.

Knock. Knock.

The door swings open. Ayden stands in the doorway. "Can I come in, Juliet?"

I nod and he steps into the room and shuts the door behind him. "I'm sorry. You and Summer come first. I've been angry with that old tosser for a long time. It seems like it has been the only constant in my life. First, his meddling with our relationship, and then his testimony at my trial."

"Can you put your feelings aside for now? We need you."

He walks to the bed and perches next to me. "Yes, I promise not to kill the old goat until after we retrieve your mom." He beams a half-smile at me. "That's the best I can do."

I stick out my hand, and he shakes it. "Deal."

"Now tell me what's going on and where we can find your mother."

I look into his eyes, and the stranger I had just met a few days earlier morphs into my father. Unfairly separated from his daughter, he missed out on so many memories, memories he can never get back. I had not made up my mind what to tell him until now; he deserves more than a bunch of lies. I have an inkling he will believe me, that he will trust me if I tell him the truth.

So, I start with my birth. He tenses up when I show him the scar on the sole of my foot, and I continue to explain everything I know. I include both the sweat lodge and the fluid from the crystal vial, explain Sicheii's theory about the Wind Spirit and Coyote and see skepticism in his eyes and in the line of his clenched jaw. I linger on Gold Tooth and Slicked Back Hair. He needs to know how dangerous they are.

He only interrupts me once, when I tell him that I alone can kill the Seeker. He pulls a .38 from behind his back. "A well placed bullet should kill the bloke."

I shake my head. "He can create a force field around himself which will stop bullets. Only my sword will penetrate." At that point, I remove the crystal hilt from Troy's backpack. When my fingers wrap around it, the blade appears. His eyes widen and he leans back on his hands.

I slash the sword through the air with a series of rapid sideswipes, upper swings, thrusts, and twirls. The blade moves in a blur, whistling as it swishes through the air. It feels slightly awkward at first, and then I let my subconscious take over. When I act without thinking, my body moves fluidly, faster than before. I finish my display, rewrap the sword in the felt, and sit beside Ayden and wait. I hope he's convinced. It's all I have.

"When did you learn how to do that?"

I shrug. "The fluid has given me that knowledge. I don't know how it works, but one moment, I don't even know how to hold the thing and the next, I'm Zorro."

His eyes turn inward as if he's calculating odds and probabilities. "This still sounds very dangerous to me. I'm sure Summer wouldn't want you rescuing her. I don't fancy you taking this on."

"It's not your choice. I want your help with Gold Tooth and Slicked Back Hair, but either way, I'm going in."

A trace of malice glints behind his eyes. "I'd be happy to meet up with those two. Are you sure you want to do this?"

I nod.

"When you do something dangerous like this, you have to be all in. You can't go halfway. You must be prepared to do whatever it takes, whatever is necessary to kill this Seeker if it comes to that." He nods at me knowingly. "Otherwise you won't have a chance. Can you do that?"

"I understand." At least, I think I understand. Either way I don't have a choice.

"When I was your age, I had to do some rough things when my brother went to jail. I was hoping you didn't inherit that proclivity from me."

"I can do this." I grab Ayden's arm with both my hands and grip it hard. "I can kill him."

The buzzer rings. He jumps.

"That must be Ella with the access card."

Time accelerates.

The Seeker is out there, and I am going to find him. For sixteen years, it was the other way around. Now I'm taking the fight to him.

Blood races through my body and my heart thumps.

CHAPTER 40

Troy holds the door open and Ella, Marlon, and Katie walk into the apartment. When Ella sees me, she darts forward and embraces me in a miniature bear hug. I close my eyes. She smells like jasmine, her favorite perfume, and I smile. For a moment, I remember what being a normal, average teenager felt like, before I became Chosen or knew about the Seeker or the sword or the Wind Spirit or before Mom was taken.

That feeling lasts exactly one and a half seconds and is replaced with the knowledge that I am forever changed. I will never again be the girl who shrinks in the back of the classroom, who tries to blend in. I will forever be the Chosen, the Seeker Slayer. I will fulfill my destiny. I will be strong. I have no other choice.

I detangle Ella from me and she frowns. "Where have you been? Are you feeling okay? What's going on? Who just leaves the hospital and doesn't text anyone?" She sounds like a breathless

261

train building up speed at a breakneck pace. "I was worried about you. How come you didn't text me?" She puts both hands on her hips and glares at me.

"I'm sorry, Ella. I had to lay low because those guys from Roundtree's house showed up at the hospital." All true, and I'm happy I don't have to start lying yet.

She gives me a quizzical look; her eyebrows arch above her eyes. "Your mom was worried also. She didn't know where you went."

"Mom's the problem. Those criminals who tried to kidnap me and clobbered Troy have taken her. We think they're holding her at the casino. They're probably camped out in one of the Villas. That's why we need your mother's pass. We need to find her."

She squints her eyes, uncertain whether to believe me. "Why don't you tell the Sheriff?"

"He won't listen to me. She's only gone missing a few hours and they suspect that Sicheii's involved in those murders."

She's about to say something, but she changes her mind and stares at me instead. She's examining me, and after a long moment her face twists in a smirk.

"What?"

"You look different," she says. "I can't put my finger on it, but you're not the same." She turns toward Marlon for confirmation.

He nods his head. "I see it too. You look *badass*."

"*Badass?*" I say.

"Right," he says. "Like how Troy's cousin, Landon, looked after he joined the Marines and got back from basic training."

"Yea, that's *it*—like you're about to bring a world of hurt down on whoever gets in your way." Ella grins. She's only half joking.

Katie steps forward. "It's probably just because she was in the hospital the last time you saw her."

From the expressions on Marlon and Ella's faces, I can tell they're not buying it.

Katie protectively wraps her arms around me and smothers me with a giant-sized hug. "I don't see how anyone can believe that your grandfather is involved in these murders. There's no way Jake could do such a thing." Katie's voice is stern. She's talking about Sicheii, but part of her is also talking about her father. With the evidence against her dad piling up and the conversation she overheard about him running, she needs faith in her father's innocence now more than ever, and the two things have twisted together for her.

"Thanks," I say, but Marlon and Ella share a look. It's only a second but Marlon's lips twist down at the ends and Ella's eyes sparkle dangerously. There's something behind that look. I'll have to ask them about it later, because Sicheii joins us from the back of the apartment.

"Does this thing with your mother have anything to do with these murders?" Ella asks.

"Well...." I don't know what to say. My newly developed ability to tap dance around the truth fails me.

Luckily, Ayden picks me up. "Summer's taking is all my fault. It has nothing to do with the murders. These guys are from my past." His face is full of remorse, with wide eyes and a deep frown. I find myself believing him even though I know better. "They are drug dealers who have issues with me from my prior life. They found out that I was released, and they're using Summer to force my hand."

Ella contemplates the new information the way she sorts out a tricky puzzle. She bites her lip, glances between Ayden and me, and makes up her mind in only a few seconds. "Okay, what can we do to help?"

"All I need is your mom's pass to the Villas. We'll take it from there."

Ella removes the security card from her back pocket but holds it tightly in her fingers. She turns toward Marlon and Katie, who both nod their heads. "I'll let you use my mom's pass, but only if we come with you and help."

"These guys are dangerous," Ayden says. "You shouldn't be involved. Once we spot Summer, we'll call the Sheriff."

Ayden's such a convincing liar I wonder if he's been lying to me. He knows we'll never call the police.

Ella twirls the pass in her hands, a satisfied smirk on her face. I know that look. It's the same expression she gets when she knows she's won an argument. She won't give up until we agree. Time is ticking away, and the pounding in my head sounds fast and angry like my heartbeats. "Don't we have some place to go?" she says.

"Okay, you guys can stay in the car at the casino. If we need to leave in a hurry, you'll be ready."

She hands me the pass.

I don't want them to come, but what choice do I have?

I jump in the white Ford with Marlon, Katie, and Ella. Ella revs the car down Route 100. When you know people well enough, looks and gestures can tell you more than words. Silent pleas like, "Let's leave this party," or "I'd like to punch you in the face, " or "Don't lie to me" are often as clear as if they were spoken.

"So what's with that look you shared with Marlon in the apartment?" I ask Ella.

Her eyes flicker across the rear view mirror and catch mine. "What *look*?" Her hands clutch the wheel tighter as she presses down harder on the accelerator. The tires squeal as she swerves around a Mercedes.

I grab the armrest, my fingernails digging in. "Slow down before you kill us. You're a terrible liar. Almost as bad as me. So, spit it out. What don't you want to tell me about my grandfather?"

The car slows, and Marlon turns to face me. "My brother says they have more evidence than just the hair and the hatchet against your grandfather for the Judge's murder."

"What else do they think they know?" I sound defensive even though that's not my intent.

"They have a witness that saw Jake leave the Judge's house around the time of the murder. He said Jake left in a green SUV." He shrugs one of his beefy shoulders. "I don't know who the witness is."

"That doesn't prove anything," Katie says. "Eye witness testimony is the least reliable kind." Obviously she's been doing some research about evidence, but she loses a little of her conviction as she goes on. "Your grandfather drives a Porsche anyway. Everyone knows that."

I slouch back. "He also has a green SUV," I tell them, my voice just barely above the hum of the engine. We drive the rest of the way in silence until we reach the casino.

Ella swings the Ford through the entrance to the resort and parks her car in the employee's lot. Sicheii pulls his SUV next to her a minute later. They stare at the green vehicle like it's a hearse. I can't blame them. I do it also.

The casino is part of a sprawling resort with one golf course, a lazy river, two pools, sixteen tennis courts, one casino, and a private stretch into the desert with dozens of thatch-roofed Villas. The main casino building itself is massive. It stretches fifteen floors high with a large ground floor for tables and games, four restaurants, and hundreds of guest rooms. I've been at the casino twice. Both times were a year ago. Mom and a friend she works with took me to the fancy Asian fusion restaurant. I thought the guy was cute and that maybe Mom had started to date him, but we later found out he was gay and just liked Asian fusion food.

We all roll out of the cars. Slung over my left shoulder is Troy's backpack, which feels burdensome with the crystal hilt weighing heavily in it. I can almost sense the weapon vibrating, calling me, warning me. I'm sure it's my overactive imagination, but it unsettles me. We need a plan and somehow I've become the leader. But before I devise one, a voice in my head seeks me out. It sounds sweet and sing-songy.

The verbalization is as clear as if I have ear buds on, but of course I don't. "Welcome, Juliet Stone. I so look forward to meeting you. I'm in Villa 11. Bring the old man. He intrigues me. Don't invite any of your friends. Your mom won't like that. Don't dawdle. She won't like that either. Do as I say, and she won't be harmed."

Everyone's eyes are on me. For a second, I assume they heard the voice also, but that's foolish. I'm sure the Seeker's message was meant only for me.

"What do you think we should do?" Troy asks.

I'm grateful for the second to compose myself. I can think of only one plan. "We should break up into two teams. Sicheii and I will start on the West side of the property on the opposite end from the gate and Troy, Ayden, and Lisa should start on the East end of the property."

Ayden objects instantly. "I should go with you, Juliet. I don't trust the old man to keep you safe."

Sicheii growls behind me.

I raise my hand. "Each team needs at least one of us who has seen these guys. I've seen both Gold Tooth and Slicked Back Hair, and Troy remembers Slicked Back Hair." I add as much conviction to my voice as I can muster. "When someone spots Mom or anyone suspicious, text everyone else immediately." I almost forgot our cover story for Ella, so I hastily add, "that way, we'll all be able to make sure Mom is here before we call the Sheriff. Ella, Marlon, and Katie will stay by the cars, at the ready if we need help."

"Why does Troy get to go and I have to stay by the cars? I should come with you," Marlon complains.

"You've never seen either of these guys before, and we'll call you if we need you. That way you can help either team. You'll be just on the other side of the gate."

Marlon huffs and crosses his arms against his wide chest, but I doubt he really wants to join us. He's probably just acting tough for Ella. We all know he's really a giant marshmallow.

Some other minor protests about my plan erupt around me like brushfires, but I march toward the employee gate and ignore them. As the sun sinks below the horizon, the lights above the security gate kick on. Ella swipes her mom's card and the sturdy black iron gate opens.

Before we split up, Ayden grabs my arm. "Be careful, Juliet. Make sure you call me if you find anything. I'll be there in a flash."

"You'll be the first to know." I lie to my father. He won't be with me when I face the Seeker, but there's no other way to save Mom. He releases me, and I feel like I'm about to throw-up. I point toward the West where I assume Villa 11 is most likely to be. "Let's go this way, Sicheii."

Troy whispers in my ear. "Be safe." His breath caresses my skin and I almost cry. His lips look like sugar. I shove him away and refuse to look at him. I can't face him. I can't be that girl. Now, I have to be the Chosen, the Seeker Slayer. I need to be strong and independent if I have any chance at all. I need to be badass.

I tromp off down the gravel path with Sicheii striding next to me.

It's right that we face the Seeker alone. He got us into this mess, and together, we're going to have to pull Mom out.

CHAPTER

I march along the path just a pace short of a jog. Flickering street lamps light our way. Little wooden posts with Villa numbers point in different directions. I hesitate at the signs to make sure we head in the right direction.

"Which Villa are we looking for?" Sicheii asks.

"What do you mean?" I respond without breaking stride.

"Obviously you know where we are headed, so what number is it?"

"Number 11."

"That is a good number. I imagine the Great Wind Spirit has spoken to you." His weathered face beams with confidence, but I can't let him believe that the Wind Spirit is directing me. That is too much and too dangerous, so I stop and grab his arm.

"I heard the Seeker's voice in my head. He said to meet him at Villa 11 and to bring only you. Otherwise, he will hurt Mom. I didn't hear the wind say anything."

He grins. "Oh, Little Bird, the Wind Spirit works in mysterious ways. Who made the Seeker reach out to you and reveal his position? I feel the Wind Spirit in this." He pulls his head back and breathes deeply. "I can smell her in the air."

I grind my teeth. "Great. The Wind Spirit wants us to march into the Villa where the Seeker and his lackeys will be waiting for us. It sounds like a stupid plan, but I don't see another choice. It's our only way to save Mom. He'll know if we bring others."

"We don't need another plan. You are blessed by the Wind Spirit, and your time has come."

A hawk circles high above us. It's a Red Shouldered Hawk, which is Sicheii's animal guide. He smiles when he sees it.

"Doesn't that hawk warn you of trouble?"

"Sometimes, Juliet. And other times, the hawk reveals my destiny. One circled overhead when I met your grandmother." We resume our trek toward the Villa.

I wish I had my grandfather's confidence, but doubt flickers like the streetlights just beneath the surface of my thoughts.

Villa 11 appears on our right. The white van is parked in the driveway and I shudder. I remember the last time I saw that van.

I can't go back now. I must be strong. I am strong.

He turns to me. "Coyote has a silver tongue. Don't be fooled by the trickster's words. He will try to deceive you through his pawn. Stay strong. You are the Seeker Slayer."

"Yes, I am." I say with a surprising amount of confidence. I dig out the crystal hilt from my backpack and tuck it into the waistband in the back of my jeans and pull the bottom of the Beatles t-shirt on top of it.

My iPhone buzzes. It's probably a text message from Troy, so I ignore it.

Sicheii puts his hands on my shoulders, his eyes wide and a little wild. "Lets go fulfill our destinies."

CHAPTER 43

The gate to Villa 11 is open. Gold Tooth and Slicked Back Hair flank both sides of the front door. We stroll up the driveway casually, our gait steady as if we are dinner guests.

They smile when they see us. Fear courses through me as I lumber up the three stone steps toward them. My body feels heavy, awkward, unsure.

Sicheii takes my hand in his big calloused one. It steels my nerves, and I move faster.

We stop when we are within a few feet of the two lackeys. A victorious grin graces both their faces.

Gold Tooth says, "You should have just come with us the first time, Love. Everything would have been easier."

"Now your poor mom is involved when all we wanted was the old man." Slicked Back Hair nods toward Sicheii.

"If all you need is me," says Sicheii, "then let them go and you can have me." He raises his arms parallel with the ground causing his linen shirt to flow loosely around him.

"It's too late for that, medicine man," Gold Tooth says. "The boss wants both of you now."

Slicked Back Hair shoves Sicheii in the back.

Energy bubbles up inside me, and I throw a right hook that lands flush against his smug little face. He falls to the ground and Gold Tooth steps toward me, but before he reaches me, I kick him in the stomach with a front kick that bends him at the waist and makes him gasp for air.

He looks up at me with shock in his eyes.

"This is for Mr. Cordingly." I spin in a tight circle and land a roundhouse kick against his head that knocks him out cold.

Slicked Back Hair moans and starts to get to his feet, so I sneer at him. "Touch my grandfather again and I'll kill you." I kick him in the stomach for good measure.

He mutters what sounds like an apology, and we walk through the front door.

Sicheii grins. "When did you learn how to do that?"

I shrug. "The Wind Spirit must have taught me when I drank that fluid."

"I'm in the living room, Juliet Stone. Stop playing with the help. I really can't wait to meet you." The Seeker sounds as if he is right next to me, whispering in my ear.

The Villa has hardwood floors and beige walls with floor to ceiling windows. The living room is off to the left so I start in that direction with Sicheii beside me. I breathe through my nose to steady my nerves and resist the urge to grab the hilt of my sword. I'd rather wait and surprise him. It's the only weapon I have.

When I push through a set of white wooden double doors, the Seeker is sitting on a bench behind a mahogany grand piano. My heart jumps. Two tall golden candles burn on both sides of the piano. A honey sweet scent wafts into the air but it barely masks the smell of rotten fish. The demon sits on one side of him and a snow white Alaskan Husky lies on the floor by his feet. The dog barely lifts his head when we enter the room, but the demon snarls at me.

The Seeker wears a white silk shirt that flows past his waist. Loose fitting navy pants touch the tops of his bare feet, which rest casually on the hardwood floor. The shirt has an insignia on the chest of a purple triangle with a golden circle inside.

His light colored skin is almost albino and appears soft and smooth, but I can't help but stare into his electric eyes. There's beauty behind those eyes and intelligence and a certain hardness that can only come from a proclivity toward cruelty. His features are perfectly symmetrical with thick lips and a strong chin. I stop breathing when I realize he's studying me much the same way I am studying him. I feel heat where his eyes pierce mine.

His lips slowly curl upward around the edges until they turn into a wide smile. "They chose a girl." He chuckles. "And a rather small, average girl at that."

My face narrows and he casually waves his hand with a flick of his wrist. Long, thin fingers beckon us to come closer. "I'm sorry, Juliet Stone, but where I come from, women are not usually put into these types of situations. I thought they would have chosen a boy. There is, of course, the story of Agatha, who some believe was the greatest warrior of our people, but she is really a myth. Even if she did exist, I doubt half of what she was said to have accomplished was real. She has become a fairy tale for children. Still, they chose you and you are before me. You clearly have courage. I'll give you that." He nods his head toward the demon. "Don't worry about my pet. He is particularly good at tracking people I want found. Since you are here with me, he won't harm you unless I command him to attack."

"Where is my mom?"

The Seeker's face turns hard, his voice terse. "Why ask me when you can tell on your own? You must be able to sense her presence."

I let my mind roam and immediately recognize her spirit. It comes from inside the house, and I can breathe. She's unharmed.

"You see, it's all the more rewarding when you discover things on your own. There are so many facts I need to tell you, Juliet Stone. I'm sure they haven't told you the whole story. They are so duplicitous in their ways, always hiding the truth, never letting anyone know the full story. They wish to trick you with falsehoods so you will do their bidding."

Doubt flits through my mind. They really haven't told me much. I don't even know who they are, not really. Sicheii believes the Wind Spirit is behind everything, but I have a problem believing in something I can't see or touch or feel. I've searched my mind for evidence that he is right. I've rummaged through my thoughts as if I were searching the Internet, expecting to find a voice that agrees with him or just knows he's right, like I do about other things, but so far, nothing.

"Don't listen to his lies!" Sicheii looks at me.

The Seeker's fingers flutter across the keyboard for a minute and play a quick paced tune, one I have never heard before. His hands stop as abruptly as they started, and he glares at my grandfather. "You have been thwarting me for years, Jake Stone, medicine man. I admire what you've done. You're a man of action. I can use a man such as you. How about you work for me. Switch sides to the triumphant."

"Never! You are evil." Sicheii's balls his hands into fists. "You are Coyote's pawn. You seek to destroy us."

The Seeker pounds out two dark chords on the piano. "Oh, seriously. You don't really believe in that nonsense, do you? I'm not the one who killed the Judge or Samuel Baker. You did that on your own."

"What?" I say.

"Jake Stone, you didn't tell your granddaughter. Shall I tell her instead?"

Sicheii glances at me, his eyes hard and unwavering. "They were weak. They would have broken their oaths before we were ready." His hands fall useless to his sides, and his shoulders slump. He looks unsteady on his feet, his age draping over him like a loose fitting jacket.

"They were your friends. They were part of your order."

"I had no choice. They knew what was at stake when they took the oaths."

I turn my back on him. I can't look at him. I don't want to see his pain or have him ask for forgiveness that isn't mine to give.

"Don't be like that, Juliet Stone. He did the right thing," the Seeker says. "Charles Roundtree was stubborn and strong minded. My henchmen could not crack him, but we would have made the other two talk. I just wish we could have beaten him to it. We could have saved some time. Not that that matters now."

"Shut up, you devil!" Sicheii lunges toward the Seeker.

I expect the Seeker to flinch or turn or react, but he stays perfectly still. Out of the corner of my eye, I see a chair fly at Sicheii. It crashes into his head and wood splinters. He drops to the ground hard, unconscious, six feet in front of the Seeker.

"Sicheii!" I yell and reach for him. I throw aside the splintered wood. Blood, thick and dark, seeps from his scalp down the right side of his face toward his ear. Air sticks in my lungs. I've never seen Sicheii hurt. He's never even been sick. Some part of me thought that so long as he was with me, everything would work out. He would find a way to make sure we were all right. Now he's still, his breath shallow and tentative.

I brush back his white hair from his wound. My fingertips touch his cheek and blood spoils them.

I glance up at the Seeker. Anger races through my body and it trembles. I bite my lip and taste blood.

"You could have tried to save him, Juliet Stone. You could have used your mind to stop that chair. It wouldn't have worked. You are no match for me, but you could have slowed it down. You let him get hurt."

My hands ball up into fists.

The demon starts to pace in front of the Seeker. Slobber drips from its jaws as it eyes me with a cold fury.

"We all make choices. Do not be angry with me, Juliet Stone. You should be irate with yourself."

I slowly rise.

"Now listen to me carefully. He's not dead. None of the people you care about are dead... yet." He smiles, pets the dog with his long fingers and closes the cover on the piano's keyboard.

I want to smash the piano over his head.

"You have a decision to make, a side to take. If you choose poorly, they will all die a horrible death. Your grandfather and mother and Troy and Ayden. I know them all. Trust me; everyone you care about will meet a grisly end. Choose wisely and a world of riches will be yours, and they all will live."

Their faces flash through my mind. My phone buzzes again, and I'm frozen.

"First, you must know the whole story."

CHAPTER 44

Truth is a tricky thing. Some people believe in absolute truths that are always correct. That's foolish. Truth depends upon your perspective. My truth might be different from Troy's, which may be very different from Katie's. Who knows what the Seeker's truth is? I'm not sure I want to know, but finding out his truth is the only way I will survive this.

He looks relaxed as he sits comfortably on the piano bench, his posture perfect. The purple flecks in his blue eyes bore into mine. Still, there is tension in his jaw and his shoulders. He's not as comfortable as he seems.

"Why should I believe you?"

"I won't lie to you. A decision based upon falsehoods is built on shifting sand. It's useless. You can see where untruths have gotten your grandfather."

My eyes tighten into slits. "He never lied to me."

The Seeker's long fingers softly caress the top of his bald head. "Lies of omission are just as bad as outright falsehoods. You know that. Don't play games." He pauses for a second and his eyes sharpen as if he's taken a whetstone to them and peers into my thoughts. "Anger is a good thing. If properly focused, it can help you achieve much. Alphians have hot blood. We've always been short tempered. Some believe extreme emotions are uncivilized, that we should *evolve* past those feelings. They're fools." He makes the word *evolve* sound dirty. "I wonder if your anger issues are Alphian induced."

"Alphian, what's that?" I have a sick feeling I already know, and it's connected to my visions.

The Seeker flattens his hands together and gently purses his lips against his fingertips. "They haven't told you much. I assumed the fusion would have informed you more. They obviously don't trust you. You see the differences between us? I will freely answer all you questions. Knowledge is power."

I shrug. I wish I understood what was going on but won't let him know that I'm lost. That would be weak. I can't be weak.

He sighs. "Alpha is the name of my home-planet. It's the first planet in the known universe to contain intelligent life—life with a soul. Humans on Earth are newborn babies when compared to Alphians. We are stronger, smarter, and more powerful than you and every other creature that has ever existed. My people split into two factions. Those of the old guard and us Deltites of the circle and the triangle." He points to the insignia on his shirt.

"There was a trial. Your kind were judged guilty." I remember the glimmering stadium from my dream. It was no dream, but a memory implanted in my body somehow.

"Not guilty, but innocent. You see, it's just a matter of perception. Alphians are superior to other life forms. It's our right, in our nature, to dominate other life, but we evolved beyond that over centuries. My group, the Deltites, wanted to bring back the old ways, the true ways, but the Elders refused. They banished us to a far-reaching part of the universe on a planet just barely able to sustain life. They should have killed us, but they were too civilized and weak and *evolved.*" He snorts, but his eyes turn melancholy.

"We lost many of our faction during the early days, until the ship came. Adam, our first leader, predicted it would come, and he was proven correct. Alphians are curious by nature and many still secretly believed in our cause. After the first ship came, the rest was easy. We grew in numbers and our power multiplied."

"What does this have to do with me or Earth?" Sicheii twitches his hand, so I shift away from him. I don't want the Seeker to notice him move.

He chuckles. "You, Juliet Stone, are a pawn in their games. The Elders still underestimate us, but others realize the threat we've become."

"Humans are the closest in DNA to Alphians in the known universe. You are weaklings compared to us, much like a pet dog is to his master." He ignores the demon and strokes the husky's fur. "But there are biological similarities that cannot be denied. Thousands of years ago, some Alphians even mated with your kind and the connection was close enough to hold. The result wasn't quite human nor Alphian, but a mix of the two. They were hybrids. Weak compared to a pure blood Alphian, but stronger than common humans. They were abominations, really, a defiling of our blood and uniqueness, but still they happened."

"Alphians have visited Earth before?"

"Most definitely! Earth is a rich planet full of resources. You're blessed with much, although you're content to throw it away in the selfish pursuit of the present. Still, we became aware of Earth only a few thousand years ago. What a pity we acted solely as observers restricted by the modern philosophies of the current Elders."

"What does that have to do with me?" Sicheii stirs, his leg shifts, so I step farther from him. The Seeker's full attention is on me, so he doesn't notice.

"Good question. Those Alphians who fear us realized we will take Earth. Earth will be extraordinarily valuable to us. Earth will help us reclaim the universe."

"By killing us and taking over the planet!" Visions of the massacre of the short and brutish people flash in front of my eyes. They were merciless. *Would it be as easy for them to conquer Earth?*

"Don't be silly, Juliet Stone." He smiles. "We won't kill everyone. We aren't going to march down on Earth with an army. Earth is too large and well populated. Besides, there are easier ways to take the planet. We are infiltrating your institutions, both political and industrial. Our leader is close to achieving the influence he wants and needs. When he is ready, we will come and humans will unwittingly welcome us with open arms. An army of humans will come in handy, which leads me to your involvement." He pauses for a second and removes a crystal hilt like mine from his pocket and places it on the edge of the piano keys. My heart falters.

"I believe they injected you with Alphian DNA when you were first born. Your newborn body absorbed that DNA, allowing you to have some of our character traits. Although meager, they make you exceptional among humans. I am sure the old guard wants you to act as their agent, help them in leading a defense of the planet against us and thwart our plans. Utter nonsense." He waves his hand as if he is shooing away a fly.

"I've lived on this planet for fifty years now as I wait for the invasion, waiting for enough progress to be made, waiting for our time to come. I still can't stand the smell." He nods toward the towering incense candles. "My wait is almost complete. Earth's time is quickly running out."

"So you want to kill me." My hand slides toward my back and my fingers inch toward the sword hilt.

"No, Juliet Stone." His voice rises and falls with amusement. "They've fused certain information with you. Information that, once we know it, will make it easier for us to take the planet and defeat whatever plans they might be developing. Once the information presents itself, you only need to tell us."

"I just have to betray my entire planet and race so you can make everyone slaves!"

"Humans are lost anyway. I will let you and your loved ones live. I'll also give you power and wealth. You will live like a queen, wealthier and more powerful than all the students at Bartens combined. Why not take our side? It is the only logical choice. Deltites are meant to rule. Choose the Alphians and everyone dies a miserable death, and we still control Earth—only more humans will die in the process, starting with your family." One side of his lips turns up in a sinister half-smile.

He will kill everyone I care about if I don't help him—Troy and Mom and Sicheii and Ayden and all my friends. What chance do I have against him? How can I stand up to him? Only one decision makes sense. If I make a deal would that make me bad?

He snaps his fingers and the husky sits at attention. He smiles at the dog. "She's a beautiful animal. Primitive but beautiful. She's happiest with a strong master. She wants to follow my directions."

I know he's talking about humans. He thinks we're no better than dogs.

"Now the demon on the other hand must run free. Only by the force of my superior power can I keep him from ripping out your throat. He chafes at my control." His smile widens as both sides of his lips curl upward. "Well, Juliet Stone, are you the husky or the demon? You obviously see the wisdom of my choice. You only have one chance to accept my offer."

The husky barks as Sicheii staggers to his feet. He clutches a stone knife in his hand, dried blood smeared against the side of his face. "You can't have her, you devil. Don't listen to him, Juliet." Sicheii's voice is rich with defiance and years of sacrifice. He lunges forward, knife held in his outstretched hand.

The Seeker moves in a blur and grabs the hilt of his crystal sword. The air shimmers, and the blade appears in Sicheii's chest as he thrusts it at him in one smooth motion. Sicheii swings his stone knife, but he's too far away to reach him. All the strength leaves his body, and the knife clatters across the wooden floor as he falls to his knees.

"No!" I scream. The world spins, and my heart feels as if it's about to explode. I can't lose him now, not when I just learned all that he sacrificed for me.

The Seeker slides his sword from Sicheii's chest.

Blood bubbles from his mouth.

"What a fool. I overestimated him." The Seeker stares down at Sicheii, his features hard like stone. He's evil. He might not be Coyote's pawn, but he's the picture of evil.

I race to Sicheii's side and press my hands onto his chest, hoping to stop the flow from the cut, but sticky blood seeps through my fingers. "You'll be okay. We just need a... doctor." My voice cracks. His life is slipping from him. I feel numb. I want to scream, but no words come out.

"Even rocks crumble eventually, Little Bird." He grabs my wrists with both of his hands. "I'm so sorry I've gotten you into this. I did what I thought was right. You're stronger than he is. You just need to see it. For all of us."

Sicheii shoots me a look right before the light leaves his eyes. It's the same look he's thrown at me my entire life. I used to be scared of that look. I feared it was some type of rebuke or reflected some disappointment that I didn't live up to his standards. Now I realize it was just his way of saying he loved me.

A hole rips in my heart and the pain singes me down deep past flesh and bone. He won't be with me anymore to teach me or show me the world in a different light. I'll miss his weirdness. I wish I had known that before.

I rise on steady feet.

The Seeker gazes at me. Blood drips from his blade—my grandfather's blood. I'm not sure when I grabbed the hilt of my sword, but I hold it steady. The crystal blade appears out of thin air.

"I see you've made your decision. You're no smarter than he was. What a pity. You are truly just a silly little girl."

"I am Juliet Wildfire Stone, Jake Clearwater Stone's granddaughter, the Chosen."

CHAPTER 45

The Seeker glances at the demon and the beast lunges at me as if it's been unchained by its owner's mind. Its nasty wings open, and I duck under it, roll just out of the way, and bounce to my feet. The demon turns and charges. I swing my sword in front in a looping sideswipe and the monster stops and rears up on its hind legs. It's just about my height when it stands on its back legs and waves its sharp front paws at me like daggers.

I dart forward and stab at its chest.

The creature blocks my sword with its left front claw and sparks fly. Without hesitating, it jumps forward.

I can't duck under the monster, so I fall on my back and grab hold of its leathery chest with my free hand. I have just enough time to use my legs to flip it over my head.

It's not as heavy as it seems, so it flies backwards and crashes into a bookcase.

The Seeker claps his hands.

I ignore him as the demon stalks toward me on all four of its legs. This time it opens its wings, and I notice a sharp edge glisten along the end of the creepy things. It looks like razor wire. I'm sure it will slice right through me if I give it a chance.

I grab a wooden chair and chuck it at the demon. The chair splinters against its head, and luckily slows the creature down. This is my chance, so I charge. Two steps and I jump. The demon swipes its left wing at me, but I cut into its black leathery skin as I jump over the creature and land behind it.

It shrieks and the rancid smell threatens to make me gag. It spins and snaps its jaws at me; I've made it mad. I back up, but I bump into a wall. The demon spreads its wings wide, which pens me in. There's nowhere for me to go.

I swear it smiles at me right before it charges. This time it wants to eat me, and in its rage it leads with its jaw.

It expects me to cower, but I won't, so I dart forward and take it by surprise. My free hand grabs its throat while I stab it in the chest with my sword. Still, it comes at me as if it doesn't know it's about to die.

I can barely hold back the teeth from ripping into my neck, and I twist the sword's blade inside its chest.

The demon howls and plunges toward my neck with the last of its strength. Drool drips down on my skin as one of its sharp claws scratches my side.

The pain rips into me, but I turn the sword one last time.

I must have shredded its heart because it bursts in an explosion of light, and the windows in the room explode. It's gone and I stagger to my feet.

The Seeker frowns at me. "You killed Damos!"

I'm breathing heavily and my side hurts where the monster ripped my skin. "I'm not really a demon type of person. I like dogs."

He doesn't give me a chance to rest and closes the distance between us with two quick steps, slashing his sword in a flurry of sideswipes. My hand moves fast, parrying the cuts just before they score. He's strong, and my arm shakes from the force of his blows. When the blades clash, they clang and the room fills with the sound of breaking glass.

I sense his confidence as he presses a dizzying attack—six, eight, ten strokes. I retreat under the barrage. Sweat stings my eyes. He dips the edge of his blade on a backstroke against my side. The edge cuts my shirt and draws a trickle of blood, and the blade feels like ice as it kisses my flesh.

Just as quickly as he started the attack, he stops and smiles. "Being fused with the knowledge of swordplay is one thing, but there is no substitute for real combat. You move stiffly and awkwardly, Juliet Stone. I fear you won't present me with much of a challenge."

Adrenaline races through me and my vision tunnels around him. I'm thinking too much. I have to let my hand move on its own, let the knowledge the fusion gave me work, unhampered by thoughts.

I dart forward and slash at his side. He sidesteps me, lets me rush past him and slices me on the leg. I stumble into the piano bench and topple it over with my foot.

He chuckles, and it sounds like fingers scraping against a chalkboard.

I breathe heavily. I want to rush him, hurt him for killing Sicheii, but next time he'll kill me. He's too good. Too fast. Too strong. I need an advantage.

I back up and start talking to buy time. "You said you've been here for fifty years, but you don't look that old." Of course, I have no idea how old Deltites are supposed to look.

The Seeker grins, his blade held steady in front of him. Candlelight flickers off its edge and the drops of blood that still cling to it. "We don't age at the same rate as humans. We are not children. We can use our minds to control our body. I wonder if you have that ability." He shrugs. "I guess we will never find out."

I scan the living room and search for something to use. I spot the candlesticks. What good will they be if the sword doesn't work?

The Seeker attacks when my attention drifts. He feints a forward side slash. I move my blade to cover. He twirls and cuts me across my left shoulder. I feel ice again and dart behind a chair, keeping it between us. My chest tightens and my eyes widen. Oxygen bursts into my lungs in uneven gasps. I can't let the panic grip me—all will be lost. Too much is at stake, too many people rely upon me, so I beat it down.

"There is no place for you to hide." He kicks the chair between us, and it explodes toward me, crashing into my head.

I see stars and stagger backward. Blood drips from a cut on my forehead and seeps into my eyes, blurring my vision.

"I'm going to kill you now, but I'm going to make it slow... for Damos." He laughs.

I fear he's right when I notice the husky standing behind him, watching us.

Sicheii's voice speaks to me. "Use the dog. Use your gifts."

I feel the dog's energy and in an instant, I am the dog. I see the Seeker's back, confident and strong. I force my anger into the animal and direct it at the Seeker. "Attack!" I command the husky and retreat from the animal's mind.

The dog launches himself at the Seeker and sinks his teeth in his right thigh, catching him off guard. He spins and the husky clamps down even harder, snarling and angry. The Seeker screeches and swings the sword down at the dog. He hacks him a second and a third time. The dog's snow-white fur turns red as he butchers the animal.

I leap forward. The sword flies in my hand, and I rake the blade against his back.

Twisting, he knocks my sword to the side. His beautiful face contorts angrily. The beauty is all gone, replaced with a vile puckered ugliness. Angry red splotches spring to his cheeks.

"You witch!"

He reaches behind his back, and when he brings his hand around, it's slick with blood. Gunshots and shouting ring out from the front yard.

"Good. Your friends are here. I'll kill them all when I finish you."

He rushes forward and our swords clash. He is so much taller and wider than me as he presses his sword down toward my neck. My body strains with effort.

I hear Sicheii's voice again. "He underestimates you. Two arrows are stronger than one."

I smile.

"Why are you smiling?" he grumbles. "I'm going to kill you!"

I feel power flow toward my hand and direct all my energy to the muscles in my arm. My strength multiplies. The sword stops moving toward me, and I bend it at him instead.

Fear jumps to his eyes. "This can't be."

He uses his other hand to push his sword against mine, but it's not enough. The edge of my blade cuts his cheek. He leaps backward, topples over the piano bench, and lands face first.

I kick the bench away and stand over him.

"Stop! I'll give you anything." The violet swirls in his eyes pulse desperately.

"Can you bring Sicheii back from the dead?"

He shakes his head, and his eyes flutter to the side of the room. Using telekinesis, he pulls a mirror from a wall, and fires it at me. I see it coming and command it to stop. The mirror hovers for a moment and crashes to the ground and shatters.

He jumps to his feet and a sly smile slips onto his face.

Mom screams from the other room.

"I'll kill her if you don't drop your sword."

The gasping sound from the other room tells me that he's using telekinesis to crush my mom's throat. If I don't do as he wishes, she'll die.

I lower my sword, and he grins. "You're weak."

"Let her go!"

The front door slams open, and Troy rushes in.

The Seeker darts his eyes toward the smashed bookcase and uses his mind to grab one of the splintered pieces of wood that's shaped like a spike.

Time slows.

I see the connection between the Seeker and the wood; a bluish energy band spins from him, circles the spike, and then he whips the dagger at Troy.

That wood will skewer him.

My body bursts with energy. I grab the wooden spike with my own mind, and my energy collides with his. The spike slows, but it still moves too fast. I concentrate every bit of power I have on the wood.

I can't let Troy die! My body shakes as both of our energy bands crash into each other. I feel his energy flood my body, and it's totally weird and creepy, but I grab hold of it anyway and try to turn it against him.

The spike reaches Troy, and I think my head will shatter.

Still, the Seeker's too strong for me. One final push and he'll drive the spike through Troy's throat. The tip touches his skin and draws blood.

I open my heart, and all the feelings I have for Troy pour out of it. I direct every bit of myself—mind and heart—at the spike, certain that all this power will shatter me into a million pieces, but I don't care. All I want is for Troy to be safe. My feelings for him bolster my energy, and the wood explodes into a shower of splinters before it impales him.

The Seeker glares at me. He must have focused his whole attention on the spike because he's no longer connected to my mom. She's safe for the moment, and my hand moves on its own.

I raise the tip of my sword and stab it into his stomach. He drops his sword, and I push my blade into him until the hilt collides with his midsection.

He stares at me, incredulous. "But you are only a little girl."

"I'm the Seeker Slayer."

I rip the sword upward, he falls to his knees drenched with blood—so much blood, a fountain of blood—and I yank my sword free from his chest.

He spits red sludge on the floor.

Maybe I've inherited more from my father than I thought. I should feel remorse, but I only feel my cold anger over my grandfather. I have become the Seeker Slayer.

When he looks back at me, respect replaces the disdain in his eyes. "I underestimated you. That was my fault, but the other Seekers won't make the same mistake." His face goes blank. "I wish I could have seen Alpha, smelled the grass just once." He sputters and falls head first to the floor with a thud.

Troy moves besides me, and Ayden races into the room with Marlon a step behind him. They freeze when they see me.

I toss my sword on the floor, and the blade disappears before it hits.

"Mom is in the back bedroom."

Ayden sprints past me.

"Are you okay?" Troy moves toward me, his steps hesitant.

I feel nothing as I stagger toward Sicheii. His face is still and lifeless. I could have sworn I heard his voice, but how could that be? His eyes are closed and he looks peaceful. He could be taking a nap, except he isn't sleeping. He isn't moving, and he will never stir again.

Strange thoughts flood my mind. Sicheii was the one who took me to school on my first day of kindergarten. Mom was sick, but I wanted him anyway. I think she knew it. He held my hand as we walked through the double doors, and I felt like I could conquer the world. I always felt stronger when I was connected to him.

Odd, but I think about glazed donuts. It was his favorite food, and he could never have just one. He never drank alcohol. He wanted to be part of the world and could never understand how others wanted to dull their mind. "It makes no sense," he told me once. "Would I want to fish without a hook?"

I laugh out loud. I'd rather laugh than cry. He would want me to laugh. I thought he was immortal. Maybe that's why I never appreciated him the way I should have. He saved me, sacrificed his life for me, and now I realize he'd been doing that all along.

Lisa storms into the Villa. "Jake!" she cries.

Troy touches my shoulder, and I fold into his arms. My head swims and I see nothing but blackness, sweet blackness.

CHAPTER

I wake in Sicheii's SUV with Ayden driving. Mom weeps next to me and Troy's arm hangs around my shoulders. "How did you guys find us?"

"When you didn't reply to my text, I called Katie. She hacked into the casino's reservation system. Only three Villas were occupied. She guessed right."

"But Gold Tooth and Slicked Back Hair were armed."

"I handled them, Juliet," Ayden answers from the front seat. "They were too busy looking in the windows to notice us sneaking up on them. Bloody careless of them."

I squeeze my mom's hand and she squeezes back.

Somehow, we end up in Dent's apartment. That's a blur, but I remember the bathroom and the gross feeling of blood on my hands.

When I leave the bathroom, Mom sits in the living room in shock. Doctor Dan watches over her, so I talk with my father alone in the bedroom. Strange how I think of him as my father now, instead of "Ayden." We talk for a long time. Mom should know the truth, but she's not ready to hear it right now. She shakes, still suffering from shock as she twirls her hair, so we invent a temporary story for her.

When she returns from whatever dark place her mind had retreated to, I tell her the voices are gone, which is only partially untrue. I can control them and understand them, so they're no longer a problem, which is all that counts anyway. Ayden spins her a tale about Sicheii getting caught up in a Roundtree drug-selling scheme. He tells her Sicheii tried to stop Roundtree, but he failed. Slicked Back Hair and Gold Tooth were dealers who worked for the Seeker. They took her because they mistakenly believed he partnered with Roundtree.

All the pieces fit well enough. Mom heard us, or at least some of our story registered with her, because she nods her head at the right times.

We have to do something with Sicheii's body, so we decide to take him back to his apartment and make it look like he died after a fight with a burglar. Troy, Ayden and I wait until late at night, wrap him in a ceremonial burying shroud, and bring him to the gallery. I act as the lookout. Luckily, we don't run into anyone.

We return to my house. Sheriff Daniels shows up first thing in the morning with his Stetson in hand and a somber look on his face. Mom answers the door, and he walks into the foyer where he tells us that Sicheii is dead.

Mom immediately breaks out in combustible sobbing even though she knew what he was going to say. Tears rain down my face also. All of a sudden, Sicheii's death is real and irreversible. I spend the entire next day weeping in a dark room. I would like to believe all my tears belonged to Sicheii. There are many things I would like to believe, but some of those tears were for me.

Sicheii will be buried in two days, four days after his death, as tradition dictates. The entire tribe will likely go and so will half the town. I won't be there, and that hurts.

I've realized what he had tried to tell me all along. I don't have to choose between my heritage and Bartens. That was always a false choice. I just have to be Juliet Wildfire Stone. It doesn't matter whether I'm rich or poor, beautiful or average, brown or white. Let others decide if Juliet Stone is good enough for them.

She's good enough for me.

The morning of my grandfather's funeral, I'm at the base of Devil's Peak with Troy, Marlon, Ella, and Katie. We sit in a loose circle on a dusty field littered with red rocks that look like they've come from Mars. The sun is out, and a hawk circles high over our heads. My eyes tear up when I see it. Sicheii is with me. I can feel him. He will help me do what I must.

I smile at my friends and try to memorize their faces, hoping to freeze this moment somewhere deep in my mind. I have just finished my story. I tell them the entire truth. Well, almost all the truth. I decide to leave out the part where Sicheii confessed to killing Baker and Brooks. Some secrets are worth keeping. Now that the truth hovers among us like a heavy fog, I have to do the really hard part.

"I'm leaving."

Katie's mouth drops, but no words come out.

"The Seeker said there were others who know about me and will come after me. I've stayed too long as it is. Everyone is in danger if I stay. I have to go." The choice is obvious, even though it will be hard.

"How will we get in touch with you?" Katie asks.

"We won't be able to," Ella says. "Any connection between us will put Juliet and ourselves in danger. She's leaving for good."

"I'm sorry I won't be around for your father's trial," I tell Katie. "Don't let them bother you. You're stronger than they are." By them, I mean the sharks at Bartens. I understand what true strength is now - strength to do what you think is right, to stand up for those who you love. Sicheii might have been misguided, but he taught me what sacrifice really is. I feel awful that I won't be able to protect Katie any more. She'll need a friend, but I see strength in her.

Katie smiles shyly. "You're not going to believe it, but Tyler sent me a text the other day. It turns out that he's into computers like me. We hung out together last night."

"When were you going to tell me?" I joke.

"Don't worry about me." Katie sighs. "I know dad's guilty. I've been fooling myself this entire time. Still, he's my father, and I love him no matter what."

"What are we supposed to do about these *Deltides*?" Marlon asks. "I mean... I don't know what comes next. There's no Snapple cap for this."

"Just because this Seeker said there will be an invasion, doesn't mean it's true," Ella says. She says this not only for Marlon, but for me also.

I nod. "That's right, and I have the feeling that whatever invasion or plan they have depends upon their leader's success. Maybe he'll fail. The Seeker said they age differently than we do, so who knows when they might show up, *if* they show up."

"They'll probably take one look at your ugly mug and be scared off," Troy adds.

Marlon gives him a hard shove, but he smiles.

"You'll give us some type of warning before space ships show up in town, won't you?" Ella asks.

"You will be the first to know," I say. "I'm sure Mom will be missing me at the viewing by now, so I've got to go."

"Only you won't be going to the viewing," Ella says. "You're leaving now, aren't you?"

I nod and hug Ella and Marlon. When I face Katie, I remove a small paper swan from my pocket. I made it last night. It contains my last words for Sicheii. "Make sure you drop this in the casket for me."

Katie takes the paper swan from me, her eyes moist. "You're my best friend. If you ever need anything, you find me. I don't care about Deltites or Alphians or the rest of it. I'll always help."

"I know," I mutter and hug her. I try hard to keep the tears from my eyes, but they come anyway. When I let go, they pile into Ella's car, and I watch them drive away.

Troy squeezes my arm.

We are close, only inches apart. "You should be going also," I whisper. The last thing I want is to be alone. It takes all of my courage and newfound strength to utter those words.

"You know better. We're in this together. I never wanted to stay in this little town anyway." He whisks a loose hair from my eyes. His fingertips brush against my cheek. "Besides, you'll spend all this money too fast without me." Troy lifts an old leather satchel. The bag is stuffed with hundred dollar bills—a final gift from Sicheii.

I glance up at Devil's Peak. It is intimidating in the hot sun. "I'd better start then."

"Why not just tell me how to climb to the top. You're still hurt. I'll scoop up the Book of Wisdom and bring it down in a flash."

I grin at him. The location of the third and final book came to me in a dream last night. The dream showed me the way up Devil's Peak—a narrow trail to the top. *Did Roundtree know the book was hidden on the top of the rock formation? Maybe that was why he protested the original site of the casino.*

"I have to do this alone." He would never understand that the climb looks hard and that the new me is much stronger than he is. "It won't take me too long."

"I'll be waiting for you right here." He leans against the Honda.

"I know."

The climb was not as hard as it seemed. The trail from my dream was accurate. There is no way of knowing of the trail's existence from the ground or even on the rock formation itself, unless you know in advance where to find it.

Sicheii had taught me how to climb, so my footing was steady. He taught me many things. When I reach the top, I find the twisted arrows symbol carved into the rock in silver. There is no obvious opening. I rub my hand against the smooth rock face and hope for a seam. There's nothing but smooth rock. When I push against the stone, there is no give.

This has to be the right place, so I sit and think. *What would Sicheii tell me to do?* Whoever left this book behind would want to make sure only the Chosen retrieved it.

I hear Sicheii's voice in my head. "Your blood is special. Embrace your uniqueness."

Could it be that simple? I pull the Wind Catcher from under my shirt and look at the turquoise stone shaped like the Wind Spirit's symbol with the etching inside. A symbol within a symbol, the Wind Spirit inside of me. The inscription reads, "You are Chosen." I close my eyes and kiss the stone. He tried to tell me all along, but I would never listen.

I remove a small pocketknife from my back pocket, open the blade, prick my thumb, and smear the blood against the twisted arrows. The arrows glow and the rock face falls away, revealing a small hiding spot with an old leather journal that resembles the box from Roundtree's house.

I grab it and place it on the rocks next to me. The secrets in this "book" will only further complicate my life. I can run away with Troy, leave it behind, blend into the world, try to be average.

That future flashes in front of my eyes. We could have a normal life, only it's a false life. I can never be average. I was never average. I am Chosen, the Seeker Slayer. My life stopped being mine the moment Sicheii injected me with the Alphian DNA on the day of my birth. I should be angry with him, but I'm not. I miss him so much already.

"I do this for you, Sicheii. I will be a rock."

I cut the wax seal with my fingernail, open the book and find a small glass vial. The vial starts to pulse red, matching my rapid heart rate.

I know what I have to do. I take the vial in my hand and tip it back. The coldness comes and then the pain a moment later and then the knowledge.

My God... there are others like me.

ACKNOWLEDGEMENTS

Many people helped us to make this book a reality. Among them are our beta readers, whether they are young or just young at heart. Their insights were, as always, extraordinarily valuable. Karen spent countless hours carefully combing through the prose, finding ways to improve on it. The end product would not be nearly as good without her help. The extremely talented author, Ruby Standing Deer, deserves particular mention. Not only did she spend the time to authenticate our Native American themes, she went beyond that to help improve the writing and shape of the story.

The great folks at Evolved Publishing continue to show what a high quality small press can accomplish. We are honored that they agreed to publish this series. Megan Harris did a wonderful job editing the book and Mallory Rock proved, once again, that she's a true artist. We would also like to thank Lane Diamond who believed in this project from the beginning and whose support has proven invaluable in developing this trilogy.

ABOUT THE AUTHORS

Jeff Altabef lives in New York with his wife, two daughters, and Charlie the dog. He spends time volunteering at the Writing Center in the local community college. After years of being accused of "telling stories," he thought he would make it official. He writes in both the thriller and young adult genres. *Fourteenth Colony*, a political thriller, was his debut novel. *Shatter Point* is his second novel. As an avid Knicks fan, he is prone to long periods of melancholy during hoops season.

Jeff has a column on The Examiner focused on writing and a blog on The Patch designed to encourage writing for those that like telling stories.

You can find Jeff online at: www.JeffreyAltabef.com Also visit him on Goodreads, Facebook, Twitter, or email Jeff at JeffreyAltabef@gmail.com.

Erynn Altabef is an avid reader, dancer, and community activist. When she's not in High School, she loves Starbucks, performing in school musicals, baking, and watching movies with her friends.

Some of her favorite authors are Veronica Roth, Joelle Charbonneau, and her dad! (That would be Jeff Altabef.)

You can find Erynn online at: Facebook.com/ErynnAltabefAuthor.

WHAT'S NEXT FROM JEFF ALTABEF & ERYNN ALTABEF?

BRINK OF DAWN
(A Chosen Novel – 2)

The second book in this young adult fantasy series is now available.

~~~~~

Special Sneak Preview: Chapter 1

~~~~~

"You don't have to do this, Jules." Troy cocks his head to the side a little, the way he does when he's worried about me.

The warm expression in his eyes melts my heart. *What would I do without him?*

He's always looking out for me. I used to get into fights, but even when they were my fault, he'd always stand up for me. Now I need him more then ever. The fate of the world is at stake, and he's still here beside me, standing up for me. He'll die to protect me if he has to, but I don't need him to protect me anymore. I need him close, to wrap his friendship around me like a blanket, to connect, to feel human.

Lately I've had a hard time feeling human without him.

"When was the last time I did something I didn't want?" I smirk, but my words ring hollow, untrue—at least for me. I'm always stuck doing chores for other people, and now there's an entire destiny to fulfill that's been thrust upon me. I'd rather be normal and have nothing to do with this future, but we don't get a chance to pick our destiny. At least I didn't.

"What's your mom going to say when she finds out?"

"Since when are you worried about my mom? You've been getting me in trouble since we were in kindergarten. Your name has been etched at the top of her *Undesirable List* since we were six. I've seen it. She keeps it posted on the refrigerator."

Troy arches his eyebrows. "Hey, your mom loves me! I'm the other child she's never had."

"Are you *serious*?" I shoot him a half smile so he knows I'm joking.

Everybody *loves* Troy. Still, he's not on the college track, and Mom wants me to go to one of the best colleges so I can make tons of money and become a big shot lawyer, like her or some other *Master of the Universe* that has no fun and works way too hard.

"Mom's back home and we're here. She doesn't get a vote."

He frowns. "It's just that... once you do this, you can't undo it. It's forever."

"*Really*. That's the point." I shove him lightly in the chest. I'm old enough to make up my own mind, but he's just trying to protect me, so I can't get too angry with him.

"What are your classmates at that fancy private school going to think when they find out?"

I pause for a second and look at him. I mean, *really* look at him, and peer past the handsome exterior: the almond-colored eyes, the chiseled chin, and the long raven hair that falls past his broad shoulders in a tight braid.

Beyond his confident shell, deep in his soul, he harbors doubts that trouble him—doubts he'll never share with me. He's making believe life will go back to normal once I fulfill this destiny—*if* I fulfill this destiny—but that's not possible. Normal has become a bad joke, but I won't shatter the illusion for him. He needs to sort events into a pattern he understands and imagine a time when life returns to what it was for us. It's how he's coping with the situation.

I need to be strong for him. I can't weaken his defenses, even if fears riddle my mind at every turn.

I straighten my back. "You know I don't care about what they think at Bartens. I *want* to do this. I *need* to do it." The wind kicks up, and the cool night air sweeps against my skin, leaving an army of goose bumps in its wake.

The almost full moon lights the cloudless sky. We inch toward the store and hesitate at the door. A red neon sign reads *Lost Souls Tattoos* in the front window. I take a deep breath and shove the door open, and a bell jingles above us.

No one's in sight. Pictures of various tattoos line the walls of the small rectangular shop. Toward the front left is a glass case with a cash register on top, and farther in the back are a massage table, some bright lights, and a chair with wheels on the legs.

A woman strolls from a back room. She's in her twenties, gaunt with sharp features, smoky gray eyes, short hair, one nose ring, and small hoops that circle the edges of her ears. She holds a half-eaten wrap as she ambles toward us. "What do you guys want?"

She wears a loose gray T-shirt and tight jeans. Brightly colored tats cover her left arm, mostly eagles and hawks, and on the left side of her neck is a teardrop the size of my palm.

"I want a tattoo," I say casually, as if ordering a cheeseburger at McDonalds.

She points to a sign taped on the cash register. "You've got to be eighteen for me to give you a tattoo, and there's no way you're eighteen."

I'm almost sixteen. In the right light I could pass for eighteen, but she probably has a lot of experience with underage teenagers asking for tattoos. Still, I feel a lot older than eighteen and that should count for something.

"No one else is here. It's late and this tattoo is really important to me." My voice whines slightly at the end. I wish it hadn't.

"Why?" She crosses her arms against her chest and arches her eyebrows upward. Two gold rings, one in each eyebrow, bob up and down.

An invisible door creaks open. I'll only get one chance to persuade her to give me the ink.

Her teardrop tattoo stands out and must be important. Grief dulls the sparkle in her eyes and shows in the muscles that tighten her jaw. She'll relate to my story, *if* it's truthful.

"I need to remember someone who died recently. He was really important to me."

"Who?"

"My grandfather. I called him Sicheii, and he raised me like a father. He died to protect me." Tears moisten my eyes. The tears are real, as Sicheii's death is a fresh wound. People tell me the pain will get better with time, but they don't know what they're talking about. They mean well, but this hurt will always be fresh. He'll always be gone, and it's my fault.

The woman's face softens. "Just for the sake of discussion, what're you looking for?"

Troy drops the satchel looped over his shoulder, smiles, lifts his T-shirt, and reveals his well-muscled chest and copper skin. Across his heart is a blue tat of two twisted arrows in a circle. Each arrow features different feathers and arrowheads.

The woman glides toward him and examines the ink on his chest. It's beautiful in its simplicity and symmetry. She clearly admires it and perhaps wouldn't mind trying to copy it.

Her eyes widen as she lingers over the details. "What does it mean?"

I hesitate. What am I going to tell her, the truth? That the symbol represents the ancient Order of the Twisted Arrows? Or that my grandfather unwittingly injected me at birth with alien DNA, which has changed me forever? Or that I'm one of four Chosen thrust into a battle for our world against a powerful enemy called from a different planet?

None of those explanations will get me a tattoo. She'd probably chase us from the store.

I settle for something bland. "It represents an old society he belonged to. It meant everything to him. It was kind of a... club."

At least it's not a lie. She's probably used to people lying to her and would catch a whiff of one right away.

She traces the circle with her finger. "Is it some weird Native American thing?"

"You could say that." Native Americans use tattoos generally to identify with certain tribes or to honor their animal spirit guide. I'm half Native American on my mom's side, and Sicheii was her father. I have long black hair, an oval face, coffee-colored eyes that are round but not quite round enough to be beautiful, and a long, pointy nose I inherited from my Irish father. I look Native American except for the ghastly nose.

The tattoo artist leaves Troy and slides in front of me. She stands close, no more than a foot away, and traces of vegetable wrap linger on her breath. I'm taller than the average person and stand at least three inches higher than she does.

She studies my face for a long moment; perhaps she's trying to see if I'm serious. "What's your name?"

"Juliet Wildfire Stone." I never used to tell people my middle name. It embarrassed me. Now I realize it's who I am, part of my identity.

"Wildfire, huh? I can see that. Where do you want the tattoo?"

I roll up the right sleeve of my T-shirt. "My shoulder would be great."

She nods. "It'll cost you two hundred cash, and you can't tell anyone you got it here."

"Done." I hand her four fifty-dollar bills.

She locks the door to the shop, guides me to the table in the back, and places a pillow on one end. "You want it the same color?"

I jump on the table. "Yep."

She gestures for Troy to come close. "Keep your shirt up. I want to get it just right."

Two hours later, she wipes my arm with a towel. "That's so weird."

"What's wrong?" My heart jumps. *Did she just totally mess up my arm and leave me with some ugly circle thing?*

Troy's smiling, so how bad of a job could she have done?

"Usually it takes a couple weeks for the tat to heal. It always bleeds a little or gets puffy, but your arm already looks perfect, as if the ink had been on it forever."

She hands me a mirror, and I smile. My tattoo is exactly the same as Troy's. Exactly the same as Sicheii's had been.

I shrug and hop from the table. "I've always been a fast healer."

My DNA's been changed, so my body can regenerate itself almost instantly. I didn't know that before. It's just another one of my *abilities*, as Sicheii would say. I've started to think of them as *aberrations*.

I have five so far: I can hear other people's thoughts and read their emotions; I can possess animals for a short period of time; I have increased strength and speed; can move things with my mind; and heal instantly. There will probably be more, but they scare me. With each new one, I become less human.

"We'd better head out."

I step toward the door, and she grabs my wrist. "Wait. I want to take a picture of the ink for the wall."

"You can't." I yank my arm away from her.

"I won't take your face. Just the ink."

"Tough." She scowls at me, but I ignore her and march outside.

When we leave the store a sharp pain stabs through my head, as though someone has taken an axe to my skull and cleaved it in two. A wild rage burns through me, and all of a sudden I'm inside a villa next to a piano.

Breath catches in my throat, all the strength saps from my body, and I plummet to the ground.

MORE FROM EVOLVED PUBLISHING

CHILDREN'S PICTURE BOOKS

THE BIRD BRAIN BOOKS by Emlyn Chand:
Courtney Saves Christmas
Davey the Detective
Honey the Hero
Izzy the Inventor
Larry the Lonely
Polly Wants to be a Pirate
Poppy the Proud
Ricky the Runt
Ruby to the Rescue
Sammy Steals the Show
Tommy Goes Trick-or-Treating
Vicky Finds a Valentine
Silent Words by Chantal Fournier
Bella and the Blue Genie by Jonathan Gould
Maddie's Monsters by Jonathan Gould
Thomas and the Tiger-Turtle by Jonathan Gould
EMLYN AND THE GREMLIN by Steff F. Kneff:
Emlyn and the Gremlin
Emlyn and the Gremlin and the Barbeque Disaster
Emlyn and the Gremlin and the Mean Old Cat
Emlyn and the Gremlin and the Seaside Mishap
Emlyn and the Gremlin and the Teenage Babysitter
I'd Rather Be Riding My Bike by Eric Pinder
SULLY P. SNOOFERPOOT'S AMAZING INVENTIONS by Aaron Shaw Ph.D.:
Sully P. Snooferpoot's Amazing New Forcefield
Sully P. Snooferpoot's Amazing New Shadow
THE ADVENTURES OF NINJA AND BUNNY by Kara S. Tyler:
Ninja and Bunny's Great Adventure
Ninja and Bunny to the Rescue
VALENTINA'S SPOOKY ADVENTURES by Majanka Verstraete:
Valentina and the Haunted Mansion
Valentina and the Masked Mummy
Valentina and the Whackadoodle Witch

HISTORICAL FICTION
Galerie by Steven Greenberg
Broken Path by Ruby Standing Deer

SHINING LIGHT'S SAGA by Ruby Standing Deer:
Circles (Book 1)
Spirals (Book 2)
Stones (Book 3)

LITERARY FICTION
Carry Me Away by Robb Grindstaff
Hannah's Voice by Robb Grindstaff
Turning Trixie by Robb Grindstaff
Cassia by Lanette Kauten
The Daughter of the Sea and the Sky by David Litwack
A Handful of Wishes by E.D. Martin
Yours to Keep or Throw Aside by E.D. Martin
Jellicle Girl by Stevie Mikayne
Weight of Earth by Stevie Mikayne
White Chalk by Pavarti K. Tyler

LOWER GRADE (Chapter Books)
THE PET SHOP SOCIETY by Emlyn Chand:
Maddie and the Purrfect Crime
Mike and the Dog-Gone Labradoodle
Tyler and the Blabber-Mouth Birds
TALES FROM UPON A. TIME by Falcon Storm:
Natalie the Not-So-Nasty
The Perils of Petunia
The Persnickety Princess
WEIRDVILLE by Majanka Verstraete:
Drowning in Fear
Fright Train
Grave Error
House of Horrors
The Clumsy Magician
The Doll Maker
THE BALDERDASH SAGA by J.W.Zulauf:
The Underground Princess (Book 1)
The Prince's Plight (Book 2)
The Shaman's Salvation (Book 3)
THE BALDERDASH SAGA SHORT STORIES by J.W.Zulauf:
Hurlock the Warrior King
Roland the Pirate Knight
Scarlet the Kindhearted Princess

MEMOIR
And Then It Rained: Lessons for Life by Megan Morrison

MIDDLE GRADE
FRENDYL KRUNE by Kira A. McFadden:
Frendyl Krune and the Blood of the Sun (Book 1)
Frendyl Krune and the Snake Across the Sea (Book 2)
Frendyl Krune and the Stone Princess (Book 3)
NOAH ZARC by D. Robert Pease:
Mammoth Trouble (Book 1)
Cataclysm (Book 2)
Declaration (Book 3)
Omnibus (Special 3-in-1 Edition)

MYSTERY / CRIME / DETECTIVE
DUNCAN COCHRANE by David Hagerty:
They Tell Me You Are Wicked (Book 1)
Hot Sinatra by Axel Howerton

NEW ADULT
THE DESERT by Angela Scott:
Desert Rice (Book 1)
Desert Flower (Book 2)
Nothing Fair About It by Linda Kay Silva

ROMANCE / EROTICA
COLLEGE ROMANCE by Amelia James:
Tell Me You Want Me (Book 1)
Secret Storm (Book 2)
Tell Me You Want Forever (Book 3)
Destined for Genius by Amelia James
Let It Ride by Amelia James
THE TWISTED MOSAIC by Amelia James:
Her Twisted Pleasures (Book 1)
Their Twisted Love (Book 2)
His Twisted Choice (Book 3)
The Twisted Mosaic – Specail Omnibus Edition 1-3 (Book 4)
The Devil Made Me Do It by Amelia James
THE SUGAR HOUSE NOVELLAS by Pavarti K. Tyler:
Sugar & Salt (Book 1)
Protecting Portia (Book 2)
Dual Domination (Book 3)
The Sugar House Novellas – Special Omnibus Edition 1-3 (Book 4)

SCI-FI / FANTASY

THE SUNDERED OATH by Ciara Ballintyne:
In the Company of the Dead (Book 1)
Eulogy by D.T. Conklin
THE PANHELION CHRONICLES by Marlin Desault:
Shroud of Eden (Book 1)
The Vanquished of Eden (Book 2)
THE SEEKERS by David Litwack:
The Children of Darkness (Book 1)
The Stuff of Stars (Book 2)
The Light of Reason (Book 3)
THE AMULI CHRONICLES: SOULBOUND by Kira A. McFadden:
The Soulbound Curse (Book 1)
The Soulless King (Book 2)
The Throne of Souls (Book 3)
Shadow Swarm by D. Robert Pease
Two Moons of Sera by Pavarti K. Tyler

SHORT STORY ANTHOLOGIES

FROM THE EDITORS AT EVOLVED PUBLISHING:
Evolution: Vol. 1 (A Short Story Collection)
Evolution: Vol. 2 (A Short Story Collection)
The Futility of Loving a Soldier by E.D. Martin

SUSPENSE / THRILLER

Shatter Point by Jeff Altabef
TONY HOOPER by Lane Diamond:
Forgive Me, Alex (Book 1)
The Devil's Bane (Book 2)
Enfold Me by Steven Greenberg
THE SYNDICATE-BORN TRILOGY by K.M. Hodge:
Red on the Run (Book 1)
Black and White Truth (Book 2)
Shadow Side by Ellen Joyce
THE OZ FILES by Barry Metcalf:
Broometime Serenade (Book 1)
Intrigue at Sandy Point (Book 2)
Spirit of Warrnambool (Book 3)
THE ZOE DELANTE THRILLERS by C.L. Roberts-Huth:
Whispers of the Dead (Book 1)
Whispers of the Serpent (Book 2)
Whispers of the Sidhe (Book 3)
Kill or be Killed: Under Cover by Linda Kay Silva

CPSIA information can be obtained
at www.ICGtesting.com
Printed in the USA
LVOW01s0231251116

514317LV00003B/105/P